CONTEMPORARY MUSING

CONTEMPORARY MUSING

SIXTEEN CONTEMPORARY STORIES FROM A SCI-FI WRITER

ROBERT J. MCCARTER

LITTLE HUMMINGBIRD PUBLISHING

Contemporary Musings

Sixteen Contemporary Stories from a Sci-Fi Writer

Copyright ©2023 by Robert J. McCarter

"The Helium Exit Strategy" © 2015 Robert J. McCarter. First published in *Life After: Stories of Life, Death and the Places In Between*

"The Disappearing Neighborhood" © 2019 Robert J. McCarter. First published in *Pulphouse Fiction Magazine, Issue #6*

"Little Greeny" © 2020 Robert J. McCarter. First published in *Creatures Featured: Thirteen Stories of Monsters and Other Creatures*

"The Dour Mr. M" © 2018 Robert J. McCarter. First published in *Anomalous Readings: Thirteen Curious and Confounding Tales*

"Laura's Magic Clock" © 2015 Robert J. McCarter. First published in *A Game of Horns: A Red Unicorn Anthology*

Except as permitted under the Copyright Act of 1976, this book may not be reproduced in whole or in part in any manner.

This book is a work of fiction. Names, places, and incidents are either products of the author's imagination or used fictitiously. Any resemblance to actual events or persons, living or dead, is entirely coincidental.

Cover image © Depositphoto.com, violetkaipa. Earth image by NASA

Version 1.0, July 2023

ISBN: 978-1-941153-81-9

Visit Robert's website at: RobertJMcCarter.com

Published by:

Little Hummingbird Publishing

P.O. Box 23518

Flagstaff, AZ 86002

CONTENTS

INTRODUCTION

I have to start this book with a confession.

Before I started writing seriously, I was a bit of a snob when it came to my reading choices. A geeky snob. I always went for sci-fi or fantasy, two genres that can be housed under the larger umbrella of "speculative fiction."

At its essence, speculative fiction asks questions and imagines realities beyond what is real for us right now.

Two things happened to bust me out of speculative fiction as a reader when I got serious about writing.

First, it is imperative for writers to read, widely and out of their comfort zone. Every writer, especially the good ones, has something to teach others who would like to write well. The genre doesn't matter. Good writing is good writing. A good story is a good story.

Second, I started writing contemporary, non-speculative stories. I didn't mean to, but because of my process, where I often have no idea where a story is going, it just turned out that way.

It was a bit of a surprise at first. Why am I writing straight-up contemporary stories? But the answer turned out to be the same as why I might write any story. Because I needed to. Because there was something to express or I was stretching myself as an artist.

I'm still mostly a speculative fiction writer, but what I have discovered is that at my heart, I am a storyteller, and whatever genre serves the story is fine by me. At this point, I don't think too much about genre when I'm writing.

Another interesting thing happened with these stories. Some of them are, I think, particularly poignant and powerful, and some are very personal. It seems some of the stories I needed to tell had to be told without any of the extra bells or whistles that speculative fiction can bring.

What unifies these stories with my other work, is me, the artist. These stories contain a lot of the same themes as my speculative fiction, they focus on character, and have crisp endings. If you like my other writing, you'll probably find something here too.

There's a host of genres: mystery, horror, family drama, young adult, romance, and some stories I don't even know how to categorize. I will warn you, a few of them might seem like they have a speculative component, but just keep reading.

A few of these stories have appeared in my other collections and a few have been in magazines or anthologies, but most of them are being published here for the first time.

As with all my collections, I have written a bit about each story, but *after* the story. That way I can speak more frankly about the story and not worry about spoilers.

I hope you enjoy my contemporary musings as much as I enjoyed writing them.

Robert J. McCarter
Flagstaff, AZ
April 2023

PART 1
THE DISAPPEARING NEIGHBORHOOD

THE DISAPPEARING NEIGHBORHOOD

"I know there was a house there," Edward mumbled, staring at the snow-covered lot, all tall pine trees and no house at all. He took a deep breath of the cold air and furrowed his wrinkled brow. It had been painted brown, yes, and small and narrow. There used to be a tiny dog door and yappy dogs would trot out and bark at him and Oscar.

"You remember, boy, don't you?" he asked his dog, but Oscar was too busy smelling the fresh smells after the new snow, out at the end of his retractable leash deciding exactly where to put his own mark.

Edward's eclectic neighborhood had been filled with empty lots forty years ago when Shelia and he had moved in. Their house had been the third one on their short street. But not anymore. All the empty lots had been taken and there was too much traffic and too few people who gave a damn about the speed limit. This house, the one that wasn't there anymore, had been here when they moved in.

Edward looked around, but everything else seemed to be in place. A variety of houses, from tiny A-frames to big modern houses crammed onto the small lots of this decidedly middle-class neighborhood.

Oscar was looking back at him, a question on his face. The dog was an Australian shepherd with ice-blue eyes and mottled brown, black, and white fur.

Edward frowned and sighed, the condensate of his exhale forming a tiny cloud in the cold air. "There was a house here, Oscar, you know it." He shrugged and walked carefully forward, making sure his feet stayed square under him on the freshly plowed street. His knees ached and the arthritis in his hands was flaring up, but the cold, at least, would be good for that. "If you aren't moving, you aren't alive," Edward said as he started trudging forward again, but winters made moving a bit treacherous. He had his ice grippers on his boots, but one fall at his age and a broken hip would keep him from moving for a good long while. Maybe forever.

And most days he didn't think that would be such a bad thing. What did he have left to live for, anyway?

"I swear there was a house there," he mumbled, shaking his head as he slowly walked away.

EDWARD TRUDGED UP THE HILL; IT WASN'T REALLY THAT steep, maybe a five percent grade. It would have been nothing even a few years ago, but now his lungs struggled to pull the high-altitude oxygen from the cold air and his knees complained at the strain. Oscar was patient, though, sniffing the now-dirty snow or looking back and waiting for Edward.

His daughter wanted him to move to Phoenix to be nearer to her, but he'd be damned if we would leave while he could still manage. He barely talked to her now since her doubt about his ability to care for himself seemed to be the only conversation they could have. And that one always ended in an argument. Retirement hadn't gone as he planned, but at least he still had his house, at least he still had Oscar.

He stopped, because he was tired, but also because there was another empty lot. How many did this make? Four? Five? He tried to remember where the first one had been, but he couldn't. It wasn't on a damn hill, he knew that, but he couldn't remember anything about it.

"Good morning, Mr. Fischer," a young man said with a wave as he walked across the street to his mailbox. He was dressed in jeans and a long-sleeved shirt. In this weather, no less, not even a hat on his head, and such short hair. The young were foolish, every single one of them, with no idea what was to come. What was his name? Matt, Pat... something short, ending in a "t," but Edward couldn't remember.

"Good morning," Edward said with a smile. It was a friendly enough neighborhood, but most of the people Edward had known well had died or moved to a lower elevation for their retirement. The young man rushed past him, but Edward said, "Excuse me, Pat."

"It's Matt," the young man said, looking at Edward in his down coat and winter boots.

"Oh...yes...sorry. I don't mean to bother you, but didn't there used to be a house here?" Edward pointed to the empty, fully treed lot next to the young man's house.

Matt was stocky and muscular, a look Edward didn't trust at all, but he had kind brown eyes. Those eyes widened, and he cocked his head to one side and stared at Edward. "No, sir. I've been here three years now. Never been a house there."

"I remember a ..." Edward began, "...a woman with long black hair and a little girl with blue eyes. Single mother. You... you liked her, didn't you?"

"I'm sorry, Mr. Fischer. I don't know what you're talking

about." He walked back into his house and Edward stood there scowling at the empty lot.

***

Oscar paced over to Edward, who was camped out on his recliner, the TV playing a rerun of *The Rockford Files*. Oscar whined, walked to the front door, his nails clicking on the tile entryway, stared at Edward, and whined again.

"No," Edward said with a wave of his hand. "Use your dog door. I'm not going out there."

Winter had dragged on, cold and oppressive, although not the kind of snow they used to get. The sun was out and the roads were clear, but Edward didn't like to walk in his neighborhood anymore. One missing house had turned to two the next week and it was eight weeks later and now half the houses in the neighborhood were missing, all of them replaced with fully treed, untouched lots. He had talked to many of his remaining neighbors about it, but none of them remembered the houses or the people, and all looked at him like he was crazy. He was beginning to think they were right.

Edward took a sip of his coffee, sharp and bitter, and turned his attention back to the TV. Shelia had adored James Garner and insisted that they be in front of the TV for each new episode. That was 1974, the year they moved into this neighborhood. "I only like him because he reminds me of you," Shelia would say with a smile. Edward never believed her, never thought of himself as handsome, but he appreciated the kindness whether it was true or not.

His grandson, Kyle, had just been over and taught him how to use Netflix. It had not been fun for either of them. Why is everything so damn complicated anymore? What the hell was wrong with on and off and channels? Edward liked *The Rock-*

ford Files just fine, but was watching it for Shelia. It helped him remember when they were young.

Shelia's chair, an overstuffed blue armchair, sat next to his shabby brown recliner, even though it had been empty for six years now. In between the two chairs was a small table with a framed picture of Sheila sitting on it. In it, her green eyes were shining and her shoulder-length gray hair was blowing in the breeze as her hands appeared to hold up the Leaning Tower of Pisa. One of those cheesy tourist things they had done while on vacation to Europe not long before she got sick. Back when there was a reason to get up besides walking the dog.

Next to the picture of Shelia was one of their whole family from about ten years ago. He and Shelia, his daughter and her husband, and their two grandchildren, teenagers at the time. Also on the table was his retirement gift from the university, a nice wooden box that he kept spare batteries for the remote in and his finishing medal for the marathon he had run at sixty-five. It was a shrine to the life he once lived that seemed more distant each day.

Oscar whined again. "No!" Edward shouted and the dog lowered his head, his ears down and his tail between his legs. The guilt hit Edward hard and he sighed, fiddling with the remote until he managed to pause the show. "Okay, okay, you win. If you aren't moving, you aren't alive. I'm still alive, so let's go."

Oscar brightened, danced back and forth in front of Edward, ran across the room to the basket that contained his toys, pulled out a squeak toy, tossed it in the air, pounced on it, and then took it to his dog bed right next to Edward's chair and chomped on it happily.

Edward smiled and shook his head. If only he could find such joy in a thing as simple as a walk. His smile didn't last long as he looked out the picture window at his street. The house directly across from his was gone. It had been a simple rectangle of a house with vaulted ceilings and a wraparound deck. A woman and her teenage daughter had lived there. What were their names? They had talked all the time. She was a kind lady, if just too busy. Audrey? Ann? Abby? Something like that. She had worked for the county, right?

Edward stood there, frozen. This wasn't right. Something was wrong. He was old, he knew that, his memory was not what it was, and the years alone had let his introverted nature get out of control, but this... He wasn't imagining this.

Oscar whined and nuzzled his hand. "You feel it too, don't you, boy? Something is happening." The dog's ice-blue eyes were unchanging; he just wanted to go for his walk.

Edward sighed, put on his jacket, and went out into the neighborhood to see if any more houses had disappeared.

BREAKFAST WAS EDWARD'S FAVORITE MEAL. IT WAS SO EASY, with glorious smells and tastes. Food was his last remaining pleasure. First the bacon sizzling in the pan, two strips only, the heavenly smell of it mixing with the aroma of brewing coffee. After the bacon, crack the eggs right into the bacon grease and put the toast down. Watch the eggs closely—a proper over easy egg is a delicate thing. Then when the toaster pops out two slices of whole wheat, generously spread on the butter, put it all on a plate, and then take it to the table in front of the picture window and eat while watching the neighborhood.

Oscar was always there, demanding his share of the bacon and the plate to lick.

One morning late in winter as Edward gave his dog small nibbles of bacon he stopped and thought, his eyes straying across to the other side of the great room to where his brown recliner sat positioned in front of the TV. He didn't know what, but something was wrong, something was missing.

He could only have one and a half slices of bacon, which was why he gave half a slice to Oscar. Any more and she would be mad. But who would be mad? Who didn't want him to eat bacon? He saw a flash of green eyes and straight gray hair, but otherwise the memory eluded him.

"It's not you, boy," he said to Oscar, giving him another piece from his open palm. The dog loved bacon enough to get a little too enthusiastic. "You want me to eat more bacon, and why the hell not?"

He shook his head, trying to clear the thought. He lived alone, he had always lived alone. He sipped his coffee, black and bitter, and stared out the window at the cold, late winter morning. Trees, so many trees and just a few houses. He just loved his neighborhood.

***

EDWARD LOOKED AT THE LEASH IN HIS HAND. IT WAS ONE OF those fancy retractable leashes that let a dog roam a bit. It was a faded blue and well used. He stopped his brisk walk and stared at it; the wrinkles on his face deepened and his brow furrowed and his lips pursed. That blue reminded him of someone, an animal, of eyes innocent and happy. The leash meant something, didn't it? It felt like it was his, but he didn't have a dog, he had never had a dog, so why would he have a leash?

Maybe he had found it, picked it up, meant to throw it in the trash. He shrugged. It didn't matter. It was a beautiful day.

Spring had finally come and Edward tilted his face to the morning sun and sighed, taking a deep breath of the fragrant air. It was the pine trees, the thick forest that surrounded him filling the air with an earthy vanilla scent.

He loved his sparse little neighborhood. Smooth blacktop cutting its way through the trees, just one or two houses to a street, rarely a car passing by, blissfully quiet. He resumed his morning walk, because if you aren't moving, you aren't alive. He had seen too many people stop moving as they aged, sitting all day, flopped in front of the television at night. Well, not him. He would walk, every single day he could.

He stopped. Who were those people he had seen give up, seen stop moving? They were shadows in his mind, flickering ghosts. They had been real but they weren't anymore.

He flexed his hands, glad to be having a good day with his arthritis. He smiled at two squirrels as they chased each other up a large Ponderosa pine tree, they as glad for spring as he. A raven squawked at him from a nearby tree and he saw some turkey vultures circling in the azure-blue air high above. He forgot his moody thoughts and resumed his walk. It was such a beautiful day.

THE OLD MAN WAS DRESSED FOR A WALK IN A T-SHIRT, cargo shorts, and his wide-brimmed hat. A long walk, a hike, even; he had a water bottle in his hand. He bounced on his knees briefly—no creaking, no pain—and smiled. He flexed his hands and they felt better than they had in... Well, he didn't really know, but he knew they felt good now and they hadn't recently.

He stood in the middle of a forest with towering Ponderosa pine trees, their dark green needles reaching towards the startling blue sky, their sweet scent filling his nose. It was warm, a perfect seventy-two degrees, with just a whisper of a breeze. He saw a squirrel jump from the branch of one tree to the branch of another and smiled again. He loved the quick, industrious squirrels with their daring acrobatics.

His stomach was full and he had just had a good breakfast. He could still taste the bacon and the coffee.

He looked around, confused. He was on a paved street and he knew that this was his neighborhood, but there were no houses here. The road led deeper into the forest and he knew that was the way he was to go, but he didn't remember where he came from. Where had he just eaten breakfast? Where had he taken a shower and gotten dressed, shaved, and brushed his teeth? As he thought on it, he realized that he didn't really remember anything, not even his name. He had a past, he knew that, but it was just a whisper, too low to make out.

He shrugged his shoulders. It didn't matter anymore. Such a beautiful day.

He walked down the road, a spring in his step, and he started whistling. He wasn't very good at it, but thought that he must have whistled a lot as a boy.

When the road narrowed into a trail that dived into a thicker part of the forest, he paused both his walking and whistling and looked back. Just a lone paved road in the middle of a beautiful forest. It had been his home, it had been his neighborhood, but no longer. He couldn't even remember what his house had looked like, what had been done there, or who he might have lived with.

He turned away, knowing he would never be back. His past was gone, truly gone, and his future...well, he had no thoughts about that either. All he had was this warm day in a beautiful forest and somewhere to go. Where didn't matter, only that he kept moving.

He started whistling a simple, happy tune and headed down the path.

BACKSTORY—THE DISAPPEARING NEIGHBORHOOD

This story appeared in *Pulphouse Fiction Magazine, Issue #6.* The editor, Dean Wesley Smith, loved the story which surprised me in the best way because this story was an experiment, and it happens to be my first professional short story sale.

This story is not fantasy, it's a metaphor, an attempt to capture what happens as we get older, as our biology diminishes, as we get closer to death, as our world gets smaller and the past gets hazy.

The idea for this popped into my head as I was walking one of our dogs through our neighborhood. We've lived here for decades, we were here before quite a few of the houses, and passing a rather old one, I wondered what it would mean if one of them was suddenly no longer there. If time was somehow going backwards and the neighborhood was regressing.

As the story matured, it became clear that it was my protagonist that was regressing as he let go of the past, of the things that used to be so dear, and let the unknown take him.

In the process, he let go of a lot of his worries and troubles.

In *Hamlet,* Shakespeare referred to death as "the undiscovered country." As happens frequently in Hamlet, he contemplates it with a lot of angst, but this story ponders taking the trip with more grace.

I guess that makes this story a hopeful metaphor of death. Or scary. I guess it's all in how you look at it.

Not that I can say what the genre of this one is. If you know, please fill me in.

This was one of the stories I wrote for my 2017 Short Story Marathon (I wrote 30 stories in 33 days). Which meant I wrote it quickly and couldn't overthink it, which is a good thing. This was an amazing and exhausting experience. I wrote about the process of writing all of these stories extensively on my blog, posting every day about it, its challenges, and what I learned. You can find these posts at *RobertJMcCarter.com/category/story-marathon*.

PART 2

THE HELIUM EXIT STRATEGY

THE HELIUM EXIT STRATEGY

I can't snap my fingers anymore. My knuckles and joints always hurt, and they look like the gnarly knots on an old oak tree. A few months ago I could snap—it hurt like hell, but I could do it. Now I can't snap at all, I don't have the strength.

I take a bite of my lunch and tell my daughter about it. The food here tastes like paste, flat and lifeless. It does have an odor to it, but it's just pretending to smell like food. We sit in the institutional dining room of the facility I live in, the tables occupied by the grey-haired elderly.

The room is cheery enough with round tables covered in white tablecloths, big windows showing tall pine trees outside. Flagstaff, Arizona, at 7,000 feet elevation, is a hard place to be old, but my daughter is here, so I'm here.

She's good enough to listen and watch me demonstrate as my middle finger just silently slips off of my thumb. But she doesn't get it. "Why does it matter, Dad? Do you need to snap your fingers?"

Of course I don't need to snap my fingers. It's not about that. It's about one more thing that has been taken away from me, one more thing I can't do, that will one day soon lead to me being unable to do something I'll need to do to stay alive.

But that is too hard to explain, especially with the paste of my lunch clogging my mouth, so I say, "I can't snap." I give her the *look*, trying to convey it that way.

She offers me a small smile and nods her head, her pale green eyes looking sad. "I get it, Dad. I can't run anymore, my knees just won't take it."

Well, that's something, but she still doesn't get it. At almost fifty she is aware that her body is starting to rebel against her, but in your seventies it's a different story. The rebellion is over, you've lost, and you await your execution.

"It's just a little thing," she continues, taking another bite of her food and pretending she likes it. "At least you're still alive."

I sigh and nod. I have to at least appear to agree with her on that. She'd freak out if she got a whiff of what I'm really thinking.

"At least I'm alive," I mumble in agreement.

<hr>

My best friend here at the Home is Lenny Armbruster. He's short, squat, and round with a blunt, gravelly voice and a sharp sense of humor.

After my daughter left—having assuaged her guilt for the week and visited her old man—we did our usual debrief. We have found it important to discuss our family visits with each other, looking for any coming disasters. And no, this isn't paranoid. The older you get the more your family takes away from you. It's not a matter of if, but when.

I sit on the bed in his small rectangular room—single-sized bed, closet, bathroom with a shower, grey-ish carpet, and a window looking out onto the parking lot. Lenny sits in his recliner.

We pick the conversation apart and don't find anything of note. Since it's 11:30, we decide to head down to the dining hall for lunch.

"I can't snap anymore," I tell him as I grab my cane. He gets his walker, and we slowly get our bodies moving.

Lenny snorts, sounding kind of like a horse, and says, "That ain't nothing, Carl. I need a goddamn presidential decree to take a piss!"

WE'VE STILL GOT OUR MINDS, LENNY AND ME, WHICH IS more than I can say for most of the folks in this hellhole. They shuffle around (well, we all do that) like they're on autopilot or something. Up in the morning, get into the shower; down to breakfast; after breakfast off to an activity; lunch; another activity; dinner; the tube, and then bed. Interspersed are the meds and the checks from the caregivers.

And we do have minds, Lenny and I. He used to be a brain surgeon—no kidding—and I was an electrical engineer.

Lenny and I are in the dining room drinking too much coffee. Frankly, at this age, I think we would both enjoy something more potent than caffeine, but we just don't have the energy to go out and find it.

Where was I? Oh, yeah, we've still got our minds, Lenny and me, but just like the rest of our bodies there is some calcification going on. It takes longer to think things through, and a lot longer to say them.

But we're at the same speed, so neither one of us minds how long it takes.

"Carl, my friend," he says. "Helium is the answer." His

faded blue eyes are glassy but intense. "We can tell them we want to throw a party."

He's referring to a reportedly painless method of suicide. If you cover your head in a bag and breathe helium you will suffocate, but it feels like you're breathing so your body doesn't freak out. It goes along quiet like. We've talked about this at least a hundred times.

It's like young people talking about their life after marriage, or middle-aged people talking about their life after retirement—we talk about how to escape the sinking Titanic of our bodies.

"But, what dreams may come?" I ask, feeling not the least bit self-conscious about quoting Shakespeare.

Lenny rubs his wrinkled face and says, "They're gonna come anyway, my friend."

I nod and sip my coffee. It's bitter and cheap, but at least it doesn't taste like paste. Since I've gone through the effort to put the cup to my lips, I inhale the scent as deeply as I can. This is what I live for: the smell of coffee and yammering with Lenny.

———

ONE PILL FOR MY HIGH BLOOD PRESSURE, ONE FOR MY HIGH cholesterol, another for my poor thyroid, one so I can poop, another to deal with the side effects of one of the others, and a huge multivitamin.

I smile at Ana—she's one of the better ones. She's got bleached-blonde hair and brown eyes with a smile worth coaxing out. She's recently divorced, the bum roughed her up. I could kill him for it. She's raising her boy, Alex, on her own, going to nursing school, and working at the Home. She's in her early thirties and has got dark circles under her eyes that never go away.

I take one pill at a time with a big swallow of water. I'm determined not to choke to death—that is not the way I want to go. And at this point in the game such precautions are very important.

"How's Alex?" I ask after the cholesterol pill.

A smile plays briefly on her lips. It's the telltale what-she-lives-for smile. Something few of us here at the Home have. "He's good," she says. "Just started second grade."

I nod and keep taking pills, searching my old brain for a joke I haven't told her before.

"How many software engineers does it take to screw in a light bulb?" I ask.

Her brow furrows and then relaxes. I marvel at how the wrinkles disappear so quickly, her young skin still elastic. "I have no idea, Carl, how many?"

"None! They won't do it, it's a hardware problem."

She rewards me with a real smile and a small laugh. I pop my last pill, that damn huge multi, and swallow it down. If it's going to kill me, I want the last thing I see to be Ana's smile.

Have you ever seen piranhas feed? Like on National Geographic? Well that's what it's like when the bus from the Home lets us out at the Dollar Store, except in really slow motion. All these slow moving, white haired, on-their-last-leg seniors move in clutching their wallets or purses looking to load up on really cheap junk. Everything's a dollar. Makes it easy, don't even need to put your glasses on to see the prices.

Normally I would go in and watch the feeding frenzy, but Lenny and I are on a mission. He heads into the store in search of some duct tape and some large plastic bags. I have volunteered to take a hike in search of helium for our exit plan. It only makes sense—I can manage okay with a cane still but Lenny needs a walker.

I turn away from the Dollar Store and peer across the street to the strip mall. There's a PetSmart, a grocery store, a laundromat, a fancy-dancy clothing store, a cheap-ass clothing store, a Bed Bath and Beyond and...

I curse and bang my cane on the ground. There used to be a Party Store where the Bed Bath and Beyond is. I was going to make the hike (and believe me, crossing the street and walking across the large, busy parking lot all uphill would be kind of like climbing Everest at this point) and scope out how to get the helium.

Now that I think of it, the Party Store has been gone for years, but in my old brain it is still there.

I turn back, but don't have the heart to enjoy the feeding frenzy in the Dollar Store, so I wander into the little pet store. It's just a little mom and pop kind of a place that somehow survives with a PetSmart across the street.

There's a young man behind the counter. He's got a practiced slouch and a thick black beard. "How can I help you?" he asks.

I see a white puppy, all fur and skin and baby fat, in a cage. "I need a couple of tanks of helium," I tell him. I'm caught in this weird place between my disappointment about the Party Store being gone and my attraction towards the puppy, and I find myself telling the truth. I tap out a little rhythm with my hands on the counter—*bud-a-bump-bump*—to punctuate what I told him. Like the drummer would do when Johnny Carson told a good joke.

"Helium?" he asks, coming from behind the counter and walking to the cage. I shuffle over after him. He lifts the puppy out and holds it. "What for?" He probably figures I don't know what kind of store I'm in.

As my hand caresses the softness, I feel a pang of jealousy for the pup. So young, so much potential, so soft, so flexible. I look up at the young man, my eyes locking on his brown. I'm in an ornery mood and want to see his reaction. "Me and my best friend want to use it to kill ourselves."

He blinks twice, but his eyes don't look away. He bites his lower lip and nods. "You'll need a big bag, some tape, and some valving to join the tanks up, too."

My hand freezes on the little white pup, whose soft tongue is licking my finger. How the hell does this kid know about this stuff?

"You sure you up for this?" he asks. "Will you be able to follow through?"

I shrug. "Only a fool would think they know the answer to that question."

He nods and smiles, like I passed some test or something. "Come back and see me next week. Bring your friend. We'll talk more." He takes the puppy and sets it back in the cage. He turns his back to me and walks through a door into the supply room.

I stand there still feeling the soft puppy fur wondering who the hell that guy is.

I POKE AT THE READING GLASSES WITH MY OVERLY LONG thumbnail, trying to scrape the little plastic sticker off. I can't get it.

I notice that my fingernails need to be clipped. I can't do that myself either, and I'll be damned if I'm going to remind anyone at the Home that they need clipping. It's too damn humiliating.

The glasses have a little piece of plastic on it that says "3.0." They are just cheap readers from the Dollar Store. I should have prescription glasses, but I keep losing them, so I buy these and they do well enough. The sticker is vexing me today because I finally noticed it there on my newest pair. I've been wearing them for a week. No one told me. No one offered to remove the damn thing. I've got my next oldest pair on, which is why I can see the sticker.

I've got my right hand holding the glasses down on the little laminate desk in my room, while I try to remove it with the nail on my left hand thumb.

I've gotten the edge up a couple of times, but that's it. I want to scream at the frustration of it, but I know they'll just give me a pill to calm me down. So I swallow it and keep stabbing at the little piece of plastic, silently cursing it.

Seems like this shouldn't be a big deal, right? Why don't I just go ask someone to do it for me? That's not the point. I wasn't always this way. I used to have a life. I used to run a small company. I used to get things done. I used to matter.

I'm late for breakfast, my stomach grumbling. I worry that someone will come and check on me before I get this done. I'm an engineer, for Christ's sake. I used to solve problems every single day. Nasty, difficult problems.

I look around my little room. A tiny bed, my little desk stacked with things I mean to read, but haven't gotten to. A small fridge and a sink. A few pictures on the wall, my late wife, my daughter, my grandson. I rip open the drawer to the desk, searching for what, I don't know. I spot a little box of stick matches. That will do.

I chuckle—that kind of thing is contraband around here. They don't want the old folks having the ability to burn the place down.

I slide it open and stare. How to get one of those tiny matches out with my terrible hands. It's a similar problem to the one I already have. I don't have time for elegant, so I spill out a bunch on the table and close the matchbox up.

After sliding one of the matches to the edge of the desk I manage to get it between my thumb and forefinger. I then hold down the matchbox with my left hand and pull the match head against the rough stripe of the striking plate.

Nothing happens. I need more pressure and more speed. I am focused now, my whole world just trying to light a damn match. I try again and get the tiniest puff of smoke. I discard that match and switch to another and give it a couple of strokes. A little smoke, no fire, but I smell sulfur.

I do another match, and another, and another. My brow is beaded with sweat when I finally get a match lit. When the flame flares up all yellow with that halo of blue at the base, I feel so damn proud. With my crap hands I did something.

The smile fades from my face when I realize I don't remember why I wanted to light the match so much. My eyes search my desk and I see the readers with the damn sticker. I take the glasses in my left hand and hold them about an inch above the flame. The glass starts to darken and the damn plastic that says "3.0" puckers.

I blow the match out and easily scrape off the little piece of plastic. My glasses are stained with black, but that is a problem I can deal with.

I get my cane and head down to breakfast, a shit-eating grin on my face. It's my best day in months. I did something.

My old heart is thumping against my ribcage, like some prisoner trying to escape his cell. I can't tell you how long it's been since I felt like that. I literally can't tell you because it's been years. The horde has descended on the Dollar Store and Lenny and I are standing in front of the pet store. The same store where the bearded young man offered to help us get our helium rig. The gear we need to exit this life on our own terms.

"He really offered to help?" Lenny asks, licking his lips,

looking up at me. Lenny is the Jeff to my Mutt. And if you don't know who Mutt and Jeff are, go look it up. Suffice it to say that I am the tall and skinny one and Lenny is built like a fireplug.

"He did," I answer. My heart is still beating like crazy and it's not comfortable, but I like it. I feel more alive than I usually do, so I let the moment draw out. "My heart..." I mutter.

"Yeah," Lenny answers, his hand going to his chest. He must feel it too. "They won't be in there forever," he adds, referring to the feeding horde next door.

We shuffle our way into the store and my heart gives one more loud thump against my ribcage before resuming a more stately rhythm. The guy I talked to isn't there. Instead a sour-looking middle-aged woman stands behind the counter looking bored. She has poorly dyed red hair with about an inch of black and grey roots showing.

Lenny whispers something to me, but I ignore him and walk up to her. She looks me over and quickly files me in the "annoying senior" bin, knowing I'm not here to spend money. "Excuse me, ma'am," I say, flashing her what is left of my charming smile. "There was a young man working here last week. Can you tell me when he'll be back?"

Her eyes are a faded brown that belong more in a seventy-year-old than a fifty-year-old. She levels that washed out gaze at me and narrows her eyes. "He doesn't work here anymore," she says. Her eyes linger on me for a moment more before sliding off to the one other customer in the shop. She moves from behind the counter towards the customer. It is clear she has dismissed me.

I look around the small store. Aisles of pet food. Cages with puppies and kittens. A couple aquariums with fish, and one with a snake in it. A linoleum floor some shade of grey, scratched and worn. A bulletin board at the back of the shop near the store-room door.

I walk back there making a show of using my cane and how hard it is to move around. The lady glances at me and I smile at her. I want to make it clear that I won't be leaving quickly. I feel Lenny follow me, but he doesn't say anything.

The little bulletin board is overflowing with flyers, as if no one ever removes them, just adds them. It's a throwback, just like this store. The Internet has taken over this function, and big box retailers have taken over for stores like this. There are the lost pet ads, someone starting a rock band and looking for a drummer, and on and on. I'm about to turn back—our ride will be leaving soon—when I hear Lenny's breath catch. I look and he's pointing at the flyer for the rock band.

Wanted: A drummer (tall and handsome) and a bass player (short and stout) for the band Helios. We play old-time rock. We plan to burn out, not fade away.

At the bottom is a phone number.

"Helios," Lenny hisses. "Helium." I nod and yank the flyer off of the board, my palms sweating, my mouth tasting like ash. There's something weird about the flyer. It doesn't have the row of all the phone numbers on the bottom for you to rip off, only the one. It asks for a short person and a tall one. I hadn't told the young man anything about Lenny.

Lenny and I quickly walk out and into the little bus for the Home. I have that flyer clutched in my hand, my heart banging against my ribs the whole way back.

* * *

My father had a theory about the human biological platform (that's what he called it—he took just enough biology in his training to be a chemist to be dangerous). He said that the human body is designed to live for sixty years, at the best. Just enough time to grow up, procreate, gain a little wisdom, and then die.

So once you go past that sixty-year boundary, things just start to break down. If it's not something quick like cancer, it's something slow like dementia. If it's not that, it's the slow crippling force of arthritis and the mental blunting of senility. Your warranty has expired, something is going to get you, no way out of it.

My father, he was such the optimist. He died at sixty-three in a head-on collision—lucky bastard.

These thoughts flit through my mind for the millionth time as I sip bad coffee and watch the breakfast crowd shuffle and wheel in. The room smells like cheap syrup and the morning light is shining in through the big south-facing windows. I sit at a table that is rather affectionately called the village idiots. I know, that doesn't sound affectionate, but we all treat those with dementia well—we that don't have it are just so damn glad. The ones with serious memory issues had magically started eating together. I think since they *all* have trouble remembering and cogitating, it's easier on them to be together. No one expected them to remember what they had been talking about at the last meal.

Lenny and I have taken to eating there some. We can talk about our plans without a real worry about the word getting out. It's not like we come out and say what we are doing, but we can talk more openly around the demented.

My stomach growls. I haven't started eating. I sit there waiting for Lenny. He's late, real late... too late.

I down the bitter dregs of my coffee and leverage myself up with my cane. I make my way to the elevator, up to the third floor, down the hall, and stop in my tracks. In front of Lenny's room stands a crowd. Not just the usual canes and walkers, but caregivers and an administrator.

I quicken my pace, moving faster than I have all year, my cane thumping down with each step, my heart beating loudly. I search the crowd hoping to see a paramedic or a nurse. But I don't. Only residents and staff. That can only mean one thing. I feel tears sting my eyes and quicken my pace further.

Lenny. Short, round Lenny. My partner in crime. My friend.

As I approach his room, my fast pace gets the best of me, my right foot catching my cane, knocking it out of my hand. I go down, my old body colliding with the floor, a sharp cracking sound startling me as my head connects.

I lie there unable to move, smelling the musty, chemically carpet, tasting fear, my tears flowing freely.

I know Lenny is dead. Nothing else explains the crowd and its makeup.

I hear shouts and people talking, but the darkness claims me. As it rushes in, cold and empty, I pray that it takes me, that I won't wake up, that I will leave this world with my friend Lenny.

CHILDREN ARE ALL A DISAPPOINTMENT AND THEY ARE ALL a joy too. Two sides of the same coin. They can't, or rather shouldn't, be everything you want them to be, so there is always some disappointment. And the joy? Well, if you look for it, it's there. From the vague, like somehow you participated in the miracle of life, to the specific, like how my daughter often indulges my addiction to red hots.

I sat in my hospital bed chewing one slowly, letting the sweet cinnamon flavor burn my mouth. She has the oh-so-worried look on her tired face. It's a look, frankly, that puzzles me. Eyes all focused, brow a bit furrowed, lips turned down. Doesn't she know I'm going to die one of these days? And "one of these days" keeps getting closer and closer. I don't know, maybe my pending departure reminds her too much of her own mortality. At her age, fifty, one does become more in touch with the reality of it.

"So, spit it out, honey," I say after I swallow the red hot and pop another one in. I eat them like I did when I was a kid, slowly. I don't get them very often, so I let them last. Besides, they help distract me from the smell of cleaning fluid and death that permeates the hospital.

She blinks, her face relaxing a bit, her eyes briefly meeting mine before looking into her lap.

"I'm just worried about you, Dad."

"Well, just stop that, honey. I'm okay."

She meets my eyes again and her need hits me like a slap on the face. "You promise."

I nod and say, "I promise." I half mean it. On the one hand, I'm not sure I can execute the helium exit plan without Lenny, but then again, I'm not at all thrilled about letting nature take its course—nature being as cruel as it is.

LENNY'S FAMILY DID A NICE MEMORIAL SERVICE, I AM SURE, but I didn't go. The thought of it made me want to puke, and besides, it's not like I got an invitation. His whole family knows me, but not one thought to invite me. Sure, Lenny and I had only been tight for a year, but we had been "tight." Like two eight-year-old neighbor kids banging around the neighborhood trying to find the right mix of trouble to get into.

And I guess I see it. I remind them of the end of his life. Probably not what they want to think about.

The Home does its little memorial, though. They bring in a rabbi—not that Lenny was a practicing Jew or anything—and I do the eulogy.

My daughter comes by early, dressed in a black skirt and

blouse. She looks nice, the black helps hide the extra pounds she keeps putting on. She ties my tie and makes sure my hair isn't flying all over the place. She, at least, understands what Lenny meant to me.

Ana comes by too and helps fuss over me. She's not even on shift. I feel so important. I feel so touched.

"Thank you, ladies," I say to them both with a little bow of my head. My eyes are all misted up and their eyes are in the same state.

From my recliner, I start to stand, attempting to leverage myself up with my cane, but my hands shake and I don't get very far.

"Do you want a wheelchair?" Ana asks, her lips turned down.

I shake my head. "I just need a moment alone. Can you two wait for me outside?"

I see my daughter look at Ana who gives her a tiny nod of her head. Can the old man be trusted to know what he is capable of, is the question passing between them. My eyes mist up even further when Ana's nod says to trust me.

After they go, I settle all the way into my big recliner until I am nestled back into the indentation my body has made into it. I've had this thing for ten years, long before I came to the Home. It's comforting.

I close my eyes and take a slow deep breath. I pretend that Lenny is there standing beside me. What would he say? "Get off your fat ass, you old geezer," flits through my mind and I chuckle.

"I'm mad at you, Lenny," I whisper.

"One of us had to go first," he whispers back in my mind.

"That wasn't the plan," I say out loud, using my anger to lever myself up and launch myself towards the door. "Together," I whisper, "we were going to hook up the helium and go together. I'm sick of everyone going before me. First Alice and now you."

My wife Alice died five years ago from cancer. Everyone asks me what variety, which you too might be wondering. I always look at them and say, "Does it matter?" The details of that story have no relevance now. Dead is dead and cancer is a bitch.

I make it out the door, and while the women look at me closely, they let me make my way down to the dining room under my own power. The suit feels strange and my hand shakes a bit, but I make it.

THE WEEKS AFTER LENNY DIES ARE REAL HARD. I FEEL THIS emptiness that only comes when someone that is a part of your day-to-day routine is gone. I keep thinking I am forgetting to do something. Everything feels wrong. I am depressed.

My daughter starts visiting twice a week instead of once. Ana comes around more and lingers longer than she needs to. But I barely notice. I shuffle through my routine, doing my best to bear the loss of Lenny.

I am no good at it.

It was worse when Alice died, but I was younger then, more capable of handling it. I start to doubt that I can survive here without Lenny. He made the place bearable. He gave me a reason to get up in the morning.

"You've got to figure this out, Carl," Ana says, the frown on her face deep. I look away, no thought of even trying to make her smile. She's got my evening meds. I don't want them. One to keep my cholesterol down, one to take the edge off the arthritis, one for my thyroid, one to keep my bowels moving, blah, blah, blah...

Is this my life? Taking pills to extend an existence I don't want anymore?

I take the handful of pills and pop them all in my mouth. They rattle around there, all bitter and biting. I take the water and swallow them down in one gulp. Ana looks at me, one eyebrow raised. She knows how I fear choking and always take the damn pills one at a time.

I feel an anger rising up in me like a volcano that's been quiet for too long. I wait until Ana has left my little room before I let it out. No need to scare the girl.

After she is gone I get up out of my recliner and start pacing, my cane thumping on the thin beige carpet. What have I got to live for? Shouldn't there be something to life? Without Lenny, how the hell am I to survive this damn place?

This is what passes for cardio for me, and I feel my breath coming quickly, my face flushing with blood. I pace back and forth in the small confines of my room. It's not much, but it's the only space here that is mine.

My path becomes a little erratic and I bump into my desk, hard. I curse and whack the cheap laminate and particle board with my cane. There is a satisfying thump, so I hit it again, and again.

As I do, the tears finally start to flow. I got all misty for Lenny's memorial, but I didn't cry. I couldn't. But now, the tears run down my cheeks, hot and salty.

There are neat stacks of papers on the desk and a cup with pencils and pens. I take my cane and sweep them all off and watch as they scatter and fall to the floor. The papers twisting in the air, the pencils spinning and skittering, the chaos that I so hate somehow comforting.

I stand there panting from the exertion, looking at it all. Junk mail, endless paperwork from Medicare, a letter from the

Veterans of Foreign Wars, cards from my birthday a month back, and the one odd flyer.

Wanted: A drummer (tall and handsome) and a bass player (short and stout) for the band Helios. We play old-time rock. We plan to burn out, not fade away.

An ungraceful sob escapes my chest as I reach for the flyer. I clutch it and cry. I cry for Lenny, my friend gone. I cry for Alice and the years fighting the cancer that eventually took her. I cry for all that I have lost: my strength, my independence, my usefulness, my life.

I weep until I can't anymore and then I lie on the mess of papers on the floor and sleep.

I WAKE UP, MY MOUTH TASTING LIKE CARDBOARD, MY tongue dry as sandpaper. It's dark and I try to blink, but my eyes are crusted up and kind of glued shut. My hip and shoulder hurt where I've been lying on the hard floor and papers, not something a seventy-eight-year-old body ought to do. I groan and roll over, smelling the acrid smell of urine. Great, I pissed myself.

I think about what to do. If I am found in this state, it will mean nothing good for me. They'll call my daughter, they may move me to skilled nursing. I don't want that. But it's dark and I could hurt myself getting up. I have one of those life-line buttons hanging around my neck. I think about pushing it despite the consequences but decide not to.

I slowly lever myself to a sitting position and look around. I see the blue glow of my clock. It's 4:00 a.m. I take a few deep breaths trying to move my aching shoulder enough for it to ease up. Okay, clock is at the back of the room by the bed, the light switch is at the other end of the room. I can do this.

I feel around and find my cane and use it to stand up. I hear the crunch of papers under my feet. I use the cane kind of like one of those sticks blind people carry and slowly move myself over to the door and turn on the light switch.

I squint my eyes against the painful light and then survey the damage. Papers, magazines, and mail everywhere. Pencils strewn about, some scratches on the desk where I whacked it with my cane.

I take a deep breath and let it out slowly. They won't bring my meds until eight. I have four hours to clean myself and this mess up.

I am about to get to work when I notice that damn flyer for a drummer and a bassist lying in plain view. It must have slipped out of my hand as I slept. But there it is again, and I can't ignore it. Lenny may be gone, but maybe that doesn't mean I can't carry out our helium exit plan. I slowly bend over, pick up the paper, and put it in a drawer, resolving to call the number. I then slowly start to put my room back in order.

———

When I call the phone number on the Helios flyer no one answers, but a message plays in the voice of that young man:

Looking for the band Helios? Well, you've found 'em, Pops. We still need a drummer so come on down to practice, okay?

It then gives an address and some dates and times.

I don't go right away. I'm sore from sleeping on the floor and the huge effort it took to clean my room up. I go about my day in a haze. Everyone gives me space, thinking it's all about Lenny. And it kind of is, but that isn't all of it.

After lunch the next day I call for the Old Farts Bus Line (they have some fancy name for it, but that is what it basically is

—transportation for the old and otherwise diminished) and have them drop me off at the mall.

No, the band doesn't practice at the mall, but there are some new apartments about half a mile away, and I'm keeping up appearances. I don't want anyone wondering what I am doing. So after the bus is gone and out of sight, I begin my hike.

Two thousand six hundred forty feet. Eight hundred eighty yards. Half a mile. Not far, right? Well, try it with a cane and a bad back and arthritis and almost eight decades on your old bones. A hike it is. I have my smartphone with me and have the address programmed in. It somehow helps to look at my progress that way. And yes, even though I am as old as the hills, I can use a smartphone. I was an engineer, remember? My issue isn't understanding how to use it but manual dexterity.

The Flagstaff Mall is in a mostly retail area—the presence of the apartments is a bit odd. I make my slow trudge and end up in front of one of them. I raise my hand to ring the doorbell and see that it is shaking. From the unusual exertion? Yes, but also from what I am considering doing.

I am not going to lecture you on the pros and cons of assisted suicide. I will say if you are one of those that don't think it's ever valid, get your head out of your ass, please. You'll be able to breathe better that way. And I won't make my own case, but you can judge things as you like from the story I present to you here.

The door opens and the bearded young man from the pet store is here. He smiles widely, and I am struck by how very white and even his teeth are.

"Right on time, Carl," he says. "The boys are all back in the living room. Come on."

He ushers me through the house, handing me a bottle of Gatorade. He also walks at my pace—an old, tired man who has just been on the longest walk he's been on in months—which is to say, very slowly. He doesn't look awkward, like he is holding back for me. His slow pace looks perfectly natural, perfectly at ease. As we take the walk I feel tension melting and breathe deeply, feeling something I haven't felt in a while—peace.

In the living room are two other old men. One has a bass guitar, the other looks like lead guitar, and there is a drum kit set up behind them. Emblazoned on the bass drum is a fiery logo that says "Helios."

I stand there blinking while my escort makes introductions, but I don't hear them. I don't know what I expected, but it isn't this. I thought maybe it would be some kind of old person's euthanasia group, not a real band. I look at the young man, he's smiling with those beautiful teeth, and I smell roses. The other two guys are smiling too. Not like they just met me for the first time, but like this is some long overdue reunion. The smiles are big and genuine. As if they've been waiting for me.

My hand goes weak and my cane falls softly to the thick carpet. I can't hear anything now, although I see mouths moving and concern blossoming on their faces. My vision waivers and my knees buckle. The last thing I am aware of is strong hands catching me and the scent of roses.

My last thought is: *Oh shit! I'm dying.*

How can you want to die and then be afraid when you think it's happening? Simple. All it takes is being human. We are often conflicted. And besides, there is a big difference between an intellectual concept and the experience of that concept.

But I'm not dying. I'm just old and dehydrated and have been through a lot.

I wake to the scent of roses and hear soft talking. I feel a bed under me and see a white ceiling above.

"There you are," the young man says.

"You... you smell like roses," I tell him. He does, and it is not unpleasant, but it is a bit odd.

He nods. "Yeah, it's my girlfriend's perfume. She used a bit much this morning before she left."

I nod back to him, glad to be talking about something mundane. Not something life or death.

"You feeling better?" he asks.

"I think so. But..." His brown eyes don't waver but stay locked with mine. They look like they have this unfathomable depth behind them, like he knows what I am going through. Like I don't have to hide from him. Like I can trust him.

"I know," he says with a sigh. "You weren't expecting a real band. What did you think? I'd have the tanks set up ready to send you on your way?" He ends with a smile showing off his perfect teeth again.

"I don't know... I..."

"Listen, Carl, I know you have questions. And we'll get to them. But for now, how about I take you out to meet the boys. They're worried about you. After that, maybe you can bang on the drums for us a bit."

I blink a few times, like I am thinking this situation will change if I just close my eyes and open them again. But it doesn't. I'm still staring into the face of the young man with a beard.

"I don't even know your name," I say.

"My name is Angelo."

I couldn't speak when Angelo first told me his name. I mean, how dumb did I have to be to not know Angelo means Angel. That this guy seemed to know stuff. That he seemed to be going out of his way to interact with me. That he knew things about me, like my name. I had never told him my name.

"Carl," he began when we made it back into the living room. "On bass, this is Herb." Herb extends his hand to me and we shake. He has good hands—no oak knots for knuckles—covered in age spots. He's short, a little taller than Lenny, with a wisp of white hair around his bald head. He looks familiar and I soon find out that he lives at the Home too. I feel a stab of grief, wondering whether Angelo had wanted Lenny for the bass player with that flyer.

"Nice to meet you, Herb," I say after the shake.

"Yeah, thanks. Welcome aboard, we really need a drummer."

I am about to object, but Angelo is introducing the guitarist. "On lead guitar, this is Brian. At sixty-nine, he's the baby of the group."

Brian is shorter than me but taller than Herb. He's got a ruddy complexion and a few strands of brown mingling with his thick grey hair. We shake hands and exchange a few words about the weather.

"Shall we get down to it?" Herb asks. He looks at me and adds, "Can you do a 4/4 beat for us? We don't get too fancy with the music."

"I... What?" I mumble as Angelo guides me to the drum kit and onto the stool. It's been almost sixty years since I did any drumming. It was a brief teenage dream to be a rock star.

Before I know it, drumsticks are in my hands, and I see Angelo smiling at me. It's a look I am not used to. It's a look that says, *I believe in you. You can do this.* At this stage of the journey, I haven't experienced that in a long, long time. Everyone expects my life to get smaller, my capabilities to diminish. No one has encouraged me to try something new (or very old, in this case) in decades.

"But, my hands," I say. "They barely work. They hurt all the time. I... I can't snap anymore."

Angelo listens carefully to me and nods. I see tears form in his eyes. "I know, Carl. I know it's not going to be easy, that there will be some pain. But I promise you this. If you do it, it will be worth it, and it will get easier."

Herb and Brian are watching, but it doesn't make me feel self-conscious. These guys know what I am talking about.

"Can't snap," Herb says. "Oh, that's a bitch. You're a rhythm guy, for Christ's sake. You gotta be able to snap."

I swear I almost lost it right there. I am not used to being related to. To being understood.

"Just try, Carl. Will you?" Brian says. "We need you."

I look up and meet first Brian's eyes and then Herb's. They need me? No one has said they needed me since my wife died. Lenny, he needed me, just like I needed him, but he's gone. But here are two strangers and this young man that smells like roses telling me that I'm needed, that they understand what I am going through.

I have such doubts. A sea of them that I could just drown in. For once I am not thinking of death by helium. I am worried that I can't do what these guys need. But, I'll be damned if I'm not going to try.

"Okay," I say, barely above a whisper, but Angelo steps back and Herb and Brian put their hands on their guitars.

I get my right foot on the pedal for the bass drum and start the beat. Herb joins in, matching the rhythm on the bass, a smile spreading on his lips, and he nods at me. It's not much. A three-year-old could do it, but it's something. It feels good.

I fiddle with the sticks, working out a loose grip that my hands will support and start on it. The bass drum on beats one and three, the snare on beats two and four. I don't even fool with the hi-hat or the toms. I just work on keeping a beat. One... two... three... four...

Herb starts working the bass line, playing around the beat I've laid down, adding texture and variation.

Brian starts riffing on his guitar in the key of C. Nothing I recognize, but unmistakable rock chords.

My hands, they hurt a lot. But I don't give a shit. I have a big grin on my face and keep the rhythm going. After a few minutes, Herb gives me a nod and I finish it up with a few bangs on the toms and some simple cymbal work.

When it's over Angelo is clapping and I'm smiling so wide I'm afraid my face will break.

"You seem happy today," Ana says as she delivers my morning meds. She looks beat, her face drawn and tired.

"Indeed, my dear. I've got band practice today."

She stops, cocks her head and looks at me. I know that look, it's the "Is he still all there" look. I hate seeing that look on her face, but I don't let it get me down.

"A rock and roll band," I add. "I'm the drummer."

"That's great, Carl," she says, but I can tell she doesn't believe me. And I can't really blame her. I hardly believe it myself. A seventy-eight-year-old arthritic man living at the Home in a rock and roll band. Yeah, I get how it's hard to believe.

As she's leaving I say, "Ana. We'll be doing a gig sometime next month. Will you come?"

She turns and smiles. "Sure, Carl. Sure."

So here is what a typical practice day is like for our little geriatric trio. I get up a little early and take a shower. I have to arrange it the night before so the caregiver can show up at my room on time. I'm not to the stage where I can't take a shower alone, but I am at the stage where someone needs to be in the room because I'm a fall risk. I hate it, I do, but not nearly as much as I'm going to hate it when I can't shower myself.

After the shower, I get down and have breakfast with the first round of eaters. I usually sit with the village idiots. Since starting in the band, I like sitting with them even more. Somehow I don't mind hearing the same stories over and over or answering the same questions. Besides, it's fun to tell them I'm in a band and see their reactions fresh.

After breakfast, I go back upstairs and get in my recliner and close my eyes. I set an alarm on my iPad (the controls are big enough for me to work pretty well) in case I fall asleep. Practice day is a big deal. I want to go with all the energy I can muster.

At 10:15 I go down to the lobby of the Home and sign out. They've got to know where I am twenty-four-seven. I then go outside and sit on the bench in front of the curved driveway. Herb usually shows up a few minutes later. At 10:30 Brian shows up in his ancient Ford Taurus and picks us up. He's the young one, he still drives, although not very fast. We make our way across town to Angelo's house.

When we get there, Angelo's got the coffee ready, and we chat about mundane things until about 11:00. We practice for around two hours and then have some sandwiches for lunch.

I get back to the Home around 2:00 p.m. I'm exhausted and go to my room and nap until dinner.

We practice Monday, Wednesday, and Friday. I miss Lenny bad and wish he'd gotten to be a part of this, because it's just heaven. Well, not all the time. Just like everything in life, sometimes it's horrible.

In our second week of practice I lose it. This is not some gentlemanly fit or mild disturbance—this is a full-on nuclear meltdown.

My hands won't obey me. I keep dropping the sticks. Angelo comes and picks them up for me each time because it would take too damn long for me to get them myself. He seems apologetic each time he returns them, so I think he gets it. I want to pick up the stick myself, but I understand the need. But more than that I just want my hands to work.

Before the band, I'd have days like this, but it really didn't matter. I would just wait it out knowing, of course, that one day all my days would be bad hand days.

But now, I'm relying on my hands, my bandmates are relying on my hands. The sixth time I drop the sticks is when I melt down. If I had been young, I would have done something stupid like putting my foot through one of the drums, but being a septuagenarian that isn't possible. So at first I just sit there unmoving, each joint on fire with pain. And then I literally get tunnel vision, I'm so mad. I then get up and walk out of the house without my cane cursing all the way.

Maybe you are old enough to understand this, maybe not, but at my age the daily betrayal of your body is a significant challenge. It is something you can't avoid, something you can't think your way out of, something unrelenting and unforgiving.

As I practiced with the band, my hands did get better. It never got easy, but it got easier. I began to believe I could do it. I began to hope that I could still do something with the tail end of my life. And then...

Angelo finds me leaning against a lamppost about fifty yards from the house. The adrenaline of my anger could no longer compensate for the lack of a cane, and my back hurt like hell.

"Hey, Carl," he says, like we are running into each other at the store or something.

I study his face. He's got a swarthy complexion like he could be Italian or Greek or Middle Eastern. His face is round and his brown eyes kind. His greeting is casual, but he is blinking back tears, like he can feel the pain I am feeling. But he doesn't come grab me or try to save me from myself like almost everyone else would do. He just stands there at the ready.

"It hurts a lot today," I say with a grin I hope is wry.

"Yeah, life is kind of like that, Carl. It hurts, sometimes more than others. What you gotta decide is if what you are doing is worth the pain."

I bite my lip and nod. He's got a point, but sometimes the pain gets so bad you don't really have a choice. I don't tell him that, but I think he knows it.

I wave him over and put my arm around his shoulder and he helps me hobble back towards the house.

"Are you an angel?" I ask.

He laughs, "No, I am not. I'm a man, just like you."

"Well, you act like an angel. You're so goddamn young and yet you seem to understand what it is to be so old."

I feel him shrug under my arm. "I've always been empathic, since I was a little kid."

"Well," I say, "if there are angels you ought to be one."

We make it back into the house and continue practicing. But the next time the sticks drop, I wave Angelo off and just keep the beat with the foot pedal and the bass drum. It ain't much, but it's all I've got. No one seems to mind.

Being in a band, being in Helios, changed me. I stop thinking about suicide and think a lot about drumming and singing instead. I stop focusing on my past and what I have lost and start thinking about my future and where I am going.

I'm not in denial about my age and the few years I have left, I know there isn't much time. But, instead of waiting to die, I start living again.

My mind is focused on the band Helios, not the helium exit strategy.

This is a full-on miracle. I am happy quite a bit, my hands hurt less, and I walk just a little bit better. We have been practicing for two months and in that time my health has improved. That just hasn't happened in a long time.

"We're happy today," Ana says, handing me my pills.

I have gotten up early and am whistling as I putter around my little room. "Yup, it's gig day, my dear."

She knows all about Helios. I have gone on and on about it. She even knows it is gig day, I have told her many times in the last few weeks. She even knows where we are playing, but she is kind enough to indulge me. "Where are you guys playing?"

I smile and kiss her gently on the cheek. She flushes red and asks, "What was that for, Carl?"

"For being so kind to me, my dear," I say, and her blush deepens. "Because you know full well we are playing here this afternoon."

The whole place is abuzz about it. Three old guys playing in a band, two of whom live at the Home. It's like Angelo told us once, "It will be as if you are all eight-year-olds, people will go crazy. Just like kids, you don't have to be the best. Just the fact that you get up there and do it will be enough."

And he's right. There is supposed to be a crew here from the local news station to film and interview us. Old people in a band are almost as cute as kids in a band.

My morning is the best I have had in years until on my way down to breakfast my mind strays into difficult territory. I want to talk to Lenny. I want to tell him how excited I am about this. I want my friend. But I can't tell him I found something better than helium, I can't share with him how my old hands are actually working better most of the time, I can't...

I suddenly feel weak and old and like a fool. I stop in the hallway and lean heavily on my cane. One of the residents goes past me in her walker on her way to the village idiots' table. The hallway narrows and I am overwhelmed with the smell of bleach —something must have required serious cleaning in this part of the hallway. I'm such a stupid old fool. Death is coming for me, just like it came for Lenny. Hell, I might not even live for Helios's first gig. And while we can belt it out, we really aren't that good. We are some novelty that people will gawk and stare at.

I decide to go back to my room. I'm going to go in and lock the door. I take a deep breath and am about to turn myself around when I see Angelo. He's striding down the hallway with so much youth and energy that I look away.

"There you are," he says when he gets close. "We've been waiting for you."

Herb lives at the Home too, and I knew Angelo brought Brian over this morning so we could go over the set, help set the gear up, do a sound check. We're old and we know it takes us longer to do these things.

I don't answer. I turn around and ignore him.

"Okay," I hear him say as he comes up next to me, his hand soft on my shoulder. "It's okay, Carl."

I feel a flush of anger as my cheeks grow hot. The bastard is so empathetic he knows exactly what I am feeling. The anger quickly twists into shame. I stop and meet his eyes, "I am a goddamn old fool," I tell him.

"And that's what I like most about you," he replies.

"I can't do it," I say.

Right then, an old guy carting an oxygen tank walks by and says, "Can't wait for the concert," his voice is coming out in a thin wheeze.

I don't say anything to him, just stare at Angelo as I blink rapidly.

"Okay," he says. "Don't worry about it, we'll figure it out. The show must go on."

I nod, a cowardly sense of relief rushing through my body. I suddenly feel weak and start to go down, but Angelo's strong arms are around me and then I am in my room and on my bed.

Angelo is there sitting on the edge of the bed studying my face.

"What will you do?" I ask.

"Oh, I've got Garage Band on my Mac. I'll just hook it up to back the boys. It'll be okay." His face is a little pinched as he looks at me.

I can't believe he's not trying to talk me into it. Why the hell isn't he trying to talk me into it? Am I really that bad that the band is better off with a computer? I sigh and turn away from Angelo. I can't look at him anymore.

I feel him get up from the bed and hear him leave without another word.

I soon fall asleep.

Unlike me, Lenny wasn't always filled with doubt. He had this sense of self-assurance that I admired. I think it was about the brain surgeon thing—you've got to be confident if you're opening up people's skulls. He would make up his mind and do what he thought right with hardly a second thought. Me, I could take weeks on my second thoughts. If we had gotten the exit via helium plan put together it would have been Lenny that didn't have cold feet.

I wake up from my nap thinking about Lenny, about what he would have to say about me lying in my bed when there is a concert going on. I look at my clock, 1:30 p.m. The concert starts at two. I groan, disappointed that I haven't missed it yet, that there is still time to second guess my second guess.

I get up and pee and sit on my recliner staring at the door. I almost expect someone to come knocking, someone to try to talk me into going down and banging on the drums.

But the minutes tick by and no one comes. I feel a stab of pain that no one cares, and then a sharp sense of guilt that I am playing such a childish game. That I want someone to encourage me, to hold my hand, to make everything all right.

I rise up, feeling my heart thumping in my chest. Everything isn't all right. I'm an old man with a body that is falling apart who has given up almost everything. No, nothing about that is all right.

I grab my cane and head to the dining hall where the concert is happening. I want to yell at Angelo, to berate him for giving me hope, for setting me up. As my cane thumps on the floor rhythmically, what I am worried about comes into sharp relief. I don't want to make a fool of myself in front of my friends.

The last time I was in a band was over sixty years ago. I was sixteen and the drummer of the Space Junkers. We played mostly covers of hits from the early fifties. It was a four-piece high school band and we never played a gig. We just holed up in Jerry Benton's garage and practiced for a year. We never got up the courage to play in front of people. At first we practiced three times a week, and then a couple times a month, and then we all just conveniently forgot to practice.

And now I want to beat Angelo with my cane. Maybe he's not an angel, but a demon. First he gives me hope, and then he sneaks this performance up on me, something I couldn't do as a child, something I never really got over.

As I enter the dining room the smell of bad coffee and the stare of hundreds of eyes assault me. Our equipment, including the drum kit, is set up in one corner. Herb and Brian are putting their guitars on. I see Ana and she nods and smiles at me as if she expects something great. My daughter is sitting next to Ana and even my grandson is here.

I stand there blinking, my jaw slack as I take in the scene.

"There you are," Angelo says as he comes up and takes my arm, gently guiding me towards the drums.

"I... I don't know if I can do this," I say, my eyes fixed on the drums with the flaming Helios logo.

"I know," Angelo says, and I believe him. "But it's time, Carl. It's time for you to play. You know what to do."

Then I'm sitting on the stool behind the drums with the sticks in my hand. Our set list is taped to the floor where I can see it. Brian is looking at me, a nervous smile on his face. The room is quiet. It feels much bigger than it is. All eyes are on us and I just sit there blinking, wishing I could throw up.

My eyes find Angelo. He's off to the side, a smile wide and bright on his face. He gives me a thumbs-up and he starts nodding with the beat of our first song.

I look back to Brian, he and Herb are both looking at me now. The room is even quieter, like church, almost a holy silence.

I look down at my hands with their swollen knuckles loosely holding the drumsticks. I know how to do this. My friends need me. Angelo's talk about using the computer was his way of getting me motivated. I feel tears of gratitude flood my eyes. I have people depending on me. I have something worth doing. Who cares if I make a fool of myself? I'd be a bigger fool not to try.

I bring the sticks together and measure out the beat. "One... Two... Three... Four..."

I HAVE TO TELL YOU THAT NOTHING FEELS LIKE A LIVE performance. You hear the audience, you see them swaying, or clapping, or, the few agile enough, dancing. You feel them as they feel the music. It's a hell of a high, I'll tell you that right now.

Our set is pretty short. We are all ancient, after all, and we finish up with the Stones "(I Can't Get No) Satisfaction."

I feel the butterflies rioting anew in my belly as I start pounding out the beat. This is my song. I sing it. And yeah, the lyrics are pretty simple, the music is easy to play, but all eyes are on me.

As I start belting out the lyrics, I think of Lenny and me and our quest for helium. How unsatisfied we were with our lives. How it didn't really feel like living to us. How much my life has changed since I met Angelo. I feed all those emotions into the lyrics as I sing. I bang on the drums as hard as I can. I vent all the frustrations I have with my life getting smaller and smaller. My wife dying. Having my car taken away. Living at the Home. Not contributing. Being a nothing.

And when it's done, I'm exhausted. The crowd is clapping and cheering and making as much noise as they can (which is to say not as much noise as a younger crowd could make). I come out from behind my drum set, forgetting my cane, my legs shaky, but usable. I get between Herb and Brian and we put our arms around each other and bow.

It's only a little gig in the dining room of the Home. But it could have been Madison Square Garden for how I feel. When we come up from the bow I see the faces looking back at me. I see joy and excitement and some hope.

Angelo's beaming at us, tears on his cheeks, his hands on his heart. He's so happy.

That day, that wonderful day, we all thought we would have more time together than we did.

THAT IS WHAT I REMEMBER NOW FROM THAT FIRST concert. The hope. It took me three full days of feeling like crap to get my energy back after that concert, but we changed people that day. They looked at us and we gave them hope that they could actually have a life in their twilight years.

Angelo did this. He saved our lives, he gave us hope, something to do, and now we give other people hope.

We've been at this for about six months now. We are up to doing a gig a week and it only takes me a day to recover after we do one. We've toured old folks homes all over Arizona. Or at least we did.

Now, as I dictate this, our future is uncertain.

I swear that Angelo is an angel. A real live angel. He recruited us, directs us, drives us, does all the heavy lifting. He is spending his life giving us a life.

Or at least he did.

Angelo died last week. He was riding his bike when a van got too close to the bike lane he was in and clipped him with the side mirror. He was sent tumbling down a hill, his head connecting with a rock.

When Brian comes to my room and tells me, I think he's kidding. Angelo's an angel, how can he die?

I stand there, my mouth hanging open like one of the sad

sacks in the memory unit. I blink at Brian, his rumpled face sagging much more than usual.

"What? Dead?" The words echo in my head, they sound hollow and I feel numb.

Brian nods solemnly and stares at his feet. Brian who still lives on his own. Brian who can drive. Brian who can still do something independently. If Angelo and this band mean that much to Brian, what does it mean to Herb and me? We're stranded at the Home. Helios is our life.

We're in my little room and I sink down into my recliner, but even it is no comfort. But at least from this position I can't fall.

"Go get Herb," I say. "Bring him here. We'll tell him together."

After Brian leaves I look up at the plain white ceiling. "Angelo," I whisper. I don't know what I'm expecting, that he'll talk to me or something? That he'll suddenly appear and assure me he was an angel all along. A sour frown forms on my face as the ridiculousness of it comes home. I'm not that kind of a person. I don't believe easily, and I don't expect miracles.

But Angelo *is* a miracle to me. He *is* an angel to me.

"What the hell is so important," Herb growls when Brian drags him in a few minutes later.

"Sit down, Herb," I say. "We're having an emergency band meeting."

"Why?"

I see the fear in Brian's eyes, he doesn't want to tell someone else the news he just told me, so I just blurt it out. Herb's thin face goes from looking old to looking ancient, his mouth opens and closes several times and then just clamps shut as his eyes well up with tears.

In that moment, all three of us know we can't do Helios without Angelo. I can see it on their grim faces. I can feel it as a stabbing pain in my stomach. All the equipment is his—he did all the physical labor. He glued us all together, made us whole.

The silence is heavy and oppressive and I can't stand it. It feels like I'm dying again, like before I met Angelo when Lenny and I were on our quest for helium.

Not this time.

"Get me my sticks and pad," I say to Brian who pulls the drumsticks and practice pad off of the desk and hands them to me. I look at my bandmates, but they won't meet my eyes. This feeling, it feels like death, and I can smell the sour scent of our fear.

I bang out the beat on my drumsticks, "One... two... three... four....," and start on the little pad. The sound is muffled, but it's a beat. "I can't get no... satisfaction," I begin singing. My voice is low, and I've slowed the beat way down. It sounds more like a dirge than a rock song, but that is exactly how I'm feeling.

Brian and Herb are both looking at me, and I give them a nod. They come in on the next line, Herb's tenor and Brian's bass harmonizing with my baritone. A smile creeps onto my face. I can't help it. We sound pretty good. Our voices aren't the smooth voices of youth, but the textured voices of age. We know what it's like to "get no satisfaction."

When the song is over I look up at them. "Angelo may be gone, but Helios lives. Even if we have to become some damn boys' acapella group."

They both nod at me, their faces serious, their old, cloudy eyes sparkling.

And right then, I feel myself promising to Angelo to continue his work. Helios will live as long as I am alive and I've got my mind. Helios will live.

BACKSTORY—THE HELIUM EXIT STRATEGY

This very personal story is my attempt to empathize with someone close to me. So this backstory isn't completely awkward, let's call them by the gender-neutral Pat.

Pat is someone that I gave a lot of my time and energy supporting. That can be rewarding and it can also be difficult. A number of years ago Pat stayed with my wife and me and it was a challenge for us all.

One day Pat told me they couldn't snap their fingers anymore. In the moment I brushed it off, but on later contemplation it became clear to me that it really was a big deal—one more thing taken away from Pat.

A year or so before this incident, I learned from my friend Jack about the use of helium to terminate your life.

Those two elements mixed together and this story was born. Since my goal was to be empathetic, the Carl character is basically me. What would I be like at that age? What would I value? How would I cope?

Unlike when I wrote this story, Pat is no longer in my life, and I am quite a bit older, making this story even more personal as a reflection of the past and a contemplation of the future.

This story originally appeared in *Life After: Stories of Life, Death, and the Places In Between.*

PART 3
LITTLE GREENY

LITTLE GREENY

Patty Jenkins is a nearly perfect creature. She's got long, thin limbs that are good for running and climbing and swimming. Tomboy is a word you might use to describe her—well, I would have until two days ago.

Her blue eyes are penetrating, looking deep into your soul. Her face has a smattering of freckles, made darker by the summer sun. Her smile is wide and her laugh loud. Her hair, long and brown, has streaks of blond from the bleaching of the sun. She's perfect and she's always been my friend, and now she's a complete mystery.

It's July 1986, and both Patty and I have just turned thirteen. Our families come to the lake every chance we get, where we play, explore, eat hot dogs, and swim. Patty and I were born on the same day, July 4, as fireworks exploded in the sky. But this year, everything is different.

I'm in the water, enjoying the cool, silky feel of it against my skin as I snorkel along. I love the water and I've been in it for a while, the cold of it seeping into me so that my lips will soon be blue and I'll be shivering. It's time to get out, but as I look up at the old wooden dock, I see Patty sitting there dressed in shorts instead of her bathing suit. Her hair is pulled back into a long ponytail and her arms are hugging her chest.

Two days ago, everything changed when Patty got her first period. Our families were having a communal cookout on the large grass lawn that rolls down from our adjacent cottages to the lake. Me, my parents, aunt and uncle, and their two kids, and Patty with her parents, grandparents, and older sister. A swarm of activity with most of the kids playing tag, except the teenagers who huddled close and talked, and the parents drinking beer and wine.

Patty and I were in the tag group. We were teenagers then, but only by a few days, and it still felt like—at least to me—that we were still kids. I do have to say that Patty was starting to look different to me. Before she was just my friend, but this summer I started to feel funny when I was around her and miss her when I wasn't. Before this summer, she wasn't a "creature," perfect or otherwise, but now she's something that seems a bit foreign to me. Mysterious.

Tag is not my favorite game. I always lose and am often "it." It's on account of my right leg. I was born with it twisted up and my foot mangled. I've had six surgeries on it and do okay now, but even in my clodhopper boot that evens out my legs, I'm not that fast.

I've been "it" too long and Patty slows down. She's making a good show of it, breathing hard and doubling over, pretending she has a stitch in her side. I think she is doing this to preserve my dignity, but I don't feel bad about not being as fast with Gimpy—that's my name for my right leg. When I touch her, she grabs her abdomen and cries out in pain.

"What did I do?" I ask. "Are you okay?"

She straightens up a bit, looks at me with her blue eyes wide, and then doubles over and screams. The chaos of running kids comes to a stop. The teenagers stare from under the big oak tree. Patty's mom comes running, and then her aunt and my mom.

I don't exactly hear what they are saying, just snatches.

Things like, "Oh my," "this is totally normal," and "...a woman now."

She's surrounded by the women as they take her back to Patty's house. I'm still standing there, my heart racing when it's all over, thinking that I did something wrong, that I hurt her.

"Come on, son," my dad says, putting his arm on my shoulder and steering me towards the lake and the empty dock. It's twelve feet long and would be where we would moor our boats if we had any.

My heart is beating even faster and I look at my father wide-eyed. My dad has curly brown hair with just a little grey and glasses. He's got a grin on his stubbly face. "You didn't do anything, Tom. It's just... you know... time." When he ends with his stammering, we're down at the end of the dock looking out over the lake.

The Finger Lakes of New York are deep gouges in the land formed during the ice age. Now they're filled with water and surrounded by homes, the hills around them verdant. The sun is getting low in the sky, but there's a water skier out on the lake, slaloming back and forth and kicking up rooster tails to the left and then to the right.

His warm hand is still on my shoulder as I watch the skier and think about what he's trying to say. As I remember how all the women reacted, it dawns on me. Not that I have a full grasp on what is happening to Patty, I just know it's part of turning from a girl into a woman. Part of the reproductive system maturing.

A shiver runs through me despite the warm evening and suddenly I understand something. Patty is changing into a woman, but that might mean that I'm changing into a man.

Could that be why I am suddenly fascinated with her hair and feel funny when she smiles at me?

"Ummm... Thanks, Dad. I get it." I turn and walk as fast as I can away from him. I don't want to talk about it. I don't want him to start in on the birds and the bees. What I want to do is get in the water, feel its support, stop thinking about Patty, about girls turning into women or boys turning into men.

SHE *IS* A NEARLY PERFECT CREATURE. PERFECT LIMBS, strong and lithe. Long lustrous hair. Big blue eyes with long lashes. She can be funny at times and shy at others. She's never made fun of my not-so-strong or lithe right leg. She's been my friend since we shared a crib by this lake that I'm swimming in.

But as she sits there, hugging her chest, she's more "creature" now. I should go up to her, talk to her, make sure she's okay. But I'm terrified. Of the fact that she's turning from a girl into a woman and that maybe, just maybe, I'm turning from a boy into a man and that's why my stomach is doing flips as I tread water watching her.

I feel something touch my foot, something smooth and scaly. I'm sure it's a fish, and I ignore it as I take deep breaths through my snorkel, steeling myself to approach Patty.

When we were eight and I got stuck in the big oak tree after climbing too high, it was Patty that talked me down before any of the older kids could find out. Or when we stole that pie from a few houses down when we were six and ate it all by ourselves, both of us getting sick, but neither of us ever telling anyone. Summers were for the lake. Summers were always with Patty.

My heart's pounding in my ears, but I swim over to the dock, pull out the snorkel and pull off the mask. "You okay?" I ask, my voice sounding froggy and weak.

She purses her lips in what is a poor excuse for a smile and nods, her arms still around her abdomen.

I clear my throat to say something else, but can't think of anything to say that wouldn't sound stupid. I don't understand what she is going through, or what I am going through, for that matter. I just know that the cold water doesn't feel so cold when her blue eyes meet mine. And that scares me.

I feel a brush on my leg again, smooth and scaly. "Must be a lot of fish by the dock today," I say, but she's not listening, and I'm not really talking to her. I put the mask back on, bite down on the snorkel and dive down. Finding out what kind of fish are here is a mystery I am up to.

I only catch a glimpse of it, the scaly thing that touched my foot. It's definitely bigger than I thought, maybe three feet long, and it looks like it has a long tapering tail, not fishlike at all. I'm scared and excited as I kick hard trying to catch up to it, but I am no match. I'm a good swimmer for a land-dwelling mammal, but I am no match for a water dweller. It's soon gone and I surface and look at the dock, spitting my snorkel out. I want to tell Patty, share the mystery with my best friend, but she's not on the dock anymore.

Our parents—mine and Patty's—are teachers in Syracuse, New York. We are not neighbors up there, but we are down here at the lake. Our cottage on the lake, small and cramped with all of us in there, used to belong to my grandparents, and they still come down from time to time, but they gave it to my mom a few years back. Patty's parents bought the cottage next to ours right before Patty was born, and our parents really hit it off, my mom and Patty's bonding over their pregnancies.

When we were born on the same day, well, that was just

more reason for our families to spend time together. Weekend summer visits quickly turned to spending the entire summer on the lake. As far back as I can remember it's what we've done. Going from our modern neighborhood in Syracuse to living in the old cottage by the lake. Going from spending our days in school and doing chores to playing by the lake and swimming every day.

The lake has always been magic to me.

My dad doesn't understand why I love the water so much. I mean, he gets it, it's because of Gimpy, but he doesn't really understand how free I feel in the water compared to the land. He's had two good legs his entire life, he ran track in college and still goes out for a jog sometimes.

One of my most cherished dreams is running. I'll be in a thick forest, a trail snaking through it past tall fir trees and mighty oaks. My breath is coming deeply as my feet pound out a steady rhythm on the dirt trail. The sun peeks through the dense forest occasionally, caressing my face with its sweet warmth. I breathe deeply of the cool mountain air and smell the pine trees and the sweet scent of decomposing leaves.

And that's it. Just running. Just being normal.

"Why do you need this?" Dad asks. He's got my brother Jimmy's set of fins that he's outgrown. Dad is trying to figure out how to alter it so it will stay on Gimpy.

"So I can swim faster," I say with a smile and a shrug. We're on the narrow porch of the cottage, the lawn in front of us and the lake beyond, boats buzzing as they drag skiers behind.

He looks at me over his glasses—he's a reader, I've interrupted him reading a Thomas Jefferson biography. He brings a stack of books down with him to the lake. I don't think he's buying it, but I'm not going to tell him there is something unusual in the lake and I am determined to find it. And that I need such a distraction because of what is going on with Patty and how lonely I feel without her with me all the time.

"Okay," he says with a sigh, using a knife to whittle back the top edge of the fin where my foot goes. Gimpy needs more room. "You'll probably have to wrap something around it to keep it on."

I give Dad my biggest smile and say, "Thanks."

The right fin hurts, digging into Gimpy a bit, but I don't care. My kicks are now powerful. I move through the water so fast that I feel like I'm flying, the cool water supporting me and sliding past me.

I haven't seen Patty today, and I take that as a bad sign. She's been in her cottage all day. Over breakfast, when my parents were out of earshot, Jimmy said, "She's got 'women problems,'" and added a knowing nod. "You know how that goes." He then rolled his eyes. Jimmy is three years older than me and acts like he knows everything and I know nothing. He also has perfectly good limbs and plays football in high school and has a girlfriend. I hate him.

The trouble is I don't really understand "women problems" and I'm sure not going to ask my brother about it. And if I ask my father it's guaranteed to turn into a long and very embarrassing discussion. And my mother? That would be the worst.

So that leaves me in the lake, trying out my hand-me-down fins, hoping to solve a mystery. Diving as often as I can, wishing I would see something more than fish and mud and algae. The visibility in the Finger Lakes sucks, so I can't see very far. What I want to see is a long scaly tail, a creature that moves fast without fins. A...

I don't know what it is. It's as mysterious to me as "women

problems." But unlike those, maybe this is something I can ask around about.

<hr>

THE MARSHMALLOW ROAST DIDN'T TAKE THAT MUCH encouragement. We've got a big fire pit on the edge of the grass right before an abrupt drop-off and then the lake. We use it quite a bit, usually on the weekends. I suggested to Dad that maybe what we all needed was marshmallows and stories under the stars. I don't think I am the only one that has been tense since that game of tag and Patty started with her "women problems."

The fire is crackling and the waves lap up on the shore with a full array of stars above us. It's not a huge group, me, Jimmy and my parents, and Patty and her parents. I'm real glad that Patty is there. The night is warm, but she's got a too-big sweat jacket on.

Dad hasn't gotten the marshmallows out yet, and things are kind of quiet. I'm not sure this is all about Patty and her "women problems," but something isn't right. And maybe it's how all the men call it "women problems," but I bet none of the women do. I get how this is mysterious to the males, but it's not an illness or anything. It's normal, right? The trouble is none of the guys seem to really know. It's a mystery so it's treated as such, but does it have to be one?

"How you feeling?" I whisper to Patty when she sits down next to me on an old picnic table bench, avoiding the smoke.

She gives me a small smile and my heart starts thumping in my chest. "Better, thanks."

That smile makes her look so beautiful. How can a smile do that? I feel real hot and look away, I don't want her to see my "man problem." I guess it's not fair to call my new feeling for Patty a "man problem," and I understand that I am not experiencing anything physical like Patty is, but I am sure experiencing something.

My father clears his throat and looks at me pointedly as if to say, *this was your idea.*

I nod and take a deep breath, feeling Patty's blue eyes on me, and feeling like the temperature just went up another ten degrees.

"The... the lake," I say, stabbing my thumb over my shoulder towards the water. "We usually tell ghost stories, but I was wondering if anyone ever heard anything about the Finger Lakes. About... *things* in the lakes."

My mom furrows her brow and says, "You mean like the Loch Ness monster?"

I nod and catch a grin on my father's face. "Well... there is Old Greeny," he begins. "Over in Cayuga Lake."

By the time he's done, I'm not so sure I want to go back into the water.

MOM IS A FEMINIST. AND YET AGAIN, HERE IS ANOTHER term that I don't really understand. I think it boils down to women wanting to be more than mothers and wives, do more than have babies and make dinner. Why wouldn't they? Obvious, right? But maybe because my mother is a feminist all this seems obvious to me.

When I learned about the women's suffrage movement, learned that women only got to vote in 1920, sixty-six years ago, and it took a constitutional amendment, that there are exactly twenty-five women in Congress, less than five percent. Well, it seems that the rest of the country was not raised by a feminist.

The next morning, after the Old Greeny stories, I'm kinda avoiding the lake, and I haven't seen Patty yet. Mom is out on the lawn hanging laundry on the line. It occurs to me then, that Mom being a feminist, maybe she might be willing to talk about what's happening to Patty.

"Hey," I say as I grab some damp T-shirts and start pinning them to the line.

"Why aren't you in the water?" she asks. "I swear sometimes you are half fish."

I shrug, glancing down at the lake and remembering Dad's story about a hundred-foot-long serpent with sharp teeth and a taste for human flesh.

She laughs. It's a bright sound and loud, drowning out the chirping of the birds briefly. "Don't believe your father. There are no mysteries in that lake."

But I know that there are. Mysteries in the lake. Mysteries out here. I nod and keep hanging clothes.

"What's on your mind, son?"

She's staring at me, her brown eyes penetrating, her hands on her hips.

I bite my lip. "I... Ummm... It's... It's Patty..."

Her face goes slack for a moment before she nods and smiles. "Ahh... And why aren't you talking to your father about this?"

"Well... I... You know, they don't really understand. They just call it 'women problems.'" I end in a weak shrug.

Her mouth forms an "O" and her eyes widen. For a moment, I'm afraid I've misjudged the situation and my mother's feminism, that this is a line that shouldn't be crossed.

"Oh. That. I see," she says, looking around, but we are the only ones in the yard. "Do you really want to understand?"

I swallow hard and nod. I do, but I'm afraid.

"I take this as a good sign, Tom. Now listen carefully."

She goes on for a while about the human reproductive cycle. About menses and menstruation. About hormones and mood shifts. About cramping and pain. In the end, I understand it as well as a thirteen-year-old boy can, but I have great empathy for the rest of the guys just calling it "women problems" and moving on. It is a process that is literally foreign to us.

I thank her and give her a hug before going to find my fins. At this point, ancient creatures in the lake seem less daunting than the realities of human biology.

***

When I head down to the dock, I see that Patty is there—and so is Jimmy. She's sitting on the dock in cut-offs and a bathing suit top, dangling her feet over the water. Jimmy is at the water's edge skipping stones, his voice sounding extra deep as he talks to Patty.

I want to skip a rock off his head.

Jimmy is three years older than Patty and me and has always considered us the annoying younger kids. He only played with us when he had to. Jimmy uses that extra deep voice on girls, when he wants to show off that his voice has changed.

Menses is not the only new thing about Patty this summer. Her chest has started to develop too.

My slow clomp down the grassy hill of our yard stops as I take in the scene. I'm barefoot and don't have my special right shoe on, so my gait is extra gimpy. Mom is done hanging laundry and I don't know where everyone else is. There are only thin clouds in the sky and the sun is hot, but I feel my face flush more than a little summer sun warrants. For all my life, summers on the lake were Patty and me. She's an only child and Jimmy never wanted to have anything to do with us. But looking at him with his perfect limbs, his deep voice, he's even started to shave. What do I have to offer Patty?

Part of me wants to protect Patty from Jimmy with his excessive talk of "boobs," the three girlfriends he had this last school year, and the *Playboy* magazines he keeps between his mattress and his box spring. And he's way too old for her. But I just stand there frozen, my left knee awkwardly bent to compensate for Gimpy. The birds seem too loud and the buzz of boats on the lake is annoying.

I just stand there and stare, like the total loser I am, and minutes tick by. As Jimmy talks in his deep voice and expertly skips stones out on the lake and Patty watches. I occasionally hear her laugh.

I want to run away, but of course, I can't. With shoes on, I can kind of run, but not barefooted. I look down at my twisted right foot and I hate it. I hate my right leg and all the challenges it's brought me. I hate that I'm a scrawny, deformed kid who has lost his best friend.

And it seems to me, right then and there, that I have lost her. Lost her to Jimmy or lost her to puberty, or something. This summer is different, and if we are to remain friends, it's going to be different. I don't want different.

Patty turns and her blue eyes find mine and she smiles and waves at me, beckoning me to come down to the dock. It's Patty with her freckled face and her perfect limbs. Patty who was born on the same day as I was and knows me better than anyone. Patty, my best friend. My knees go weak and my face must be beet red as sweat trickles down my back.

I don't understand any of this. My whole freak out about Jimmy talking to her. How her smile makes my knees weak. How suddenly it matters that Patty is a girl and I am a boy.

I start my clomping steps down towards the dock without really thinking about it. Like she's a magnet and I'm a piece of metal. I have no choice.

"Nice fins," she says when I get there, patting the dock next to her, inviting me to sit down. Jimmy has wandered off and it's just the two of us.

"Yeah?" I'm not sure they are so nice with part of the right one carved out and the dangling shoelaces I use to tighten it up.

"Yeah," she says.

I stand there for a moment, not knowing what to say. Staring at her. She really is a nearly perfect creature.

"What's wrong, Tom?" she asks.

I shake my head, feeling my cheeks burn. Her face darkens, and I'm sure she thinks I'm freaked out by her getting her period. And truth be told, I am a little freaked out. Mom's demystifying of it hasn't helped.

Seconds tick by and I know a line is being crossed, one that we can't uncross soon. "I saw something in the lake," I blurt out. "The other day, when you were sitting on the dock and I was out swimming."

I sit down next to her and tell her everything I can about Little Greeny—that's the name that pops into my head as I talk to her.

I tell her how worried I've been about her. I use the term "menstrual cycle" and tell her I can't imagine what it must be like. I tell her how crazy I felt seeing Jimmy paying attention to her and how useless and different I feel with Gimpy. I tell her how scared I am of things changing, of summers not being the same with the two of us anymore.

It all spills out of me in this inelegant display of verbal diarrhea. My face is hot the whole time, and I am sweating so much I am afraid I must just stink.

After it's over she's just sitting there, swinging her legs above the water, staring down into it. I've screwed it up, I just know it. She's going to take those beautiful limbs and run away from me as fast as she can. She's not going to talk to me for the rest of the summer. She's—

"You're sweet," she says, her face suddenly close to mine. "You've always been sweet."

Her breath smells... well, it smells like her, I can't really explain it, but suddenly I love that smell.

"I... You know... we..."

She kisses me on the cheek, just a tiny peck, and my face is so hot now I think I must be as red as a cherry. "I think I'll be able to swim tomorrow," she says. "Can we go looking for Little Greeny?"

I'm left mutely nodding as Patty Jenkins takes her nearly perfect self and heads back towards her cottage.

SLEEP? FORGET ABOUT IT. WHAT'S SLEEP WHEN PATTY Jenkins called me sweet and kissed me on the cheek. I swear I can still feel where her lips touched my skin. I will never wash my face again, lest I remove part of her.

All night, Jimmy is in the bunk bed below me snoring—which I usually hate—and all I can think about is that freckled face, the long brown hair with strands of sun-streaked blond, those long, perfect limbs.

In the morning, I wolf down my Apple Jacks and am down to the pier before it's even warm enough to go swimming. Patty, of course, is not there yet. I plop down on the dock and pull my sweat jacket close.

I'm crazy. I am literally crazy. It's like I've been infected with this virus that is rewiring my brain, changing how I behave. My "boy problems." And honestly, I wouldn't change it if I could. I like feeling this so much, especially about her.

I'm still there two hours later when Patty makes her way down to the dock. She's dressed in jeans and a baggy T-shirt. She can see the disappointment on my face as she sits down next to me.

"Not today," I say.

She shakes her head. "But you go in and I'll stay here and keep watch. You can tell me what you see."

It's not what I want, but it's Patty and me doing something together and that makes me happy. No, happy is not the right word. More like "ecstatic."

What is this strange disease I've contracted? I smile and nod and get my mask and fins on, shuck my sweat jacket and jump in.

The water is cold and I come up gasping and see Patty smiling at me from up on the dock. I wonder if she would mind if I just treaded water and stared at her all day. But I don't. I know she would be creeped out, and so would I, for that matter, but the force that is driving me is irresistible. Suddenly all the movies and TV shows I've seen where people falling in love did the stupidest things makes sense. It's this biological insanity.

"Can you toss me my snorkel? I forgot it—" I'm cut off by the feel of scales against my foot. Just like I felt before. Patty tosses me the snorkel and I catch it. "It's here," I blurt out before biting down on the snorkel and getting my face in the water.

The water has algae and particulates in it, so you can't see very far. But there it is. The swish of a tail disappearing. I fill my lungs and dive under and kick hard with my fins. I don't think about Gimpy or Patty or anything else. I swim as hard and as fast as I can. It's Little Greeny, I just know it.

The tail starts to resolve and it's attached to a body with clawed feet. It's big, much bigger than I first thought, bigger than me. But still I swim hard, ignoring how the fin bites into Gimpy, ignoring my lungs as they start to burn from a lack of oxygen. I go faster and deeper and then I see it. All of it. It stops and twists around and looks at me. Its mouth slightly parted, its triangular-shaped teeth showing. Its eyes yellow with a vertical slit like a snake.

For a few seconds we're both still, we're both staring at each other. Little Greeny has scales, several shades of green, clawed feet, gills on his neck, and is about six feet long from nose to the tip of its tail. Some kind of huge lizard that breathes water?

It swishes its tail and moves closer, those eyes looking so strange, so foreign, but there seems to be intelligence in there.

I'm freaking out. Maybe because I've been down too long. Maybe because a six-foot serpentine creature with sharp teeth is examining me. It then dawns on me that those teeth scream carnivore. You don't have teeth like that if you eat weeds all day.

That does it. I surge straight up. I spit out the snorkel and suck in air, feeling dizzy from being under too long—and from seeing Little Greeny. The first thing I notice is that I'm out away from the dock quite a ways. I feel a swell of pride at how far I swam under water, I made it past the buoys that mark this part of the lake for swimming. The next thing I notice is Patty. She's standing up waving her hands and shouting. My ears are full of water and I don't quite make out her words. She is very excited about something—maybe it's Little Greeny. I then hear the thrumming buzz of a boat and turn. It's coming in fast right at me.

<hr>

"Are you okay?" Patty asks, her face close to mine, her breath smelling sweet. I'm on the dock exhausted and panting for air. That boat didn't see me. It would have run me right over, but I dove down and away from the boat and it missed me. Turns out Little Greeny is not the biggest danger in the lake —it's the boats and boys like me who don't pay attention to where they are.

I nod, but can't speak yet. My lungs are burning and my limbs feel like rubber.

"Talk to me!"

"I'm fine," I manage to gasp out between pants.

"I'm going to get your mother."

"No." I push myself off the wood of the dock into a sitting position. "Please."

Patty turns towards me, her hands on her hips in a gesture that seems to be universal when exasperated females are dealing with males.

I rip my fins off and get myself into a standing position. "I'm just worn out." I stick my arms out and turn around slowly. "See, no damage."

She takes a step back towards me, her lips pursed. Another universal female signal, one I don't recall her doing before.

"We can't tell anyone about..." I nod back towards the water. "Little Greeny."

She rolls her eyes, turns on her toe, and marches away.

I sit there for the longest time, letting the sun warm me as my body recovers. Gimpy has a bright red welt where the fin dug in too deep, and I am just exhausted.

I run through the conversation with Patty and for a while think I'm better off without her if she's going to do the arm-crossing, lip-pursing female thing. I watched her go and she didn't go to my house, but hers, so at least she's not telling on me. At least for now.

But why is she so mad? I don't understand.

SHE'S AVOIDING ME AND IT HURTS, LIKE SOMEONE CUT MY arm off or something. At dinner we're in the yard, a couple of picnic tables pushed together, and she sits next to Jimmy, laughing at his stupid jokes, stabbing little glances at me from time to time. She's doing it on purpose. After I spilled my guts about how I feel, she's trying to hurt me. I don't understand.

My father tries to talk to me after dinner—I was getting lots of sideways glances from the adults—but I shrug his hand off my shoulder and walk down to the dock.

They all give me space, which is just as well. I don't understand what is happening, why I even care who Patty Jenkins talks to. It's just those perfect limbs and sun-kissed hair and constellations of freckles on her cheeks.

The sun sets as I sit there pondering all the problems, woman and boy.

"Do you want to talk?"

I jump, my heart is in my throat and pounding hard. I look back and it's Mom, her arms folded across her chest. God, are they all going to do it to me today? She's got my sweat jacket and hands it to me—it's getting chilly out. She sits on the dock and dangles her legs over the water next to mine.

"So?" she prompts me.

"Do I have to?"

She shakes her head. "About you and Patty, no. About the boat, yes."

My eyes are wide as I stare out onto the lake. I swear I must look like a deer in the headlights of a car.

And then my face flushes red and I am so angry at Patty. I don't care about the freckles or the infectious laugh, or even that she's a girl. I want to punch her in the nose.

I look around hoping for an excuse to escape, like the Jenkins' house being on fire, or a Sasquatch lumbering down our yard. But no luck.

"Did she..." I manage to spit out.

Mom shook her head. "I gave her the chance, asked her how the afternoon went, but she kept her mouth shut."

I swallow hard. The anger fleeing and my stomach feeling heavy around the burger and potato salad. I just want to run. I stare at Gimpy, my weird twisted foot, and wish I was someone else. Anyone else. "How?" I manage to ask.

She laughs—it's brief and full of irony. "The kitchen window faces the dock, you know. I'm always keeping an eye on you."

For a moment, I imagine what my mother must have felt, seeing me go under and then stay under for so long. Watching Patty get nervous and searching the water for me. Seeing me pop up out of the buoyed area right in front of a boat, but too far away to do anything about it.

I take a deep breath and slowly let it out. "I'm real sorry. I..." I trail off, trying not to tell her why I was under so long. She smiles and gives me the smallest of nods, but her lips are pursed. She waits silently and then her eyebrows raise, a signal clearer than words that she wants me to continue. "I saw something, something strange. I was chasing it."

"And..."

And then it just tumbles out. I tell her about Little Greeny, about why I wanted the fins, why I asked for stories over the fire, why I was under so long. How I don't want anyone to know because people will try to catch him—somehow, I think Little Greeny is a boy—and examine him.

When I'm done, it's pretty dark out and the crickets and bullfrogs are putting on their evening concert and the fireflies have come out to play.

"Thank you for telling me, son. I appreciate it." With that she gets up and leaves me there on the dock.

OF ALL THE MYSTERIES IN THE UNIVERSE, I THINK WOMEN (and girls) are the greatest when it comes to men (and boys). It's like the words we exchange, the things we say, are only a small part of the signal being transmitted. There is this whole other universe of information when it comes to communicating with women and girls. The things not said, their posture and inflection, and things I can't even imagine. The trouble is the communication is lost on most of us boys (and men).

Patty getting mad at me down at the dock. My mom mysteriously walking away without delivering any punishment.

And the crazy part is, I think they both wanted me to understand them based on those subtle signals. They seem to natively understand them, and I sure don't. And the worst part is, Patty used to be a lot more straightforward in her communication, until this summer.

The next morning, I get up late and creep downstairs for breakfast. Jimmy and my parents are at the table chatting and eating pancakes. "Good morning," I say, which is echoed by my parents. I sit down and start eating, waiting for it to come—the scolding, the grounding, the worrying—but it doesn't. After breakfast, my father takes Jimmy and heads to the hardware store because the screen door isn't closing right, and I'm left there alone with my mother.

I help her clean up, admiring the view from the kitchen window down to the dock, thinking that now it's going to happen, now that we're alone I'll learn what my punishment is. But after everything is clean my mom is just sitting at the table sipping coffee as content as can be.

"I don't understand," I say.

"Hmmm. You'll need to be more specific than that." She knows exactly what I'm talking about, but wants to hear me say it.

"The boat! Aren't I grounded or something?"

"Do you need to be grounded?" she asks, her lips pursed again.

I stand there blinking.

"Did you learn something?" she asks.

And this is it, this moment here will decide my fate. Did I learn something? I learned that there is a serpentine creature living in our lake—and that's what is important about the whole thing to me. The boat... well, it sure did scare me, but it wasn't something I was trying to do. I know better than to go out past the buoys and I never would except for chasing a legendary creature—which in my mind is worth some risk.

"Yes, ma'am. I learned that nothing is worth that kind of risk." Yes, I lied to my mother, who was being really cool as far as parents go. But maybe one of those invisible signals made it to me and I figured out what she wanted to hear. I also realized that she didn't believe me about Little Greeny. She thought that I had just seen something and mistaken it for an amazing creature, inspired by campfire stories. I also realized that she had discussed this all with my father and had planned this discussion.

She stood staring at me for the longest time before she finally spoke. "Well then, I guess you don't need to be grounded."

***

I'VE GOT MY FINS ON AND AM IN THE WATER BEFORE SHE can change her mind. I dive repeatedly, searching for Little Greeny, but no luck. After an hour of this, I come up and see Patty standing on the dock, her arms crossed, a bathing suit on. I smile at the bathing suit, but worry about the crossed arms.

"Sorry about yesterday," I offer, figuring a blanket apology might be enough.

"Are you?"

"Yeah," I say, swimming closer and treading water below her. My talk with my mother has given me some insight. "That boat, such a close call, it must have been awful for you to see that."

Her face darkens, but she nods and sits on the dock. "Have you seen him today?" she asks.

I shake my head. "Want to look? You can use my mask and snorkel."

She smiles and jumps into the water and we take turns diving and looking for Little Greeny. It feels almost normal, the two of us playing in the lake. We used to play tag in the water, or see who could stay under the longest, or play Marco Polo and stuff like that. This time we're doing something that seems more important—searching for Little Greeny—and we're not the same kids we were last summer. But it's almost like normal. Almost.

WE SPENT WEEKS LOOKING FOR LITTLE GREENY, BUT WE never did see him again. For the rest of the summer I wondered about the changes we were both going through, and was fairly distracted by her, but we are still Patty and Tom swimming in the lake as much as we can, enjoying our summer away from the city.

I've come to a conclusion—some mysteries shouldn't be solved. Little Greeny can stay a mystery as can Patty Jenkins. I mean, what fun would it be to find out that what I saw in the lake was just something common, something everyone knew about, and not this tantalizing mystery? And what fun would it be to have Patty all figured out, to understand every nuance, every gesture, every emotion?

I'm content to keep looking for Little Greeny, but I will never try to catch him (or her). And I'm content for Patty to be my best friend and to spend as much time as I can with her. We're only thirteen, there are a lot more changes to come, and a few more summers together before those changes send us off on other adventures that don't include spending the summer at the lake.

Our last morning there, Patty and I walk down to the dock to say goodbye to the lake and the summer. There are things to be said, but I don't have words for it, and she doesn't seem to either. So, we just stand there and look out at the lake.

"Come on, guys," my dad calls from the car, honking the horn.

"I guess we should go," I say, looking at Patty's face, which now seems so beautiful to me.

"Wait!" she hisses, grabbing my arm and pointing out to the lake, just inside the buoys. And there he is, a flash of a long tail, just a glimpse, and Little Greeny is gone. It is like he's saying goodbye to us.

Patty's face is bright as she smiles at me. She has finally seen him.

"So, I guess we'll resume the search next year," I say.

She shrugs her shoulders and says, "I guess," but a smile plays on her lips. A little of the new Patty and a little of the old Patty.

Patty Jenkins is a nearly perfect creature, and not just because of her perfect limbs or long hair. Not because of her adorable freckles or infectious laugh. She's a nearly perfect creature because she's my best friend.

BACKSTORY—LITTLE GREENY

"Little Greeny" does a good job of capturing the spirit of this book. It's non-speculative, a coming-of-age story, and different from most of my work.

It's also a powerful, lovely story (at least to me) that explores that oh-so-awkward time of life when we are in the liminal space between childhood and adulthood.

Personally, I love a good coming-of-age story. It's a universal experience for us humans and, I think, something that happens more than once if we live a long life. Maybe I should write some coming-of-middle-age stories or coming-of-old-age stories. Actually, I probably have, but you get the idea. We go through multiple periods in our lives as we pass through these one-way gateways that change us forever.

And that makes those kinds of transitions fertile ground for storytelling.

This story first appeared in *Creatures Featured: Thirteen Stories of Monsters and Other Creatures.*

PART 4
MOUNTAIN DRAGON MAN

MOUNTAIN DRAGON MAN

The man stumbled down the sidewalk, his gait exaggerated as if the cement was moving beneath his feet. His dirty brown hair was overlong, hanging in front of his green eyes, and his filthy winter jacket had holes with the stuffing leaking out. His beard wasn't long, maybe a week's growth, but scraggly and ungroomed. There were a few strands of grey in the brown of his beard and a few crumbs of food nestled in it.

People driving by tried not to look at him, lest they feel guilty for what they had and he didn't, or worse yet, feel like they should help him but not being able to because of the busyness and chaos of their own lives.

His mouth moved as he mumbled sentences that were strings of words, but didn't go together. Like, "He Mountain Dragon Man went over under but not too far, you know."

Spring had slipped into summer and the cool of morning was gone. He was sweating beneath the heavy jacket, but he didn't take it off. It was his, and if he put it down, well, he knew someone might take it, or he might lose it, and then he would be so cold at night. Or the witch might tell him he's not supposed to have it, and although she was a good witch, she didn't really understand. Besides, he would need it as armor if he ever, finally, found the dragon.

He stopped and stood on a busy corner with a stoplight and cars streaming by. He stood swaying, his hands fumbling with the zipper, his mouth moving. "Mountain Dragon Man will divide the veil, you know." He stumbled towards the busy road, barely stopping himself in time, a black pickup honking at him. "Mountain Dragon Man!" he yelled, and then quietly added, "you know."

It took time, getting the zipper down. The jacket was old, the zipper had some broken teeth. His fingers fumbled to find the zipper pull and then would slip off, but he was determined. It was the most important thing to do right then, the only thing to do. So, he stood there swaying and worked it until it was done. Time didn't matter. Nothing else mattered.

When he finally accomplished the task, he stood there smiling, showing off perfectly straight, healthy teeth underneath his chapped lips. He turned to the north and his breath caught as he saw a great snow-tipped mountain rising into the sky, but it was far and he had no idea how to get there.

"Good morning, Mountain Dragon Man," a young man said, nodding at the proud, disheveled man as he stood and waited to cross the street.

"Good Mountain Dragon Man after dogs, you know," he replied, giving a slight bow. The person talking to him, how nice that he was, must be a college student with his youth and backpack and quick pace. But he looked familiar with his black hair and green eyes. It stirred something in him, something not comfortable. He knew, no, had *known* someone with black hair and green eyes like that. But younger, a boy not a man. He blinked and swayed and stared.

"Here," the young man said, handing him a granola bar.

When the crosswalk sign showed the white man, he added, "Have a good one, Mountain Dragon Man," and quickly crossed the street.

He followed slowly, although the white man left to be replaced by the red hand, and the horns honked. That young man was a sign sent to lead him on his quest. The dragon had taken something, hadn't it? Something precious. And the young man had called him Mountain Dragon Man. Was that his name?

AS HE WANDERED THROUGH THE COLLEGE CAMPUS, HE named things and pointed at them. "Mountain Dragon Man *car*, you know. Mountain Dragon Man *building*, you know. Mountain Dragon Man *woman*, you know." Everything had a name. Some names covered broad territory, like tree, which applied to many different kinds of trees. Others were very specific, like a single person's name. What was "Mountain Dragon Man?" If it was a name, was it like tree or was it like one person, him? And in any case, it was a strange name, but he felt it in him. He had to say it.

The day was growing hot and he craned his neck at the tall buildings, wondering at the beautiful perfect grass, watching the streams of students, so fast on their feet, while he lurched along. And they stared at him, the students. Some smiled and he smiled back. Some looked away and so did he. Some looked afraid. Some pointed. These actions he did not repeat. Fear should not be spread. That he knew for sure. Dragons spread fear. He was no dragon.

When he got to the north end of the campus he stopped. He liked the old buildings made of huge, red-brown sandstone blocks. He liked the ancient trees reaching into the blue sky. He stumbled up the stairs of one of the beautiful old buildings, turned, and saw it. The mountain. Tall and beautiful, rising up out of the forest with two snow-tipped peaks.

"Mountain Dragon Man, you know," he said with a smile.

The trees were very much in the way and he wanted a clearer view of the mountain. He stood there for a few minutes, resting for the quest ahead, and ate the granola bar the nice student had given to him. He had followed in that student's wake and found his way here, found the way to the mountain. And somehow, he knew it wasn't just a mountain, it was *his* mountain.

As he lurched his way north off of campus, he saw two men dressed in grey uniforms walking quickly toward him. They had serious looks on their faces and they were staring at him. He didn't care, though. This was a celebration. "Mountain Dragon Man adventure way, you know." He emphasized by nodding his head vigorously and pointing in the direction of the mountain he could no longer see. The two serious men kindly escorted him the rest of the way off campus.

"Just keep going up this street," one of them said, pointing in the direction he wanted to go in. "There's a shelter there. They'll help you."

He smiled broadly, glad to see the man was not just serious, but kind too. "Mountain Dragon Man happily ever after, you know," he said with a wave after they parted.

HE WAS IN A PARK ON A HIGH PLATEAU WITH DIRT TRAILS and people walking and running on those trails. Out front stood a statue of a buffalo. This place was familiar, he had been here many times. He stood there, breathing in the warm air, his arms wide. In front of him was a craggy-faced mountain, but not his mountain, and farther away to the north and west was the big snow-tipped mountain, his mountain.

"Mountain Dragon Man!" he shouted, and then somewhat embarrassed to have to, he followed it up with a quiet, "you know."

People stared at him, but he didn't care, the view was spectacular. He could see the glorious big mountain with its little brother, smaller mountain. The air was warm and clean. He was hot, he should take his jacket off, but he would just lose it. And now there was nothing but forest between him and his mountain —at least it looked that way—and he was ready to go home. But then she was there. The witch.

"Come on, Hal," she said. "Time to go home."

He hadn't noticed her at first, she had been pacing on the trail back and forth in a tight loop. She was tall and thin, fairly young, but with worry on her face making her look older, making her brown eyes sad. She was thirty-two, he knew, thirty-three next month. Her name was Tiffany. She was a witch.

"Mountain Dragon Man row all the way, you know," he said.

She smiled and nodded, patted him on the shoulder. "You did good."

"Mountain Dragon Man quest taker, you know." He pointed to the two snow-tipped peaks.

Tiffany sighed. "Hal, we have to get you home. I've been worried sick. You've been gone six days this time. The cops couldn't find you. You usually get up here much quicker than this. You need your medicine." She smiled, but it was a sad smile. She pulled on his jacket and added, "Where did you find this thing? It's too warm for that. Come on, let's get it off you now."

Hal held his arms tight so he would not lose his armor.

"Please, Hal. I..." Her eyes welled with tears and he felt scared. Tiffany was a witch, but he knew that she was his witch.

He held his arms out and she took the jacket off. He sighed in relief as the breeze started to cool off his sweat-covered body.

Hal pointed at the mountain and nodded his head urgently. He knew it then that Hal was his name, but then what was Mountain Dragon Man? It was important, it was part of him, but his mind couldn't quite grasp it. Maybe it was an honorary title bestowed upon him by the queen. The mountain, the dragon, the witch. It all went together, if only he could understand how.

"Mountain Dragon Man and witch, quest like doves, you know." He pointed to the mountain again.

Tiffany sighed. "Okay, okay. You win, dear. We'll go to the mountain. We'll find your dragon. But..."

Hal smiled widely, cutting Tiffany off. Finally, he would go to the mountain and find the dragon.

———

"Mountain Dragon Man bug rider, you know," he said after pulling his face in from the open window, his hair wild, his green eyes bright.

"Yes, dear," Tiffany answered. "You always did love this car. Insisted we get a Beetle."

He looked around and saw the ratty jacket, his armor, was in the backseat. If he were to face the dragon, he must have his armor. And something else? What else would he need? "Mountain Dragon Man sword play, you know," he told his witch. He had his armor. He had his steed, a mighty and quick bug, he would need a sword.

Tiffany pursed her lips and shook her head. She pulled into a turn lane, turned onto the road that climbed the mountain and then pulled over.

"What are we doing, Hal? I need to know. Right now."

Hal nodded solemnly. Witches were powerful creatures, to

be respected and honored, especially when they were your witch. He took a deep breath, wanting to tell her, but he didn't really know himself. He just felt pulled to the mountain. He sought the terrible dragon. The dragon had something of his, something important, something he needed back. The beautiful witch had found him, and that was good. He looked into her brown eyes and felt his chest tighten. He was the cause of her worry, he was the reason for her fatigue, he had made those lines in her forehead. He didn't know what had happened. He only knew that he had to be on that mountain.

With his shaking hands, he grabbed her hand. "Mountain Dragon Man trust, you know. Mountain Dragon Man quest, find lost, you know."

Tiffany was fighting back tears, he could see that, and she held his gaze for the longest time. Then she sniffed, nodded, and reached across him and opened the glove compartment and fished around in it. She pulled out a small metal cylinder, Hal knew that it was for tires, something about pressure, but it didn't make any sense to him. "I know it is small right now," she said, "but in your time of need it will become the Sword of Destiny." She carefully placed it in his hand and bowed low.

Hal sniffed and nodded. He was grateful to have Tiffany as his witch and that she was finally listening to him. They could not fail.

The mountain rose above them, its snow-covered tip thrusting proudly into the bluest of skies. The kingdom of Arizona was laid out for them to see with the forest of the mountain eventually disappearing as the land folded its way down to desert.

Hal had put his armor back on, for the wind was cold and he

knew the dragon was near. He held the witch's hand in his left hand—she had insisted, and he didn't mind. He held the Sword of Destiny, still the small silver cylinder, in his right hand, his eyes seeking the dragon.

They were standing in the parking lot and Hal took them forward, towards the mountain which had many long stripes of grassy earth as if a dragon as big as the mountain had raked its claws along the slope, removing the trees. There was a contraption, the word "lift" flitted in his mind, that was slowly running, taking people up the mountain in metal baskets. He knew that people put sticks on their feet and slide down the gashes in the mountain when they were snow covered. He had vivid memories of Tiffany and him doing this together with cheeks red from the cold, but happy smiles on their faces. And they had done this with someone else, someone with green eyes like his, but his mind recoiled from that memory.

"Mountain Dragon Man and his witch quest all the way, you know," he said, pointing to the top with the tiny metal cylinder.

Tiffany nodded, a pained look on her face. "We'll take the lift to the top, Hal. But after that, promise me we will come down, we will go home."

Hal nodded and squeezed her hand. There, at the top of the world, he was sure his quest would be complete.

<hr>

THE AIR WAS COLD AND THIN, AND HAL THOUGHT THEY must truly be on top of the world. Mountains, canyons, cinder cones, forests, lakes, deserts all were spread out below them. Dark green to brown with rare spots of blue water. Cuts on the land for the roads, the houses and buildings of Flagstaff. They were as high as the clouds.

"What now, Hal?" Tiffany the witch asked.

He held the mini Sword of Destiny in his hand, held it at the ready, but he didn't see the dragon. He wasn't sure what to do.

He shrugged his shoulders and shook his head. He had felt the mountain call to him, pull him. He turned and looked, they were at the top of the lift thing, but not at the top of the mountain. That is where he needed to go. But the witch, she would be so mad.

He let go of Tiffany's hand and moved as fast as he could in the thin air.

"Wait!" Tiffany yelled. "Hal, please don't. Please."

He knew that with his unsteady gait the witch was faster than him, that she could catch him, put a spell on him if necessary. But she didn't chase him, and the sound of her crying was worse than any spell.

He turned and saw the tears streaming down her face, her arms wrapped around her body. She did not bring a jacket with her.

He stopped and stared, his heart beating hard and his head dizzy. He had hurt the witch, his witch. He nodded slowly and turned around and walked back. He took his jacket off and wrapped it around her and pulled her into his arms.

"I don't know what to do with you," she said in between racking sobs. People were staring at them, but she couldn't see them, and he was used to it.

The witch wanted him to take the pills that made him calm, but he hated the way they made him feel. Like he was small, trapped, like he was nothing. But the witch was his wife too. The mother of his...

And then the flood hit him, wave after wave of memory and emotions. Their son Drake, with green eyes like his and unruly black hair. Drake who loved fairy tales and fantasy movies, and dragons most of all. Drake who at eleven years of age had a spinal cord tumor that was cancerous.

"It's just a dragon, Dad," Drake would say of his cancer. "It's sitting on the top of a mountain. We are men. We're gonna climb that mountain, we're gonna slay that dragon, I know we are."

But they didn't slay the dragon. Drake died just before his twelfth birthday.

"Tiff," Hal said, holding his wife close, his voice turned wet by his own tears. "I'm here, I'm here, you know."

She held him tighter and cried harder. How long had it been that the fantasy had held sway on him, how long had he been under its "spell," hiding from his grief in a fantasy land he used to play with his son in?

Dizziness hit him, and he leaned against the smaller woman for support. He felt insubstantial as if a breeze could blow him away, and his stomach was gnawingly hungry. How had Tiffany survived the death of their son and the madness of her husband?

"I'm sorry," he whispered as he slumped down to the dry ground, a shiver passing through him. He wrapped his arms around his chest and could feel his ribs. He had lost so much weight. He felt his bearded face and how lean it was. He could hear the words that doctor had said that he hadn't understood at the time. "He's had a psychotic break from reality, retreating into this fantasy to protect himself."

"I'm sorry... you know," he said again, feeling his cold face flush with shame.

Tiffany wiped her face off, her brown eyes seeking his. "Are you back? Can you stay with me?"

He shook his head, he didn't know. Being Mountain Dragon Man was easier. It involved escaping from his own home and then nights in hiding as he tried to find his way to this mountain. But Mountain Dragon Man was on a quest he was so sure would result in victory, not living a life without the thing he cared about the most.

And that felt unfair to Tiffany, and his shame deepened.

"Mmmm.... Mountain... you..."

"Damnit, Hal. I need you. I need you." She was shaking him, her voice shrill. Drake had needed him, they had tried everything, but they had failed. And now she needed him, but he needed to escape. He needed to feel anything but the hollowness his son's absence brought and the burning shame of knowing of how his absence had hurt his wife.

"Stay with me, Hal! You have to stay with me."

But how could he live with it? How had she lived with it? She must be so much stronger than he, and his shame deepened again.

"Mountain Dragon..." he began.

She sniffed and nodded, still squatting in front of him, her voice steadying, her face hardening. "I love you, Hal. I can do this." She took a deep breath and gently touched his face. "Yes, I can do this. You go if you need to. I understand. I promise it won't take me so long to bring you back up here."

Hal shook his head, snapping it back and forth, his jaw locked and his hands clenched as his fingernails dug into his palms. His breath came quick and fast and his dizziness made the world spin around him. There had to be more to him than this. He had to be stronger than this. He felt the confusion of his fantasy calling, it was sweet, it promised succor. Tiffany had given him her permission, he could go, he could resume his endless quest, forget about his dead son.

He slowly stood, his legs shaking, Tiffany helping him. He held the tire pressure gauge out to his wife, his hand shaking. "I... I don't need this anymore. You... you know."

"Are you sure?"

He nodded his head and pressed the gauge into her hand. It was no Sword of Destiny. He was no child. "No. I don't know how much control over this I have, you know. But I will fight. For you, for us... I... I will fight."

Tiffany nodded and took his hand, squeezing it hard. "One step at a time."

He smiled and took a deep breath. "I'm really hungry, you know. Can... can we get some food?"

Tiffany laughed, it was strained and shrill, but it was a laugh. She nodded and they walked towards the ski lift, both eager to leave the mountain.

BACKSTORY—MOUNTAIN DRAGON MAN

This story is an attempt at empathy.

Empathy is fundamental to writing stories about characters that are not you, characters that view the world differently than you do. You have to get into their heads and try to understand them.

This story started with me driving through Flagstaff seeing someone who looks very much like the protagonist in this story and wondering what it would take for that to be me.

Every homeless person has a story, and I think those of us that are in a better place like to believe that it can't happen to us, but of course it can.

None of us are unbreakable. We want to be. We hope to be. We may even pray that we are. But that's just not the nature of the world. Fate does what fate pleases without regard to our desires.

We are not powerless, we can prepare, we can fight, hard, but we are not all powerful. Maybe it takes more strength to recognize our limits than to think we are untouchable.

This story was me imagining circumstances that might put someone like me on that street corner. Like several other stories in this collection, "The Dour Mr. M" and "Laura's Magic Clock," it is the psyche of the protagonist that adds the "fantasy" element to the real world.

PART 5
NOT A SUPERHERO

NOT A SUPERHERO

*W*HAT IF THE SUN COULD SUSTAIN ME? HE THOUGHT, HIS lean face turned toward the just-over-the-horizon sun. He stood alone on a ridge with pine trees behind him, the land slumping down in front of him, rolling off to a deep valley below. *Then, I could just walk away. Find some water. Be fed by the sun. Leave all this.*

He took a deep breath, wishing he could breathe the photons in, feel more power than just the warmth of the sun driving back the cold fall morning. Like one of the superheroes he wrote about. Maybe Photonman or Lightman or... No, those were all lame, and besides, he hadn't written anything of substance lately, had he?

He sighed, watching the cloud of condensate form from his exhalation and then quickly dissipate. The years were beginning to weigh heavily on him; his thin, lanky frame sometimes hard to keep erect. He was starting to want less. Less work, less responsibility, less structure. Middle age had settled on him like a fall cold that jumped from throat to sinuses to lungs and back to throat and seemed it would never go away.

But just as that cold would finally pass, so would middle age, only to be replaced by the tenuous frailty of old age. Fall to winter. Middle age to old age, the seasons of his life tumbling forth quicker than they used to.

When he was a boy, summer seemed to last forever, filled with forts and friends and sprinkled with boredom. This last summer had flicked by faster than one of the photons flying through space to warm him, with not a moment of boredom. Just work, responsibility, worry.

He closed his eyes and turned towards the sun, imagining the photons hurled from the nuclear furnace that is the sun feeding him. Making him confident and bold and strong. He breathed in the yellow/orange of the first light of the day, imagining that faraway fire lighting a flame deep in him. A passion that would get him through his day at his cubicle writing software that didn't matter, would carry him through to visiting his incoherent mother at the memory care unit, would take him home to deal with bills and the other problems of the day, with maybe a nice moment or two with his wife or a call from his daughter.

He needed the power of the sun, he needed passion, but it felt like he couldn't keep the flame going anymore. Maybe it was his age, the "middle" of it sucking his energy. Maybe it was the juggling act of work stress, caregiving stress, and life stress that was just too much.

He rolled his shoulders and stretched his neck, trying to dispel some of the tension, but that didn't help either. He turned from the sun and walked back down the narrow trail to his car. His few moments were over, time to do what had to be done.

Not a superhero, not Photonman, just a middle-aged human on planet earth trying to get through the day.

THE CLACKING OF KEYBOARDS, TOO-LOUD VOICES ON THE phone, muffled music bleeding through headphones, the pad of feet on worn carpet. The office was mostly about sounds. Photonman paused from his work and let the soundwaves wash over him. And he knew sound was not psycho like light. While light was sometimes a particle, sometimes a wave, sound was always a wave, a pulse of energy traveling through space and matter.

He closed his eyes to concentrate on the sounds. Cars on the street outside. The hum of the heater. The whish, whish of the copier.

It's been a week since his morning on the hill when he had first thought of Photonman. He still found the name awkward, particularly the "n" followed by the "m"; it didn't just roll off the tongue. But he had embraced it. Part of him knew it might be a dangerous thing, psychologically, but it seemed to help. A superhero could handle these days, he could not.

His legal name, Brett Evans, which he found too bland to even think of anymore, was that of a middle-aged man being squeezed between overwork and eldercare, neither of which he could escape. He couldn't quit his job—there was a mortgage, car payments, credit card debt, and a daughter in college. He couldn't leave his mother because... well, he just couldn't.

So, by day he was a mild-mannered programmer and by night... he was a husband and father. But in his mind, day or night, he was Photonman. He could absorb the power of the sun. He didn't need a house or a job or food. He just needed water and the sun and that was all.

Not much of a superpower—photosynthesis, something so banal every plant possessed it—but independence is what he dreamed of. If he didn't have to work, didn't have to care for his mother, that somehow made this all bearable—barely.

"Come on, Brett, meeting time."

Photonman tried to suppress his revulsion at that name, keeping his shoulders from rising too high. He swung around in his office chair and gave the speaker, Robby, a small smile. "Oh boy! More requirements gathering."

Robby snorted and nodded and walked towards the cramped conference room. Photonman followed, pausing in front of one of the office's few windows, taking a deep breath, and soaking up the power of the sun.

"So why don't you write it?" Ann asked as the vegetables fried in the skillet and she chopped some broccoli. The aroma was intoxicating, and Ann's cooking would be one of the most difficult things for Photonman to give up. To watch Ann cook was to watch grace in motion. She seemed so happy and called it her "therapy."

Photonman shrugged and took a small sip of his red wine. The work day was finally over and this was when Photonman and his wife had a few minutes to talk. "It's too derivative," he said. "Superman is powered by the sun, that territory is quite thoroughly claimed. There is no room for a Photonman."

She shrugged her shoulders. "Who cares? The Egyptians had Ra, a sun god. Isn't everything derivative to some extent?"

He smiled and took another sip of wine. He told Ann everything... well not "everything." There wasn't actually enough time to explain the insanity of his day or all the strange twists of his mind. He had told her about Photonman, about the idea of a simple humanistic story of a man who only needs water and sunlight to survive and tries to walk away from his stressful life. But he hadn't told her that he had begun to think of himself as Photonman. Wished he was Photonman. He couldn't tell her that. She wouldn't understand. No one would understand.

She paused in her chopping and turned to him, a quizzical look on her face. "But this isn't really a superhero story with people in silly costumes and over-the-top villains. Superman isn't relevant. Write it." She went back to her chopping, and for her the discussion was over. It was clear and simple. But to Photonman it was anything but.

Photonman stood in the parking lot, his eyes closed and head tilted toward the sun, letting the light strike his face as the cool breeze played with his short brown hair. Well, it wasn't so brown now, the grey having a good foothold, and it never did used to be this short. He started buzzing his head a few years back as part of a "grey reduction program." Looking in the mirror had become more and more disconcerting as his self-image diverged from reality.

The two-story building had a small and crowded parking lot with a covered entryway with a few rocking chairs out front. Two old women in motorized scooters were smoking cigarettes and staring at him.

He took another deep breath, trying to draw in the energy of the sun, and then walked under the covered entryway. "Good morning, ladies," he said with a strained smile as he headed into the care home. The ritual was deep now. Stop and sign in, exchange a few words with the woman at the front desk. Go to the bathroom—the thought of using the toilet in his mother's room gave him the creeps. Say hello to any caregiver he passed by name—they had a tough job and it was important to him to relate to them as humans. Ring the bell to the memory care unit and avoid looking at the forest mural painted on the double doors; the cheerfulness of it was too incongruous for him. Wait until one of the caregivers popped out the left door—which only could be open briefly lest an alarm sound—worked the keypad on the wall, and let him in the right door. Then, down the hallway, greeting residents by names, the ones that still knew their names and could respond, and then take a right four doors down into his mother's room.

There, anything could happen. She could be asleep or watching TV—at least her head pointed towards it—or crying and frightened, or in the dining area, or watching TV in the communal area right off the dining room.

Today she was in her room, slumped in her blue recliner, her short grey hair disheveled. When she saw him, recognition lit up her eyes and she raised her shaking hand. Her lips started moving, only pronouns escaping as her eyes darkened from some unknown terror. "They... he... I..."

It was going to be a bad one. Irrational fear brought on by the damage to her brain caused by her dementia. Fear that couldn't be negotiated with and which often devolved into last resort medication that left her barely able to walk, unsafe on her feet, and at risk of falling.

Photonman wanted to run away, but he didn't. Superheroes didn't run away. "Hey, Mom, good to see you," he said as cheerfully as he could.

THE MONTHS SPUN BY IN A HAZE OF THE INESCAPABLE. Work. Mom. Life. Everything he did seemed to be the things that had to be done, or time flopped on the couch in front of Netflix out of sheer exhaustion. He was losing weight. He wasn't sleeping well. Ann was stuck in the same cycle with him, the strain of her job and his mother's care was wearing on her too. They both looked ten years older than they had six months ago, and drank more wine than they ever had. They would sometimes talk about it, but the conversation would follow a tight loop like this:

"I can't stand this. I can't do this anymore," one would say.

"We have to help her," the other would reply. "She needs us. There is no one else."

"And we have to keep working, bills to pay, college for Beth, retirement to save for," the first would add.

"Don't we have to find some time for ourselves?" the other would ask. "You know, beyond eating way too late and falling asleep in front of the TV. Maybe we can watch a movie tonight."

"I'm tired, can we go to bed early?"

"Sure."

His retreat into his alter ego, into Photonman, made sense to him. Too much sense.

<hr>

THE SMOKE WAS BLACK AND ACRID, PHOTONMAN'S EYES watering as he watched the fire with a morbid fascination. It was the office building next to his, just across the grassy area he often ate lunch at. It was on fire, alarms blaring, sirens approaching, people shouting and running.

His building had been evacuated and he had streamed out with the rest of his coworkers, but stopped once he could see the fire. His mind was sluggish, thinking about fire and photons. Fire is a chemical combustion with oxygen resulting in heat and smoke and light. Light is photons. If he was Photonman, shouldn't he be able to do more than just live off sunlight and water? Shouldn't he be able to manipulate photons, pull them out of the fire, robbing it of some of its energy?

The fire crackled and popped. The sound seemed evil to him, like the fire was alive, like the fire was something, wanted something. Like the fire was a villain.

He was exhausted. Too much work, too many late-night calls from the care home. His mother had been getting disruptive and it wasn't clear if they would be able to continue to care for her. If they couldn't, then what? Would he have to quit his job and bring her home? And if he did, would he and Ann survive, would their marriage survive?

He took a step towards the fire, his tired mind still thinking about photons.

"What is wrong with you?" The voice was shouting, but he could barely hear it. "Brett, come on, they're evacuating the whole complex." He glanced away from the fire and saw Robby, short, young, with glasses, his face full of fear. Robby lived in the cubicle next to his.

Photonman shook his head and took another step towards the fire. It was beautiful in a way, the orange-yellow flames dancing as they consumed the building, producing heat which he could feel on his face, heat that was hotter than the summer sun. The fire was shooting photons at him, calling to him.

He coughed, the wind carrying the black smoke to him, but he kept walking. He was Photonman. He was a superhero. He had to be; otherwise, how could he survive his life? How could he walk into the care home after work? How could he get up in the morning? And if he was a superhero, shouldn't he be doing something to help?

Robby said something else that he didn't hear and then was gone, and soon Photonman was at the front of the five-story building, flames roaring out of the third story above him, the sirens now loud and close, the crackle of the fire nearly deafening, the heat becoming painful.

He heard something through all the noise. A voice. A cry. Someone was in trouble.

He didn't stop to wonder how he could hear a voice over the roar of the fire. Maybe Photonman had enhanced hearing, maybe it was his imagination, maybe it was real. He opened the glass door and walked into the burning building.

———

Photons with their schizophrenic, quantum nature could be a wave or a particle and could travel at nearly three million meters per second. Photonman would be nothing like Superman. He could travel to the sun in eight minutes, he could change his body into pure photons and pass through the smallest of spaces. His kryptonite would be mirrors, which if perfectly sealed around him, could trap him. A much more interesting weakness than a green rock from an alien world. Brett Evans, aka Photonman, thought of all of this as the smoke assaulted his lungs, as the intense heat made him sweat, as the weak voice called to him.

He realized that Photonman's powers would go far beyond the ability to survive on light and water, be far greater than the ability to live without a soul-sucking job and heart-breaking responsibilities. Photonman could travel to the moon in seconds, could escape from any form of restraint, could manipulate his body at the quantum level. Photonman would be an interesting superhero to write about.

He found the timing of all of this somewhat amusing. His creativity had been barely registering since things had gotten intense with his mother, and he hadn't actually finished any stories in close to a year. He kept finding himself writing scenes with tall, slim, middle-aged men facing implacable enemies in the starkest of landscapes. He was tall and slim and middle-aged, facing an implacable disease and living a life that felt bleak and seemed more than a little untenable.

He also realized that light wasn't the only thing that had been schizo lately, he had. He wasn't Photonman, that was just a fantasy to get him through the day. He was just a middle-aged human being that wrote software for a living and wrote fiction on the side to make himself happy, was married, had a daughter, was trying to do right by his mother while her dementia regressed her back towards childhood and ravaged her brain. His mother was facing a villain worse than Lex Luthor or The Joker, locked in a battle she couldn't win. There were no heroics or happy endings as far as his mother went.

"Help! I'm hurt. I can't walk. Can anyone hear me? Help me!" He could barely hear the voice over the roar of the fire two floors above him.

It was coming from the stairwell on the other side of the lobby, and Brett was afraid. He looked back at the front door, only six feet behind him, the heat making it difficult to move while sweat flowed from all his pores as his body desperately tried to keep him cool. His heart was pounding hard in his chest and his mouth tasted of smoke. He coughed, the smoke was getting worse.

"Please! Someone, help me, please."

Through the glass windows he saw three fire engines arriving. This was their job, not his. He had wandered in here in a sleep-deprived fog, fueled by his overly creative mind and his desperate need to escape his life. But they might not get here in time. They had to set up, assess the situation, determine if it was safe to enter the building—at this point, he was quite sure that it wasn't.

But here was someone in the real world that needed real help. Not from Photonman but from a fellow human.

He didn't hear the voice anymore, but heard a weak pounding on the door.

He shook his head, trying to clear it. Unlike his mother's dementia, here he could do something. He jogged across the deserted lobby, around the glass reception desk and to the stairwell. By the time he got there, he was dizzy and could barely stand up. He took his shirt off, wrapped it around his hand and turned the doorknob.

Smoke came flooding out the door and he couldn't see anything or breathe for a few moments. When the smoke cleared, he saw an unconscious woman lying on the floor. She was young, maybe thirty, with long dark hair, and a blue skirt and jacket on. Spilled papers were all around her and her right foot was twisted at an unnatural angle. She was unconscious, and must have stayed too long, trying to take the paperwork out with her. She must have tripped and fell down the stairs and couldn't get the door open.

Smoke continued to pour out of the stairwell and the roaring sound of the fire had gotten even louder. As he continued to cough, he crouched down and grabbed her by the collar of her dress jacket and started pulling, keeping low to the ground.

Suddenly the thirty feet across the lobby to the front door seemed like a marathon. His hands were slick with sweat, his eyes burned, his throat tightened, and he could hardly breathe.

No more thoughts of Photonman, or his work, or his mother, or the villainous disease that was ravaging her mind. Just one thought. Get to the door. Survive.

He almost made it, but too much smoke was pouring into the lobby, and no matter how low he got, the air wasn't breathable. He almost abandoned the woman—he didn't know her name, but had seen her on sunny days at lunchtime. They had exchanged a few words. She had two young children.

If he had left her behind, he would have made it. He knew this when he collapsed three feet from the door, gasping for air. As he lay there, he thought of Photonman, how if he was writing his origin story this would be the perfect kind of event to catalyze his powers.

But there were no superheroes, there was no escape, and the

only villains in this world were selfish, greedy people and implacable diseases.

As things grew dark, he thought of Ann and Beth and wished he could see them again.

And then another thought occurred to him, a dark spike of energy that he hated. *I'm free now.*

DEATH IS A FREEDOM, THE FINAL END. NO MORE JOBS THAT turn something you love into something you hate. No more taking care of a mother who has turned into a geriatric child and will never get better. No more facing days that seem unfaceable.

And death means the end of hearing his daughter's voice or holding his wife's hand. No more watching March madness, no more barbeques with the old man.

Freedom yes, but no more anything.

Brett woke up to the beep-beep of a monitor, a mask on his face, and rough sheets under his skin. His mind was foggy, thinking of endings and villains, superheroes, and photons. He felt a warm hand in his and heard a sharp intake of breath.

"Oh, thank God! Brett, can you hear me?"

He could hear the tears in Ann's voice and he no longer hated his name. He loved it.

He swallowed hard and nodded his head.

"How?" he croaked, his eyes still closed and his voice muffled underneath the oxygen mask.

"The firemen found you, pulled you out, right before the building collapsed."

"The woman?"

"She's still unconscious, but they think she will make it." There was a pause as Ann took in a shuddering breath. "What the hell were you thinking? Why did you do that?" The relief was tinged with anger and still he could hear the tears. He slowly opened his eyes and smiled, seeing the brown eyes and hair of the woman he loved.

He shrugged and said, "I wasn't quite myself."

She nodded as tears rolled down her cheeks. She understood. Neither had been themselves lately. They both had jobs that they still needed to do. His mother still needed their help, even though there was no last-minute rescue coming for her.

***

FLAKES OF SNOW DANCED IN THE GREY SKY AS BRETT EVANS once again faced the daunting entryway to the care home that housed his mother. Things were getting worse, her fear and paranoia had come to dominate, she couldn't manage her clothes well enough to go to the bathroom anymore, and she needed help feeding herself.

This afternoon, three smokers were out on the porch staring at him as they puffed away on the cigarettes, huddled into their jackets against the cold. There was no sun to warm his face, no bright ball of burning helium to lighten his mood, no pretending he was Photonman. There was only hard reality to face without any fantasy to protect him.

He took a deep breath, the cold air stinging his nose and the wind pulling at his hair. He was letting it grow out, no more "grey reduction program," no more hiding from the inescapable.

The visit was going to be hard, they were all hard now, but he had Ann helping him, and Beth would be visiting for Christmas soon. He was back to writing, not very much, but enough to get him by.

He smiled, not the pure kind of smile kids have when you put a bowl of ice cream in front of them, but not a forced smile either. Maybe you would call it a realistic smile. He was daunted by what was in front of him, but happy to be alive, grateful there was something—no matter how small—that he could do to comfort his mother.

"Good morning, ladies," he said to the three smokers as he headed in.

BACKSTORY—NOT A SUPERHERO

Most stories are personal in some way. I think that is the nature of art. This one is personal in a lot of ways. Too many, really. Some of the stories I write are about exploring the hard things in my life and I wrote this one not long after I had come through a very difficult period.

This story is about an exhausted middle-aged writer wrestling with the difficult problems that come even with a rather privileged life, problems that don't exactly contrast well with the characters he writes about.

That was where I was when I started writing this story, this line is particularly telling: "...a middle-aged man being squeezed between overwork and eldercare, neither of which he could escape." It's not autobiographical or anything, just taking that feeling, twisting the circumstances around a bit, and exploring it.

Finding our way back to ourselves isn't always easy, but it is often necessary.

PART 6

THE THREE THINGS YOU MUST KNOW ABOUT YOUR NEW COMPANION

THE THREE THINGS YOU MUST KNOW ABOUT YOUR NEW COMPANION

THE INSTANT I OPEN THE DOOR TO MY HOME, I KNOW something is wrong. There's no squeal, no sound of scampering nails against the hardwood floor, no excited panting.

This has been a bad day already. If anyone ever "woke up on the wrong side of the bed" it was me. Today. A malaise I don't understand haunting me all day long.

My brain kicks into overdrive before my eyes adjust from the bright summer sun to the dim house. Where is my pug, Brutus? He seemed a little off this morning too. Is he sick? Did he run away? Did someone break into the house and steal him? What will I do without him? How will I get by? Did he finally figure out that I'm not good enough for him?

Time seems to slow as the questions reverberate in my mind, making me nauseous. My well-honed ability to worry and question myself ramping up, becoming a power, a force of nature, like a haboob rising up over the desert, the winds starting to race, the sands starting to fly.

That's when it's time to run, but I can't run from myself.

My brain is built for this kind of overthinking. I have an

excellent memory and a sharp imagination. I build scenarios for gaming companies, multi-branching scripts for video games. From dungeon crawls, to pirates on the high seas, to space armadas, I have to think all the moves through.

Where is Brutus with his beautifully smushed nose and comically heavy breathing and curled tale?

It's 6:28 p.m., exactly thirty minutes to sundown, and I'm right on time, the summer heat washing into my century-old home. Out of habit, I grab the leash off the hook right by the door, my eyes adjusting to the light and I see him.

Brutus is just staring at me. Like I'm a stranger. Like I'm not his everything.

What did I do?

What's wrong?

What if there's an intruder and he's trying to warn me?

What if he's having a stroke, he's three now, but that's not that old.

His wrinkled mouth is slightly open, his tongue lolling a bit to the side. His nose, ears, and mouth are black, with a few white hairs invading at the chin, the rest of him a lovely tan. He just sits there and stares at me softly panting.

Where's the rambunctious greeting that makes my day worth living? Where's the eager panting and dancing once I touch the leash, the soft gurr of excitement? Where's the snuffling at my shoes and pants as he hoovers up any scents I might have brought home?

He's just sitting there, staring at me.

This isn't right. My brain is exploding.

What if none of this is real and I'm just a simulation designing simulations for a simulated company? What if Brutus isn't real, was never real, a trick of my mind. What if he's been a robot all this time? What if this is a glitch or a test or a...

Maybe this will sound silly to you, but of all the beings on the planet, Brutus is the most important one to me. The one that keeps me going.

My mind spins out of control with worry.

BRUTUS WAS A GIFT FROM IRIS. HER LAST GIFT AS MY WIFE. She brought him over the day the divorce was final. The day my heart was empty, and I sat on the couch for hours rewinding our relationship and trying to figure out at which branching point I chose the wrong scenario, took the wrong turn, didn't ask the right question.

My mind raced trying to fathom living without what I knew I couldn't live without. Her. Us. This amazing woman that had somehow learned to love my chubby, bespectacled, geeky self.

Netflix was streaming some Marvel show turned down low that I wasn't watching, just so there was some noise in the house and I couldn't hear the old walls creak. The living room was nearly bare, with just a brown overstuffed couch on the worn hardwood floors across from the big flat screen and Xbox. I let Iris take everything she wanted. She wanted a lot of things, just not me.

The divorce decree was stuck to the refrigerator with magnets. I had left it there for the last week because I didn't want to forget the day.

We humans exist in space-time and while I am always firmly rooted in space, time is something that seems elusive to me. I'm not a time traveler, or any such nonsense as that, it's just that I don't remember dates. I'll forget what's on my calendar five seconds after I look at it. This was only one of the many problems Iris and I had.

I was so deep in my head that the knock on the door was a shock. I blinked against the sunlight when I opened the door. A woman was standing there, she looked tired and in need of a shower. It took a few moments for my mind to engage and recognize her.

"Here, Henry," Iris said unceremoniously as she put the wriggling, licking, bundle of puppy in my arms. It was maybe three months old with endless curiosity and energy. It felt like a foreign thing in my hands. Something I couldn't understand just like the woman that was no longer my wife.

Iris's face was stained with tears and her brown hair was a bit greasy and pulled back in a tight ponytail. "I know you don't think you need this, but you do."

The smell was the most striking thing about the warm puppy. Sweet and earthy, it seemed to slow my beating heart and my mind changed gears. I had never had a dog before and I had no idea what to do or how to care for them.

What if I failed with the puppy like I had with Iris?

What if the dog hated me and added its miserableness to my own?

What if I end up loving this thing and then it dies? That would be...

I opened my mouth to speak, but she continued. "Supplies and instructions are in the basket." She pointed to a large wicker basket on the stoop piled high with dog food, dog cookies, a ratty towel, chew toys, and more.

Iris wasn't me, but she was a lot like me. Behind my back, I'm sure people whisper "on the spectrum" in reference to me and some might do that for Iris too. She's not normal, not as this world defines normal. She can see math in her head, how the numbers flow together in such beautiful ways. We thought our not-normal similarities would help us stay together, but I guess it wasn't enough.

And then she was gone, and I was left with the puppy, his

sharp teeth gnawing happily on my knuckle. "You are a brute, you know that?" I said, laughing despite myself.

I couldn't refuse Iris's last gift. And maybe, I thought, she had solved the calculus of me and this puppy was the solution. I smiled, went inside, and put the animal down where it proceeded to pee on my grandmother's Persian rug.

I DON'T UNDERSTAND PEOPLE, ME INCLUDED. I DON'T understand the big things, like why (or even how) I fell in love with Iris. I can play back the memory with ease. We met up at the ski resort in Flagstaff. I stood staring at the mountain refusing to ski, disgusted when I realized the unnatural strip of snow was made with reclaimed water. She made fun of me when I told her. That had led to drinks and her coaxing me out onto the slope and then more. So strange that such a small thing had turned into a life-changing event.

I don't understand the small things either, like why I can't go to bed until I've checked the locks on the doors twice and the windows once—never more, never less or I won't sleep.

I don't understand why we are all so irrational while pretending we have perfectly rational motivations that we mostly make up to justify what has already happened.

And I don't understand how we got this way... well, you can either claim an omnipotent god did it for some reason or another or the messy chaos of evolution just landed us here. Neither is satisfying.

But I do understand Brutus. Or, at least I thought I did.

I ignore the hot air washing in and get down on the hardwood floor. He has always liked people better when they are down on his level.

"Hey, boy," I say softly. "What's going on? Did something happen?"

My mind is still racing, along with my heart, but I don't let any of that out. Sometimes I do let my difficult emotions out and Brutus just looks at me like he finds me as unfathomable as I do most humans, but not today. He doesn't want to hear how worried I am.

He sits there, staring and softly panting.

I scan the room. Everything is in order. His dog bed sits next to the couch and it's slightly out of place which happens when he turns and turns in a circle and digs at it like its grass, guided by some genetic programming.

The Blue-rays are in their place in the shelves by the TV, alphabetized and each case pushed all the way in. The Xbox is put away and the plants are in their exact right spots. The latest copy of *Wired* magazine sits in the center of the coffee table.

Through into the kitchen, I can see his water bowl and his empty food bowl next to the back door with his dog door.

I see nothing out of order.

Dogs like routine. No, dogs *love* routine, and Brutus loves his even more than I love mine. Thirty minutes before sundown, I get home from work and we head out for a walk. He walks on leash through this old Phoenix neighborhood past all the single-floor cinderblock homes, until we get to the park. Then Brutus really fires up his nose and I let him choose his way. Routine is important and so is variety and stimulation.

There is a small dog park there, and we usually end up going in and I unleash him, and he socializes with ease—something that I know he needs but makes me quite uncomfortable. I do try to socialize with the other dog people (not dog "owners," I don't own Brutus) but it's never with ease.

Then, when the sun dips below the horizon, I fetch him—he's never ready to go—and we head home for dinner.

This is his favorite part of the day. Well, I *think* it's his favorite part, I *know* it's mine. Partially because this time with Brutus assuages my own loneliness, but more because I am able to do something so simple that makes another being on this planet so very happy.

Humans are not easy to make happy, but he is.

Brutus loves his walk. Then why is he sitting there staring at me?

My mind has been rushing through the possibilities and has discarded the intruder scenario—there is just no evidence—which leaves me thinking of all the maladies or diseases he might be suffering, which leads me quickly to his eventual demise not being so eventual, which leads me to...

I can't even go there. I just can't.

***

"I don't understand him," I said to Iris. This was three days after she dropped him off and the first time I'd been able to get her to pick up the phone. She had answered a few texts, but it was usually answers like, "google it."

"Interspecies relationships are hard," she said dryly, her amusement still clear.

"What? Interspecies?" I stared at the little, still-unnamed puppy as it merrily gnawed on my slipper, which was still on my foot.

She sighed. "Didn't you read the note I left you? The worst thing you can do is treat your dog like a human. He's not."

It was obvious, but somehow I had been speaking to the animal expecting it to understand me. Expecting it to be civilized. The thought of a dog as an "alien" was delicious to my geek brain, but that is not what stuck in my head. "My dog?" I mumbled.

Iris laughed, a real laugh, it wasn't much, but it was the first I had heard in so very long. "Yes, Henry, he's *your* dog."

"But..." I started, but then stopped. In my heart, in a place where I dared not look or admit, I was hoping that it was "our" dog. That this was some kind of test, that if I could care for an animal then Iris would want me back.

"Okay, okay," she continued. "That might be a bit misleading, that 'your' thing."

My heart thumped in my ears and the world and the puppy gnawing on my slipper nearly disappeared as I waited for her to continue, hoping... no wishing... no, *needing* her to use the word "our."

"You don't own the dog," she chuckled. "It's going to be more the other way around. But he is yours in the same way a family member is yours."

I sucked in a breath and slowly collapsed to the floor, that secret I was trying to keep from myself was now naked before me. Of course this wasn't about us getting back together, even though that is what I needed.

There had been too much silence, so I said, "You used to have a pug, right?"

"Pomeranian, well a mix, but mostly Pomeranian. When I was a kid." She paused, her tone getting serious. "He needs you, Henry. I didn't just go to the pet store. He's a rescue. The other important thing to remember about a dog, is that it's not about you."

"Wait. What?" Surely this dog of all dogs was about me. She had given him to me to ease the grief of our separation, hadn't she?

"It's not about you," she repeated slowly like I was a slow learner. "If you make it about you, this won't work. You are there for him, he is not there for you."

It didn't make sense, the concepts not quite fitting together, but I said, "Okay. Not about me. Got it."

Had that been the problem with our relationship? Had I made it about me instead of making it about her? Was she trying to tell me something?

"Listen, Henry, I've got to go. Keep googling, remember dogs are not like us..." her voice trailed off and then she sniffed. "They are much simpler, much purer. Just let this happen, okay?"

"Yeah," I said not knowing what else to say as the puppy continued to happily chew on my slipper.

"Read the note," she said before hanging up.

I rooted through the basket and found it written by hand in her ornate cursive:

The Three Things You Must Know About Your New Companion

1. *It's not about you.*
2. *Interspecies relationships are hard.*
3. *In many ways that matter, your dog is smarter than you.*

As I search the house, giving Brutus a wide berth, he just stares. Sitting there. Only his head moving.

Interspecies relationships are hard.

It keeps running through my brain and Iris's tone when she said it.

Brutus has his reasons, but he can't talk and today I don't understand them.

My bedroom is fine, a round pool of wrinkles towards the bottom of the bedspread—Brutus had taken a nap. While I smooth it out—sorry, I would have had to make the bed before evacuating the Titanic—I noticed the spot was warm. He had just been here.

The bathroom is fine, the spare bedroom, and the kitchen. His dog door is operational and the folded towel under his water bowl is damp—that I can leave, I switch it out once a day.

I hear his nails clicking on the hardwood. He has moved just far enough so he can see me.

"What is it, buddy?"

He takes a deeper breath and sighs.

I used to wish that he could talk, but that thought is only a fleeting one these days. Just because you can talk doesn't mean a relationship is any easier. Sometimes, I think, it's the opposite.

I step outside and check the yard and find one brown pile. Using a plastic arm-length claw, I carefully moved it to the little metal can I keep his waste in.

The house, his world, is just fine. But he doesn't seem to be.

All of this restless activity on my part is about avoiding Brutus and his behavior which I just don't understand. Now that I know his environment is okay that leaves only one thing. One unthinkable conclusion.

He's not okay.

<hr>

Puppies are teething. Puppies are young. If you don't give them things to chew on, they will chew on things you don't want them to chew on (and sometimes, they'll do that anyway).

It's not about you.

This was one of the first things I figured out about the wriggling bundle of energy and hunger and joy that was the puppy Iris gave to me.

Most of his behaviors are due to his alien nature. Cause and effect.

Puppy and teething (cause) = incessant chewing (effect).

I was so proud. His behavior was about him not me.

Not that it wasn't in almost everything I read, but once I had absorbed it, applied it, and seen that it worked it was like a revelation. And a disappointment, because I wanted human relationships to be that easy.

The puppy's home while I was at work was the kitchen with pads for peeing, water, and lots of safe things to chew on.

I stood there at the baby-gated entrance to the kitchen, a smile on my face. This balanced out the damage to my couch a bit.

"Good boy!" I said. After all, positive reinforcement is really the best way to train an animal. So said the book I was reading.

It had been a bad day on top of a bad month on top of a bad year. First the divorce and now the puppy had taken my attention away from my work and my project had fallen behind. My boss had used long sentences and very serious words when he spoke to me today, his face looking tired and serious. I have always strived to stay out of the principal's office and then out of the manager's office. I don't underperform. Ever.

I stepped over the baby gate and the puppy pounced on my shoe and started gnawing it.

"No! You brute. No!"

He didn't listen. He was not a human. He didn't understand the word yet, but he did hesitate, so he was starting to understand the tone. But then I felt bad, he was just lonely.

I had spent some time at work sketching the scenarios out as if I were writing it for a video game, trying to get into the head of the character (the dog in this case).

Dogs are pack animals. Dogs don't like to be alone. Puppies have excessive energy and little self-control. Puppies need lots and lots of exercise.

I got down to the floor and grabbed him, breathing deeply of that sweet puppy smell. It wasn't the kind of scent I would normally enjoy, given the animal would lick anything and everything, but I had come to really like it.

He immediately started to chew on my finger, his sharp, new teeth decidedly painful.

"Et tu, Brute?" I asked the puppy, but of course he didn't understand Latin any more than he understood English.

He didn't care, and I didn't really either. I would have to wash my hands, of course, to remove all the dog saliva (we all know where that tongue has been) but it made me laugh.

"Brutus, that is your name."

I grabbed my phone and Brutus moved his attention to my shoe and I took a picture and texted it to Iris telling her his name.

This was the one thing that she would still talk to me about, the one way the lines of communication were still open.

The void I felt with her gone was worse than the pain of our fighting and separating, and I needed something, anything.

A few minutes later the text came in: "Good name. Now you two are a family!"

I sat there, hearing nothing but the pounding of my heart in my ears for the longest time while Brutus chewed a hole in my shoe.

THIS HAS NOT BEEN A GOOD DAY. I HADN'T SLEPT WELL, IRIS filling my dreams. That day we met in Flagstaff at the ski resort. My sheer delight at finding that she was in no way "normal," that she lived in Phoenix too. Those first few tentative dates that were nearly a panic attack for me to get up the courage to ask for, much less go on.

It was all the early stages when I felt for her what I didn't think possible, what I had seen in movies, but had never believed in. She was all I could think of, memories of her taking my brain over like a computer virus, replacing all the thoughts that used to exist there with thoughts of her. She was my world.

I had woken with an exhaustion that coffee couldn't touch. I couldn't concentrate. My food tasted like cardboard. It's like I wasn't even in the correct life, everything just off.

The divorce is three years in the past and I'm actually liking my life, making the dreams all the more confusing.

And now that I'm home from this awful day, Brutus is just staring at me.

"Please," I say to Brutus, back by the front door with the leash in my hand. "Please, boy. I need this."

He just sat there, staring. I could pick him up and haul him outside, but that wouldn't be right. I could leave, go on a walk without him, but that would just be spiteful.

It's not about me. I have to make this about him, put myself aside for a moment and find out what he needs.

I rack my brain trying to remember all the early lessons, before I understood Brutus. I'm missing something, if only I can remember it.

———

BRUTUS AND I WERE A FAMILY. IRIS AND I WERE NOT, BUT the pug was the one thing that still linked us together.

As I figured Brutus out, I would text her about him and she would respond with an emoji or a few words.

We had been a bit of an "odd couple" during our marriage. She was a slob and I was fastidiously clean. I was a chronic overthinker and her insights came to her in bursts of startling clarity. I needed rigid structure and yet couldn't remember an appointment to save my life. She hated structure and wanted to be spontaneous all the time.

There was love and we tried to keep it going, but I think we tried too long. I think we burned each other out.

When Brutus was about one, we were out at Encanto Park on a hot, but not roasting, fall day, walking near the pond under the palm trees, the trace humidity in the air refreshing for Phoenix. Encanto was not near my home, not at all, but I had taken to trying a new park with Brutus every weekend. We needed the comfort of structure and we needed the stimulation of variety.

As I walked him, I saw a couple on a bench holding hands. We were coming up from the side on a path and they were gazing at the pond and didn't see us. The woman was willowy with long brown hair dressed in a powder blue sundress, the man muscular with close-cropped black hair.

It was Iris. I opened my mouth to say "hello," excited to show her the fully grown and well-behaved Brutus when she laughed, said "Oh, Tom," and they began kissing.

I felt like vomiting. It had been a year since the divorce, of course Iris had been on dates. I knew this logically. I had even been on a couple disastrous blind dates, but I hadn't actually seen her in nine months and now this...

My mind exploded with thoughts of the past, worry about all the things I had done wrong, how my inflexibility had driven her away. She was intelligent. She was beautiful. She had moved on and I hadn't. I didn't even know if I was capable of moving on.

"Nothing here for us," I said to Brutus as we turned around.

"Let's try this," I say, walking over to Brutus and snapping the leash on. He sniffs my hand but doesn't move. I step away, the leash growing taut, but still he doesn't move.

My mind is full of Iris. There is something there, I was just missing it, too lost in the past to see the present clearly.

I put the leash down, go to the ceramic cookie jar and shake it, the bright sound ringing through the house, but he doesn't come. I take one to him and he eats it, but it is clear by his lethargic affect that he is only doing it for me.

I sit down with a sigh and check his nose which is moist. I look him over again and don't see anything going on. It will be time to haul him to the vet soon, but I've come to trust Brutus. There is a message here, I just don't understand it.

I sit there and stare at him as he stares at me.

ONE EVENING WHEN BRUTUS WAS ABOUT TWO, HE DIDN'T go outside as I was preparing for bed. He had a dog door and was very comfortable using it. We both had our little rituals and I found the slap-slap of him going out the dog door while I was brushing my teeth a great comfort.

He still had a fondness for my footwear, but otherwise had become a fine companion.

I still felt the scars of Iris and our failed marriage, but it was fading as time passed. Brutus had done what she wanted him to do: given me a reason beyond work and family. Given me a good reason to come home every night. Given me love.

It seemed hollow at times; I lost a wife and gained a dog, but Brutus liked my strict routine and made a whole lot less messes than Iris had. I could make Brutus happy just by being with him. I knew it was important to not let him be my everything, that would put too much of a burden on him. In fact, I had recently asked a coworker named Jill out on a date. Just coffee, but she had said yes.

But it was Brutus that grounded me and made the hard days bearable and the good days better.

"What's wrong?" I asked. He was in his dog bed next to the couch, staring through the kitchen at the back door. Recently, I had finally made the house whole following Iris's exodus by putting in some bookshelves and a few chairs to go with the couch and a coffee table.

I sat down and pet him, checked to see if his nose was warm and tried to prevent my brain from leaping to the worst-case scenarios. Maybe he just didn't need to pee. Maybe he had peed earlier, and I just hadn't heard the dog door.

But he was staring at the door. Something wasn't right.

I got a flashlight and headed towards the door, the click of Brutus's nails on the floor behind me.

I went out and knew something was wrong. The normally bland scent of the Phoenix night had turned foul, smelling vaguely of burned rubber.

"What is it?" I asked, looking back at Brutus whose hackles were raised. He surged forth barking and I saw the skunk just before it sprayed both of us.

You know that smell of skunk that roadkill puts off? Being sprayed is a hundred times worse. It smells chemically, like some kind of toxic waste, and burns like pepper spray if it gets into your eyes.

The next day after I had cleansed myself, Brutus, and the house I called Iris and she actually answered.

After I told her what happened, she said, "Well, you know, Brutus is smarter than you."

"What?"

"He knew there was a skunk out there. That's why he didn't go out. He only got involved because he was trying to defend you." I could tell she could barely keep herself from laughing.

"Well..."

"It's true," she said, her tone becoming serious. "In many important ways dogs are smarter than we are. It's on the note I brought with Brutus."

The house still smelled of skunk and I was sitting on the couch on an old blanket I had thrown over it with Brutus curled up next me, his loud pug breathing a comfort. "I don't know about that," I said defensively.

"They are, Henry. They rest when they need to. They don't hold a grudge. They experience joy and give love readily. They don't dwell on the past..."

Her voice trailed off and my heart started pounding, my brain running scenarios. Something was up. She had answered the phone. She was about to tell me something, something I didn't want to hear.

"Just say it, Iris," I said.

She paused, and I heard her sniff. "I'm seeing someone, Henry, and... I... I think it might be serious."

My mind seethed with jealousy, but I said, "I'm happy for you, Iris." Because this too, wasn't about me.

Brutus woke up and looked at me, his brown eyes sorrowful, and he put his chin on my leg and let out a long sigh.

I was learning to be a better human from my dog.

THE SUN IS DOWN AND THE NEIGHBORHOOD QUIET, ONLY the sound of an occasional car going by and the distant warble of a siren. My mind has finally calmed down, has run through all the worst-case scenarios and I had given myself some time to remember.

If Brutus is sick, it is just probably an upset stomach, not an emergency. But I don't think that is it.

I remember the lessons I learned. Brutus is smarter than me

in many ways that count. Interspecies relationships are hard. It's not about me.

As a human with an ego, it's that "not about me" rule that has taken me the longest time to understand. It is really more about a Brutus-first approach and getting out of my head. The greatest joy in having an animal isn't what they do for you, but that you can serve them, make their lives wonderful, giving them what they need. And that, in turn, pays off handsomely.

And I think of Brutus with every decision I make. How long I will be away. What kind of vacations I take (they are much better with him), what kind of things I bring into the house. How I exercise and rest. Who I date.

I'm still seeing Jill. She loves Brutus... if she hadn't, that would have been a deal breaker for sure. But we've taken it very slow. I don't know what the future holds for us, but it's nice to have someone to talk to.

In many ways my life orbits Brutus's, not the other way around.

But maybe this time it is about me.

Maybe this is about those dreams of Iris and our courtship and marriage that had stuck with me through the day, a thick malaise that is only now breaking up.

I get up and go into the kitchen and look at the old-fashioned paper calendar. It is attached to the refrigerator with a magnet and I put things on it that I don't want my phone reminding me of or things I really wanted to remember. It sits there next to Iris's three things.

Scrawled at the top of today is "Iris's Wedding #2."

Iris got married today.

That explains the dreams and my funk.

My calendar-challenged brain and my grief-shy heart had kept the thought out of my mind, but my body knew it and Brutus knew something was wrong with me.

A dog knows how to take care of themselves. Maybe that's what he's demonstrating to me. I need to withdraw for a bit, let the feelings come out, not hide from it. Maybe it's time for a break from the routine to take care of myself.

I get my phone and text Iris, *Congratulations Iris! I am so glad you are happy. Give my best to Tom.*

I collapse onto the couch with a sigh. Iris and Tom have been engaged for eighteen months and during that time she has allowed our friendship to slowly come back. There was even an extremely awkward double date. Our friendship is no longer restricted to Brutus. And while it's been hard, that is good.

I then text Jill. *I've had a tough day and can't wait to see you tomorrow.*

She quickly texts back a thumbs-up and a heart—she loves her emojis.

"How about a sappy love story?" I ask Brutus. "I think I need a good cry."

Brutus yawns, shakes, gets up onto the couch and burrows his head under my hand. I laugh and pet him.

Brutus is smarter than me, so much smarter than me.

BACKSTORY—THE THREE THINGS YOU MUST KNOW ABOUT YOUR NEW COMPANION

A few years back, after we had lost our beloved and brilliant spaniel named Madison, I went through a phase where I wrote a bunch of dog stories. My wife and I were without a dog in our lives for the first time in decades and we were both grieving. Writing stories that featured dogs was one of my ways of dealing with that grief.

During that time, I contemplated writing one of those annoying blog posts that have a list of things you just have to know that serves as click-bait. I didn't want to write this for the traffic, but because I had some things to say.

Fortunately, being a fiction writer, many of those things came out in the stories I wrote in that time frame, this one the most clearly.

This story was selected for an anthology that, unfortunately, was canceled because of the COVID-19 pandemic.

PART 7
APRIL AND ALAN

APRIL AND ALAN

I don't know anything.

The darkness of doubt has overtaken me, and I don't know anything.

She's dying. The only "she" there ever has been for me. Decades of April and Alan versus the world. Us two clinging together through the madness of the external world and the chaos of our internal worlds. Marriage, the death of a child, the death of our parents, jobs, recessions, illness, cancer…

I don't know anything.

Well, there's gravity and death and taxes, so not knowing anything is clearly hyperbole. I know my heart has to beat for me to live and I must eat and drink and rest. I know beginnings fold into endings before you know it. I know that the expression of love is the most powerful force in the universe.

But it *feels* like I don't know anything.

And feelings are what this experience of life is about. And April has been my life for over forty years.

She's dying now, and I don't know anything.

HER HOSPITAL BED IS IN THE LIVING ROOM, FURNITURE pushed aside to make room for it. She wanted to die at home. And I don't blame her, would never even whisper a word to her about this, but after she dies I'm going to have to move. Right away.

If I don't, I think the memories will destroy me.

The one-story house is big and breezy and more than we needed, but we liked the neighborhood and our knees were old enough that our two-story house was getting to be a problem. Three years ago, we started looking and April rejected each house the realtor took us to within two minutes, except for this house.

"This one, Alan," she had said, taking a deep breath in that living room for the first time. It was empty, with off-white carpet that was worn and stained.

"I don't know, April," I said. "It's more house than we need. It's..." I didn't continue. We didn't need four bedrooms, Kyle would never come visit us. We only visited him when we took our monthly outings to the cemetery.

This was the kind of house for a new family or for retirees if they knew their kids and grandkids would come visiting.

"Oh, come on," she said, sweeping up to me, still graceful enough with her long grey hair caught back in a ponytail, a bit of a sparkle still in her hazel eyes. She put her warm hand on my chest. "It's two miles away from our existing house. Same area. An easy move. No more stairs. We can afford it."

She was like that, answering all my objections at once, leaving me nowhere to go. "It's too much," I said. "I don't want you cleaning all the time."

"I like to clean." She swept into the kitchen and started talking about the marble countertops and the new stove, but I wasn't really listening. I stood in the living room just watching her, a smile lighting up her face.

April is my older woman. I am a gentleman and won't tell you her age, but I'm over seventy now and she's a fair number of years older, age having wrinkled her beautiful face and finally succeeded in slowing her down. The move would be hard on me, but harder on her.

I stood there kicking at a stain in the carpet while she went on about the kitchen.

She had survived Kyle's death, had beat breast cancer, I knew we would survive the move. I just felt this dread that had slowly built up over the years. Our bright beginning was nearing its inevitable end and I was starting to fear change, knowing one day one of those changes would be a death.

I sighed, shook it off and looked at my beautiful wife. The lines of age had taken over her face, but not her beauty. I would always watch my beautiful April every chance I got.

In truth, I didn't care much about houses, or granite countertops, or how big the fridge was. The house had a garage, which I did care about, and the one floor, which my knees cared about.

"Look at this view. It's perfect, Alan!" she called from the kitchen.

I smiled and nodded, walking into the kitchen. I couldn't say the house was perfect, I've never found anything in this world to be perfect... except for April.

HOSPICE IS A COMPASSIONATE PROCESS. IT'S THE ONE AREA in medicine when it's all about the journey, not the destination. The destination is set—death—so the only thing to focus on is the quality of the journey. Before that, the focus is on doing anything and everything to avoid that final destination as if it's not the most inevitable of things.

"Thirsty?" I asked, standing near the hospital bed. The TV had an old sitcom playing that she loved, and the house was too warm at 82 degrees.

She shook her head, her hazel eyes barely flicking up to me.

This was different and terrifying. Not just the weight that was dropping off her, not the gaunt face and hollow eyes, this withdrawal into... well, I don't really know, but she was withdrawing, going deep within, as her body rocketed her towards that final destination.

She didn't take her eyes off the TV but patted the bed and I nodded. I pulled a chair up and took her cool hand. The house was overheated so she felt comfortable under her blankets, while I was in shorts and a T-shirt.

The bed had her in a half-sitting position, which was good for TV viewing and for when the coughing came. A winter pneumonia had landed her in the hospital where she caught some drug resistant crud which led to the ICU and major antibiotics.

Three weeks in the hospital. Three weeks being by her side as much as I was physically able. Holding her hand when she was awake and asleep, when she was coherent and when she was raving from the effects of the infection. Endless consults with doctors who didn't know what else to try. Awkward visits from friends who wanted to either have their good-bye time with April or wanted desperately to help me but had no idea what to do.

Many, though, looked at me with such fear. Fear that asked, is this going to be me one day? Will I be so terrified and helpless?

April's dry chuckle at the show turned into a barking cough. I got a tissue for her and offered her some water after it was over.

She sucked the barest amount through the yellow straw, only to please me, I suspect.

I thought of asking her whether she was done with water, or more brazenly, whether she was ready to go, but she was past long conversations and I needed to make this journey about her and not about me.

Things will be left unsaid. When there are endless things to say, this is inevitable.

Dreams will be left unfulfilled. With a heart full of dreams, this has to happen.

Regrets will be there. In a life actually lived, there are mistakes and there are regrets.

Endings can be such bitter things.

WE MET IN THE MOST MUNDANE OF WAYS, AT THE GROCERY store. This was before you could order almost everything online, before the internet, thank God. In the internet era, I just wouldn't have left the house and missed my chance to know sweet April.

I was battered by my first marriage turning into a complete disaster in the first year. I had gotten married too young, one year out of college having studied accounting and business administration and having married Mary Toulson, my college girlfriend.

We were too young, Mary and me. But I kind of think that no one is old enough to get married when they get married. Sharing your life with someone, being intimate physically, financially, and emotionally—how do you prepare for that?

Mary and I even lived together for a full year before marrying, but even that wasn't enough. In the cliche-filled year of our marriage, she fell for my best friend, had a torrid affair with him, and eventually came crawling back to me.

I divorced her.

And that long aside was to get me back to that grocery store in 1972. I was twenty-five and still felt like a bit of a fraud shopping for groceries. Mary had cooked, had loved to cook, relegating me to barbeque duty and Sunday morning French toast—both skills I learned from my father.

I was pushing a squeaky-wheeled cart down a worn linoleum aisle under the bright fluorescent lights. The back-right wheel was the troubled one, it flapped like a fish out of water when I pushed, making the path of the cart not only noisy but a bit unpredictable.

I was feeling disconsolate, thinking I deserved to have the worst cart in the store, deserved to have lost my wife and my best friend, deserved to... No, I didn't deserve this damn cart. I gave the cart a good shove while I stared down at the wheel, which suddenly turned straight, and the cart escaped my grasp and went rolling down the breakfast cereal aisle. Squeak, squeak, squeak.

Its path was a little wobbly, but basically straight. It made a beeline for a woman who appeared to be deeply lost in thought, choosing between Apple Jacks and Raisin Bran and didn't see the cart.

"Watch out—" I began as the cart connected with her hip. She had brown hair and was quite pretty, with a navy-blue skirt, a white blouse, and a string of pearls around her neck. She let out a small cry and her angry face looked down at the cart and then at me.

"I'm sorry. The wheel... It was... I...." I stammered as her brown eyes bored into me. "I'm just so sorry."

She took a deep breath and then her eyes wandered down to my cart which was filled with Hungry-Man frozen dinners, Folgers Instant Coffee, a loaf of white bread, and a bunch of bananas.

When she looked back up, her anger was replaced by pity.

She was a bit older than me, I couldn't have told you how much, but a few years at least. She was still young enough that she didn't really look that much older, it was more how she carried herself. Her cart had a variety of food in it including fresh fruits and vegetables.

"Bachelor," she said with a small smile.

I nodded. "Look, I really am sorry. I swear that cart is possessed" I extended my hand. "My name is Alan."

Her intense gaze continued to take me in. I was sure she must have thought me a boy, immature. And I certainly didn't think so then, but from the perspective of the long years in between, I know I was but a boy in a man's body.

"April," she said, looking at my cart and shaking her head. She took my hand and... well, no fireworks, no sparks of electricity, but I was intrigued. She was beautiful and kind and was wrapped in the mystery of an older woman—a denser mystery than the normal mystery a woman is to a man. "Maybe you should learn how to cook, Alan."

"Maybe you should teach me, April." I gave her my best smile, wide and bright, a smile I hadn't tried out for many, many months.

My stomach seized up on me and my face flushed hot. I was so embarrassed by my bold statement.

She let go of my hand and put her hands on her hips and I felt my heart fall. I had gone too far, been too forward. And then she laughed. It was a bright sound and warm, out of place under the hum of the fluorescent lights above us and the bland ugliness of the linoleum below us.

"Tell you what, Alan," she said, her head slowly shaking. "Go put those awful TV dinners back and I'll show you how to shop for real food that is easy to cook."

I stood there with my jaw hanging open. I don't know if I

had been expecting a date to come out of my bold questions, but I can tell you I wasn't expecting what looked like a motherly lesson on how to shop.

"Well?" she prompted.

I almost told her no, but then I got a little bit lost in those hazel eyes. She really was quite beautiful.

"Be right back!" I said, grabbing my errant cart and shoving it towards the frozen food section.

APRIL'S HAZEL EYES LEFT THE TV AND MET MINE FOR more than a moment, finally. Her brow furrowed, deepening the already deep lines there, and a smile played briefly on her thin, chapped lips.

Her cool hand was in mine and my butt ached from being in the chair so much. I longed to go out and feel the sun on my face, breathe some air that wasn't thick with the dank smell of impending death. But I couldn't leave her, not longer than it took to go to the bathroom, or shove some food in my mouth, or get something for her.

"I was just thinking about how we met," I said, my voice quiet.

She smiled, a real smile, but only briefly. She licked her lips and swallowed awkwardly. I grabbed her water glass off the little table next to her bed and presented the straw. She took a small sip.

"TV dinners and instant coffee," I said with a smile as big as I could manage... which wasn't that big.

"Bananas," she croaked.

I smiled. "My one concession to fresh fruits and vegetables."

"Cute."

I stared at her, trying to get her meaning. "I was cute or that I had bananas was cute?"

She nodded.

"Both?"

She nodded again and smiled.

Her eyes wandered back to the TV. That was it. She was done talking to me. Two words, "bananas" and "cute." At this point it was a treasure, but it felt weak and mean compared to my forty-year-old memories, compared to our decades together filled with long, rambling, philosophical conversations.

And my memory isn't that good. I remember meeting April, because... well, that's the day my life truly started, but the memory is old, well worn, and badly faded.

But even it was vivid compared to the two words that amounted to a long conversation at this point in our journey.

She closed her eyes and was quickly asleep. I turned the TV off because I just couldn't stand the babble of it anymore and put on classic rock music, real low. She loved the Beatles and Rolling Stones and could listen to them forever. I didn't know if it would be too much for her in her current state. I had to trust that if it was she would find a way to let me know.

Fatigue hit me hard and I moved to the couch, in sight of my sleeping wife, and was soon asleep myself.

***

THE MOMENTS, THE INTENSE MOMENTS, THAT CHAIN together my life... well, after meeting April at the grocery store, most of them include her.

Our first date, which almost didn't happen.

I was mad about her. Completely, but I didn't know if I was ready for a relationship and she didn't seem to be either... or she just wasn't interested in me. I didn't know, and I wasn't strong enough to find out. I couldn't ask the question.

Lessons in the grocery store turned into my first dinner party —she brought her sister. My best friend from work and his wife also came.

And then putt-putt golf with a group of friends. And movies. And picnics. Always with a group of people. We became friends. I was fascinated with her, this kind woman that had taken pity on me with my basket full of frozen food. I was fascinated by her feminist rants and her stories about being an ER nurse. I was puzzled that she didn't have a husband or a boyfriend and hadn't been married.

"It's going to be stupid," I said, my opening salvo in kind of asking her out. I couldn't stand the thought of going to my company's cheesy Christmas Party alone. "But there will be excellent eggnog—the only area where I know my boss excels— and plentiful food."

We were in the hospital cafeteria having lunch. It wasn't far from where I worked and a very public place. We had taken to doing it once or twice a week. She would call me at my desk, where I would be buried in ledgers, doing my most boring accounting job, when the phone would ring. "Ten-minute warning." That was it. No hello. No "How about we go to lunch." Just a brief countdown.

She worked in the ER. They're busy. Breaks are unpredictable. I never minded and was always happy to leave my adding machine.

Some days I couldn't leave, and she would eat alone. Some days when I got there she had been sidelined by some emergency and I would eat alone.

It didn't matter.

I was crazy about her.

I was just afraid.

During that early December lunch, when I asked her, she stopped, a bite of salad halfway to her mouth, the murmur of the busy cafeteria swirling around us as she stared at me.

It had been over six months since the grocery store. These lunches would be hard to call dates, but a Christmas party? That was a date.

My heart beat hard and I started to sweat. "It... well... I know it will be much better if you are there," I said, finishing the invitation.

She blinked and bit her lip and I felt like throwing up. And I felt silly for it. I was no teenager. I had been married and divorced already. Why was I afraid of April?

"A date?" she asked, her voice even.

This was a test. We had never so much as held hands or been alone. Our friendship had been decidedly platonic. I didn't even know how old she was yet.

The noise and the jangled smells of the cafeteria faded and all that was left was April. She was in loose blue scrubs, hiding her fine curves. Her long brown hair was pulled back into a tight ponytail with a few wisps of hair having escaped along her forehead. Her face had the barest of makeup, just a little eye liner, and her hazel eyes were bright.

"I hope so," I said quietly.

She held my gaze for two more seconds and then looked down and shook her head slightly, a sigh escaping her.

I felt like someone had just punched me in the gut. All this slow-build-friendship stuff had been because my heart was so tender from Mary. The same reason I hadn't formally asked her out before, and this one was really an accident. I blinked hard, my mind going back to the night Mary admitted to the affair, to how desolate and lonely I had felt.

I looked away, my cheeks burning hot.

"I like you, Alan," she said, her voice barely loud enough to hear. "But..."

And then the shame began to twist into anger, more at me than at her. "But what?" I said, my teeth gritted together. I had never had a friendship with a woman like this before. It seemed to me like a fine foundation for a more intimate relationship.

"I'm... I'm..." she stammered, and I looked up and met her eyes, seeing fear there. "I'm thirty-seven years old, Alan."

All the anger flew out of me. Thirty-seven. Twelve years older than me. I blinked and swallowed hard. I had known she was older, had often been so happy to go see my "older woman" thinking it was five years, maybe seven, but twelve?

"I don't care," I said, the words rushing out before I had truly thought them through. "You are the most amazing woman I've ever met. I look forward to our next meeting every moment we're apart. I just want to..." I trailed off, seeing the fear in her eyes. I reached my hand out to her across the table and she took it, squeezing it hard. "What is it, April?"

She sniffed, her head down as she slowly shook it. "I'm too old for you."

"I'll be damned if you are." Her sureness of this just strengthened my resolve. Twelve years was a lot. I could almost see my mother's shocked face if I were to tell her. But older men are always with younger women, with many more years between them than us. Where was April's feminism now? "Look at me April, please."

She slowly looked up and the tears welled up in her eyes nearly undid me. I sucked in a deep breath and forged ahead. "It's just a date. Just a Christmas party. Just one evening. Can we do that? Take just one more step together? Go on a nice friendly date?"

She sniffed and nodded and my heart pounded from hope and from fear.

I woke with a start, my cheek wet, drool having pooled on the couch's throw pillow, my head full of April in that hospital cafeteria, April thinking she was old when she was only thirty-seven—so young—my nose still filled with the jangled smell of too many foods in that cafeteria.

I was smiling, my twenty-five-year-old fears and concerns seemed quite quaint.

But the smile didn't last long as my eyes found the hospital bed dominating our living room, and I felt the aches of my age and the difficulty of this time descending on my body.

"Don't Fear the Reaper" was playing softly, and I regretted my choice of music.

I could see April's wrinkled hand, it was dangling off the side of the bed, her wedding ring with its small diamond visible.

Was she gone? I stared at her hand looking for some small sign. A pulsing vein, a whisper of movement... anything.

Suddenly I was sure she was gone, that I hadn't been there for her, instead dreaming of a happier and simpler time. "Just be with me," April had said, her eyes sad when we had decided it was time for hospice.

Just be with me.

I scrambled off the couch, my heart beating hard, a flash of dizziness hitting me, forcing me to sit back down. I bent down and took deep breaths, tears stinging my eyes. I wasn't overreacting—one of these days she would be gone. We only had days left. This could be the day.

And then what would happen to me? A seventy-two-year-old man waiting for his own death alone. I forced the thoughts out, breathed deeply, and got my dizziness under control.

I got up slowly and walked over to the bed. I almost fell over again when I saw April looking at me. She had this beautiful smile on her face and she somehow looked decades younger.

"I love you, Alan," she said.

"I love you, too, April," I said, nearly collapsing into the chair. She was back. Maybe for only a moment, but she was back.

And then I remembered what the hospice nurse had said. "There is often a rally, where they are themselves again, right before the end."

"You were dreaming," she said, her voice feather-light, like she was far away. "What were you dreaming about?"

"About my beautiful April," I said, sitting by her and taking her hand. "About our very first date."

For that first date, April insisted on meeting me at the company Christmas party. I didn't know where she lived. I found her waiting in front of the steel and glass doors to the high-rise. The street was thick with cars, the honking echoing off the buildings. The air was cold, our breath hanging between us, little clouds of condensate. I didn't know what to say.

She had lipstick on and rouge, pulling out her lovely cheekbones. She had a dark wool coat on, but I saw a glimpse of red underneath. She also had red heels on and pantyhose. I caught a whiff of something floral over the smell of exhaust.

She had never dressed up like this during our friendly outings.

"You... umm... You look lovely," I managed to stammer, my heart in my throat.

Her cheeks were already red from the cold, but I swear the blush deepened.

"Thank you," she said, not meeting my eyes. "You look very handsome."

I felt like I was thirteen years old asking Sally Kinderman to dance at the winter formal, feeling like I had no idea what I was doing, thinking that everyone was staring at me, knowing Sally was going to say no and I would be embarrassed in front of the whole school.

What was it about April that did this to me?

"It's," she began, her teeth chattering. "It's cold, do you mind if we...?"

"Of course." I shook it off and opened the door for her. We were quiet as we walked through the big lobby, our footfalls echoing off the marble floor. I pressed the up button at the elevator and we had another long, awkward pause. This was our first date, but we knew each other fairly well. My mind was slipping, like a car with a bad transmission, and I couldn't think of anything to say.

Muzak played in the elevator on the ride up and I stared straight ahead, not daring to make eye contact.

In the office, after she took her heavy coat off, I just had to stare. The dress was a bit old-fashioned, red with lace at the neck and sleeves. It went down to her knees and all the way up to her neck, but it fit her well, putting her fine figure on display.

Her eyes widened, and her hand went to her neck. "Is it... Is it okay?"

"You are so beautiful, April," I said, my tongue finally untied. "You are the most beautiful woman here and I couldn't be happier than I am right now."

She smiled brightly and this time I am sure that she blushed.

Later that night after dancing and eggnog, we kissed for the first time under the mistletoe.

And that was it, just one kiss, but it was the beginning of April and Alan versus the world.

"I was terrified to kiss you," I said to April in our hot living room, the smell of her illness stifling. I tried to chuckle, but it came out strangled.

She was no longer a young thirty-seven, healthy and bright, but an old eighty-four, near death. We've had almost forty-seven years together and I know I should be grateful... Actually, I am grateful, but it's not enough. It will never be enough. Even if our end was centuries from now, it wouldn't be enough.

"I was already in love with you," April said, her voice low and husky. "But you were too young..." She paused, a smile forming on her face. "You still are."

I tried to chuckle again, but her smile, executed on her emaciated face, was terrifying. The end was here, and it was bitter.

"Tell me about it, old woman," I said, doing my best to smile. This time was for her, about her.

"Shut up, boy," she said.

"Cradle robber!"

"Juvenile! Why, I should—" She was cut off by a wet, racking cough, and our banter, what little we had managed, was at an end. I tended to her, my heart heavy.

Later, while she slept, I stepped outside into the fall morning, the maples ablaze in our front yard. I sucked in the fresh air, getting it as deep into my lungs as I could and let the cold air cool me down. The tears came, and I could not stop them, a bitter torrent that racked my entire body. I kept as quiet as I could, my back pressed against the side of our house as I slid to the frost-covered ground.

I had sent friends and family away, all of them. It was just me and the daily visits from the hospice nurse. People left food for me on the porch, which I dutifully carried into the refrigerator, would even peck at a bit, but I wasn't really eating. My pants were cinched on with a belt and my stomach always felt hollow, an appropriate companion to my aching heart.

After I got myself under control—the neighbors were kind enough to not stare, at least not overtly—I shuffled back to the front door. There was a small package wrapped in plain brown paper with my name scrawled on it in big black letters. It said, "Alan, for your time of need."

I blinked, my mind not working. This was my time of need, wasn't it? My April was dying, how could I be in more need than this? I took a breath and it came out as a shuddering sigh as I realized there was a time where I would be in more need than this. After April was gone.

I picked up the package and set it on the narrow table in the hallway where I put my keys and dumped the mail. I peeked at April, she was still asleep, so I headed to the bathroom for a quick shower, not giving the package another thought.

———

ROMANCE, THE MEETING CUTE, THE GETTING TO KNOW each other, the first missteps when you realize the other is truly human... well, that's just the very beginning of a relationship.

After that Christmas party, April and I executed those steps, rather awkwardly. Me, I was gun-shy from my first marriage. Her, she had some abuse in her past which made it very hard for her to trust any man.

By the next summer, a year after our meeting in the grocery store, we were inseparable. We had come to really know each other—warts and all—and still loved each other.

Life, though, threatened to subsume us in its unrelenting urgency. Her father got sick and she had to fly to Chicago often to help out. I was diagnosed with type 2 diabetes which sent me into an obsessive spiral where I would analyze everything I put into my mouth. It also quickly defeated the "I'm invincible" feeling of my twenties—not that I had much left after Mary.

But on that day, on the anniversary of our meeting, I reserved us a table at our favorite Italian restaurant, and promised not to obsess about what I ate. On the way there, I insisted on a stop at the grocery store.

I took her hand and pulled her over the worn linoleum, under those harsh fluorescent lights to the cereal aisle, right where my cart had run into her a year earlier.

"What are we doing here, I thought— Oh..." Recognition blossomed on her face when she saw the Apple Jacks and Raisin Bran, the sweet smell of it almost overwhelming the scent of floor cleaner.

Barry Manilow was playing, barely heard above the chattering noises of the store. I got down on one knee in my suit and she gasped, her hand flying to her mouth.

"April Tully," I said, my voice shaking as I held up the small box and opened it revealing the ring inside. "Will you make me the happiest man in the world and agree to be my wife?"

Romance is full of overstatement. It seems to be required. "Happiest man in the world" is a beautiful sentiment, but unmeasurable and unverifiable. My life finally made sense having April as my partner and lover, that is what I should have said. Or told her that I am my best self with her, even my happiest self. But the romantic overstatement just slipped out.

It didn't matter. She squealed, got down on the linoleum with me and threw her arms around me, the tears on her cheeks rubbing off onto my cheek.

"Yes, Alan. Yes!" She kissed me hard, her breath coming fast.

There was a bit of applause—we must have gathered an audience.

And maybe in that moment, I was the happiest man in the

world because I had just gotten what I wanted most in the world —a commitment from the woman I loved to go through this life together.

It was a beginning, a beautiful one for us, we had no thoughts of endings back then.

OUR LIFE, APRIL'S AND MINE, WAS PRIVILEGED WITH GOOD health care, good jobs, enough money to get by. But our life was hard, even with all of that.

And this is because life *is* hard. There is no getting around it. Strife and suffering are things to be contended with, minimized as much as possible, but they can never be eliminated.

This, really, is the benefit of finding your partner. Not that you won't suffer, not that there won't be hard times, but that you won't be alone.

That "Happily Ever After" stuff is complete and utter nonsense. No one is always happy.

"What?" April asked from the hospital bed, her breath smelling of something dank and rotten. We were nearing the end of her rally and she wasn't awake much, but when she was, she did engage.

I took a deep breath and smiled. "Just thinking about our first anniversary of meeting." Yes, I lied. I had been thinking of that, but my thoughts had then turned rather dark, looking ahead to the coming loneliness, not back to our new love.

A smile cracked her face, twisted and ugly. It was not her fault, it was a genuine smile, the best smile she could do in her current state.

She moved her hand towards me slightly and I took the hint and grabbed it and squeezed gently. It was all bones and paper-thin skin and arthritic joints now, not much left there.

"Good to remember," she said.

I nodded, doing my best to smile, but fearing it was not much better than hers. I had lost weight, not nearly as much as she had, but I was worn from this time, tired in a way that is so all-encompassing it is hard to describe.

"We were so young," I said.

"We still are," she whispered, a tear forming in her left eye.

I looked down and nodded. I understood what she meant. At seventy-two I still saw out of the same eyes I looked out of at twenty-five when we met. The "me" that was twenty-five was still here, still looking out through my much older eyes.

"Younger," I said, meeting her tired eyes. "I know a hell of a lot less now than I did back then."

She looked away and nodded.

The young believe there are answers and a solution for everything, the old know that there is not. Acceptance, yes, answers, not always.

"Tired," she said, turning from me and closing her eyes, and I could feel the rally and what was left of my April slipping away.

———

ROMANCE MUST BE EARNED, IT MUST BE FOUGHT FOR. After our first anniversary, I began to learn that. April was working four twelve-hour shifts a week. I would barely see her those days, nothing more than a late dinner when she was often too exhausted to speak.

My days weren't as long as hers, but it took me most of six days a week to get the work done, so I usually worked Saturday afternoons.

That left us Sunday as our day. At first, I couldn't fight the fatigue I felt on those days and wanted to do nothing more than sleep in, read the paper over coffee, watch football or baseball on TV, maybe barbecue and go to bed early. Find some small amount of rest to fortify me for the coming week full of ledgers and balance sheets and client meetings.

The tyranny of the urgent will suck you dry if you let it. Job. Bills. Taking care of the house and the cars. Keeping up with family. Fighting back the flu. Trying to stay healthy, getting some exercise.

Our lives get so filled with the things we must do, it's so easy to let go of the most precious things.

"What should we do today?" I asked April one sunny spring day as I sipped coffee and read the *New York Times*.

She shrugged and smiled, her fingers deftly wielding a sewing needle as it bobbed in and out of her needlepoint. She wore an old blue robe and fuzzy pink slippers, proper Sunday morning attire.

The needlepoint was a piece of white cloth stretched on a small round frame, the words "Home is where the Heart is" slowly forming with flowers all around.

"A drive, maybe?" I offered.

She looked up at me, but her hazel eyes flicked away and back to her work. She could still be shy, even after our two and a half years together. She didn't call herself old much anymore, but about other things she could be shy.

"Let's go down to old town and do some window shopping," I said. "Let the sun kiss your beautiful face. Find a nice place for lunch."

She smiled, nodded, but didn't look at me. She put her needlework down and walked to the bedroom and closed the door.

I sat there staring at her needlepoint for the longest time. Although she was still shy sometimes, my April was no prude. She had something on her mind.

Later as we strolled hand in hand, I felt quite proud of myself. Rising above my own lethargy had provided ample bene-fit. The air was still a bit cool, but the sun was warm, the sky an azure blue. I felt unaccountably proud that day. Proud that April was by my side. Proud that with her my life had some meaning.

Later in the park, sitting on a bench watching kids play on a jungle gym, April leaned over and whispered what had so been on her mind. "I'm pregnant."

She had just turned forty and during our engagement she had told me, rather emphatically, that she was "too damn old to be bearing a child."

I sat there for a moment, my heartbeat echoing in my head.

At first, I worried about her, about the strain on her body. This was 1975 and forty was quite old to be having a baby. Next, I worried about us, how we would manage our busy lives with a child added to the mix. And then I stared with wonder at the children playing, shouting and laughing, and I wanted nothing more than to be a father.

I looked at her and she was silently crying and my stomach clenched. I had no idea what it meant, so I fell back on the truth. "I am terrified, my love," I said, "but so happy."

She nodded, the tears flowing freely and pulled me into a fierce hug.

I REMEMBERED MORE AS THE RALLY FADED AND APRIL slipped into a coma. I remembered our year-long engagement, our marriage by the lake with the pine trees and bright blue sky above us. I remembered our joy when she got pregnant and the miracle of our son Kyle. I remembered our precious eight months with him until that morning when I went to check on him and he was dead in his crib.

As I remembered, I was sitting with April, my hand toying with the "In your time of need" package, still wrapped in plain brown paper.

They called what happened to our baby Sudden Infant Death Syndrome, basically their way of saying your child died suddenly and we're not sure why.

April wasn't waking anymore, and her lungs were slowly filling with fluid, her breathing a wet, disturbing rattle that I longed to escape, but I could barely leave the room now, afraid that she would die when I wasn't here. And that was… I don't know why, maybe it's because of Kyle, but the thought of her dying without me next to her was terrifying.

My stomach was an empty gnawing knot and I stank from a lack of bathing. I was keeping myself awake by drinking way too much coffee, my hands shaking slightly as I toyed with the package.

My time of need.

How many of those had I had? Had we had?

Kyle's death and that grief that followed and the years it took us to get back to being "April and Alan."

April's aggressive breast cancer, chemo, mastectomies, and reconstruction.

My traffic accident that put me in a wheelchair for six months with all the horrible PT as I learned to walk again.

How many "times of need" does a human go through?

April's sister's unsuccessful battle with cancer. My brother's addictions and suicide. The dementia of my father and her mother.

Aren't we always in need?

The package slipped from my fingers and fell onto the charcoal-colored carpet. One piece of tape had come loose, and I could see a bit of the box underneath. It too was plain and brown, it looked used, like it had through the mail a couple of times.

In my time of need.

What the hell does that mean?

Who sent it?

Why?

I leaned down to pick up the package but froze, something wasn't right. The room was still and quiet, the smell of it dark and heavy, the only thing I could hear was the barely perceptible hum of electricity running through the house and the sound of a car on the street outside.

No disturbing wet rattle of a dying person.

April wasn't breathing.

I froze, the room suddenly feeling small, and getting smaller, like the longer the silence lasted the smaller the room got and soon I would be crushed by it.

It was only a couple of seconds and then she dragged in a wet, rattling breath, and still I couldn't move.

The hospice nurse had told me this would happen. That she would have long gaps in between breaths until there were just no more breaths and she would be gone.

My hands shook like leaves and my head spun. The end was here.

I reached down farther and grabbed the damn "in your time of need package" and ripped the paper off.

This was my time of need. After might be more of my time of need, but I wasn't there yet. I was desperate now. April was dying.

I don't know how to describe what it was like finding Kyle, our baby, dead. I don't think I can, not in any way that would make sense.

I will say that the demarcation between life and death is a wickedly sharp one. I had been up at 3:00 a.m. tending to the fussing child, an alive bundle of what I loved most about this world. When I checked on him at 5:30 a.m., just a peek before getting ready for work, I could tell something was wrong.

Kyle had his own room, the walls painted blue with clouds along the top that April and I had dabbed on with big sponges. There was a rocking chair, a changing station, and his crib.

I paused in the doorway... something didn't feel right. I could see that he had rolled onto his stomach and was perfectly still. But it wasn't that. Something else bothered me, something subtle, something just out of reach.

I smiled and shook my head, knowing that it is usually better to let sleeping babies lie. I took a step back into the hallway, but then turned around and walked right up to the crib and froze.

It wasn't the way he looked, and at first it wasn't the utter lack of movement. It was something else. Something missing.

I looked back to the hallway—April was still sleeping. She was doing late shifts at the hospital so she could be with Kyle for most of the day.

I reached my hand into the crib and froze, my heart clanging in my head. I stared. He wasn't moving, was he? Could he be that deeply asleep?

The moment stretched out as I stood there, leaning against the crib, my hand not quite touching my precious son. In that moment he still "could" be alive, but part of me knew he wasn't. Sweat beaded on my forehead and my breath started coming fast, and still I stood.

Most of me knew that he was gone, but I wanted to preserve that sliver of doubt, that tiny possibility that I was wrong, that he was fine, that soon he would be wailing for his diaper to be changed.

Change. I wanted to hold it back, delay the tsunami of change that would strike us if my fears held true.

But the moment couldn't last. I touched him and felt his unnaturally cool skin. Kyle wasn't there anymore. It was just cooling flesh and stilled blood in that crib.

A BIBLE, A GODDAMN BIBLE, THAT WAS WHAT WAS IN THE "in your time of need" package. One of those pocket-sized editions that someone with my old eyes would have a hell of time reading.

When I saw it, I surged up out of the chair and walked away from my dying wife. I was so furious that my vision tunneled in and the world became flat and two dimensional.

How was a Bible to help me now? Let me do something between the growing gaps in between my wife's dying breaths?

I threw the book across the room and it bounced into the kitchen and went skittering across the tile floor. I knew who sent it, of course. Young Polly Benjamin—well, forty seems young to me these day—who was one of those neighbors who worried and prayed for us when she realized we didn't go to church. She was kind, nearly half the casseroles in the fridge that I couldn't eat were from her.

Neither of us were ever much into church, but after Kyle died... well, believing in a god that would allow that seemed wrong. Don't get me wrong, we wanted to believe that our baby was in heaven, that all of this had some kind of purpose or meaning, but we just couldn't.

The air was hot and closed in around me and without thinking I shuffled out the front door into the cold night air, panting from the effort, my head throbbing with each heartbeat, wondering if all that caffeine and all this stress was about to give me a heart attack.

I stumbled out to the grass and collapsed onto it gasping. My chest tightened, and it seemed like I couldn't breathe. I looked at my watch, an old windup Timex, at its steadily tick-tick-tick and just tried to breathe, tried to will back the vise I felt closing on my chest.

I slowly sucked in a breath for four seconds and let it slide out for four seconds. In and out.

In and out.

The vise slowly let go of me and my head stopped throbbing.

I kept breathing, slow deep breaths in, long exhalations.

Is this what I was supposed to do after April died? Stare at my watch and use it to calm the panic attacks that were sure to come. The first day I woke up alone. The first Valentine's Day without her in forty-six years. Her birthday. My birthday. Kyle's birthday.

It made more sense to me than reading stories about a god that let little babies die in their cribs for no apparent reason.

The thought of weathering Kyle's birthday without April, even all these decades later, was too much. The tears I had long held back came flowing out in a bitter, salty torrent.

I wailed and cried on my front lawn and was so lost in my own suffering I didn't have a self-conscious moment thinking about what the neighbors might think of me, Polly Benjamin among them, if my crying woke them up.

How long it lasted, I couldn't say, but by the time I was done, I felt drained and cold, and not ready, but able to go back inside.

As I rubbed my wet face with my sleeve, I realized that I had been out here for quite some time. What if April had breathed her last breath without me?

I surged up and stumbled back in, the Bible and everything else forgotten.

I KNOW WHAT IT IS LIKE TO LOSE THE MOST PRECIOUS THING in the world. To be so bereft you don't even know who you are.

I know what it's like.

After Kyle's funeral we came home, April and I, to a house that felt foreign without him. No, that's not the right word. It felt empty and evil, like something had twisted and perverted something we loved into something we hated.

We shut the door to Kyle's room and didn't go in, not for a very long time, but it wasn't enough. The smell of baby powder lingered in the air, the pantry had a shelf devoted to baby food, his windup swing was in our living room, and the general untidiness of the house spoke of his presence here.

Everywhere we looked were signs of him. Everywhere. There was no escaping it.

That night we sat on the couch and stared at the inert TV. We didn't touch. We didn't talk much, just mundane things: "Are you hungry?" "No, not really." "Okay."

There was no being okay. No being right.

After a time, we went to bed. We didn't say goodnight. We didn't kiss.

Months flew by as we numbly stumbled through our lives. Both of us worked a lot, too much really, but having something urgent outside of ourselves was the only thing that was any kind of balm, the only thing that got us through, kept us moving.

We had no fight left in us.

We had only our grief.

But we couldn't show it. Couldn't process it.

When we saw friends we would smile, tell them we were

getting through it, accept their hugs and their condolences, but it was all a sham. We weren't all right and we couldn't be.

One winter day when the snow piled up so much we didn't dare leave the house, didn't dare go to work, we both ended up at the kitchen table after breakfast. I had coffee and a newspaper, April picked up her long-abandoned needlework of "Home is where the Heart is."

When she did, I just stared at her. That needlework was it, the moment where I decided romance needed to be earned, the day when she told me she was pregnant.

My mouth felt stale and bitter and I just stared at her.

"What?" she asked when she caught my gaze.

Romance must be earned.

I couldn't say it. I didn't even know if I thought I deserved love. I had been given the most precious thing in life you can be given and somehow lost it. Fatherhood must be earned, and I hadn't earned it. I had let my baby die.

"Are you okay, Alan?" April asked, reaching out and taking my hand.

We had been coasting through our lives, doing what we must but not really living. It didn't feel right to live.

"No, I am not okay," I said, my voice nearly breaking.

She sniffed and nodded. She didn't need to ask me why. "I'm not either," she said.

I took a deep breath. "What do we do?"

She shrugged and looked down at the flowers and twirling script of the letters of her needlepoint. Her finger idly traced out the word "Home."

When she looked up, tears were silently flowing down her cheeks. "I don't know," she said.

And then she was in my arms as racking sobs took her. And then I was crying too and holding her fiercely.

We didn't have Kyle anymore, but we did have each other.

It was a long road, but that was the day we started to be "April and Allan versus the World" again.

I held April's hand, my mind fraying, from remembering griefs of the past and anticipating the tsunami of grief about to land on me.

Well, not about to land, it was already crashing on me. We grieve when we let go of something, and April and I had been letting go of each other for a while as her health degraded. She was going to die. I was going to keep on living.

A world without April and Kyle in it... I didn't know if that was a world I wanted to live in.

I held her hand, which was warm for once, and sat on the hard wooden chair next to her hospital bed. The gaps between her breaths were irregular but had grown longer. Each time, I would feel panic rising until she noisily sucked in the next breath.

This wasn't like Kyle where I was dealing with a fussy baby and a few hours later he was gone. This was the slow and lingering death of the old.

The room was only dimly lit by a single lamp, and staring at her face, it almost seemed like she was young again. Like the years between then and now were just a blink. When April was so worried about the twelve years that separated us, worried that I wasn't mature enough for her, worried that the years would drive us apart.

And I guess the years were driving us apart now.

"I love you, sweet April," I said. My voice was weak and rough. I had not been talking much at all.

"I know there has to be an end of us," I said quietly. "All that live must die, even relationships, even love. We know this. Kyle taught us this."

I paused and licked my lips. I was hungry and thirsty and needed to go to the bathroom, but we were too close now. I couldn't leave her, not for anything.

"It's okay," I lied. "It's okay, April. You can go." I whispered to her as if she were a sleeping baby I didn't want to wake. "I'll be okay. I'll find a way."

Lies have their place, even in a relationship like ours. But I was lying to myself, not just her. I didn't think there was a way for me without her.

I stared at her hand—I couldn't even look at her sleeping face. Well, she was in a coma now, is that sleeping? Her hand was thin and boney, age spots decorating it, her veins visible under her thin skin.

She had changed so much since we met. Not that I hadn't, it's just that I felt largely the same (give or take the aches and pains and the slowing down). But she looked so different, sometimes it was a shock. In my mind we were both about the same age as when we met, but looking at her or looking in the mirror challenged that.

Time withers us, it is the price we pay to be alive. Every beginning has an end. Every story has to stop. The curtain draws on every romance.

April let out a long shuddering sigh and then... nothing. My eyes snapped from her hand to her face. The gap was back. Was this her last breath or one of her last breaths? Was this the moment that would leave me bereft of the love of my life?

I glanced at my watch's second-hand ticking away, as the gap lengthened. Five seconds, ten, twenty. I tore my gaze away from the watch and back to April. This was it. I could feel it. She had let go of her last breath, let go of her life.

And then I hated those twelve years between us. And not

just in some intellectual way. I hated them with all my being. I loathed them. I wished that we had been closer in age, that time's withering embrace had not been so different for each of us.

I wished fervently that we were the same age, April and I. That our journey through this world was more inline. We had walked our forty-six years, side-by-side, together. I wished we had more.

Just a few more years.

A few more days.

One more conversation.

Anything.

The gap lengthened. Thirty seconds, forty seconds, and then I couldn't look at my watch anymore. I ripped it off and flung it away.

Time didn't matter to me anymore.

April was dying.

April was dead.

I held her hand, for how long I couldn't tell you. I wasn't a creature of time anymore. I was a creature of grief. Part of me marveled at it, a tiny piece of me in the back of my mind. I had loved her so much that her loss just might destroy me, and I was fine with that.

Life at any cost was never a concept I subscribed to.

Love at any cost, now that was something I had aspired to.

There came a moment, minutes after that last breath, where I felt something. A breeze in the still house when the heater wasn't running. A tingle in my hand as it held her slowly cooling hand. A sudden stuttering of my weary heart.

And I knew she was gone.

Not just her body, but April, I felt that the essence of April was gone.

I WAS A GHOST IN MY OWN LIFE FOR THE NEXT NINETEEN days, stumbling around numb, barely aware of what was going on, doing what needed to be done. Waiting for the mortuary to come get her body. Calling relatives. Arranging for a "celebration of life." Receiving more casseroles from kind neighbors. I lied and thanked Polly Benjamin for the Bible, told her it comforted me in my time of need.

I didn't taste food, what little I ate. I didn't remember anything I saw on TV. I slept, but never felt refreshed. I cried and never felt relieved. I showered and never felt clean.

I was a ghost in my own life.

Knowing April was dying, trying to imagine what it would be like without her, having been through the traumatic loss of my son, none of it prepared me for the reality of it, for the winding and torturous course my grief took.

And honestly, this is the way it's supposed to be. Grief remembered is not the same as grief experienced. If it was, I don't think we would survive. Time doesn't heal grief, not the big ones, but it does mellow it. And if there is a god, I thank them for that small kindness.

We had a church service for April, in a big, breezy Lutheran church—the last one we had attended together. It was almost three weeks after her death that the service was held, I just couldn't do anything very fast. The church was packed. April was loved. People said kind things, some said things that sounded wise, but I can't give you any more details than that. It's all a blur.

I didn't sell the house, like I swore I was going to do after she died. I'll probably keep it. Memories here, you know. And besides, I just don't have the energy.

After the service, close friends and family came to the house and we ate and drank and talked and remembered. And that was good. I found myself smiling and laughing, being a little bit less of a ghost.

Soon they were all gone except for my sister and her two daughters and I felt something.

I sat in one of our dining room chairs that had been moved into the living room, the configuration of it still odd, with things pushed to the side, but the hospital bed missing. Someone had spilled wine and the smell of it was starting to sour. My sister was quietly talking to her daughters as they rushed about cleaning up. I could hear the sounds of dishes clinking in the kitchen and the comforting sound of running water.

I felt a warmth to my left, in the chair next to me. A comforting warmth that felt like April. I looked over and it was empty, of course. I may have felt like a ghost, but I didn't really believe in ghosts.

I didn't really believe in anything anymore.

Part of it was losing April, but part of it was all the years and all the loss. I have seen my own beliefs to be wishful thinking way too often, so I have come to look on them suspiciously.

I won't say that April's spirit or ghost or whatever was sitting next to me, but I won't say it wasn't. It could be my memory of her or it could be something outside of me. It doesn't really matter.

There are some advantages to not knowing, not believing.

"Hi, honey," I whispered to the warm space next to me.

The warm space didn't reply, but I felt acknowledged, nevertheless.

"I love you. I miss you," I said, feeling emotions shifting in my chest like glass was embedded in my lungs, each movement inflicting damage, but it wasn't something I could turn my back on.

I felt a whisper of a sensation on my cheek like the gentlest of kisses and the tears came and I let them flow unchallenged.

These tears felt like the kind that could provide some small comfort, some small relief, not like the ones I had cried so far.

"You okay?" my sister asked, suddenly sitting on the other side of me, her warm hand taking mine. She's my older sister, but defiant of her years, keeping her short hair brown via the aid of chemical assistance.

"No," I said.

She nodded. "Thank you for not lying."

"I may never be okay."

She paused, her faded green eyes searching mine. "Yeah. I get that. But maybe not too much truth right now, eh?"

She said it playfully so I smiled as best I could.

"Can I get you anything?" she asked. "A casserole. You have plenty, you know."

I shook my head, but smiled, grateful for her gentle attempts at humor.

"You really should eat."

"I will," I said, but that didn't mean I would eat today or even tomorrow. I would eat when I was hungry, whenever that was. "Right now, I'd just like to sit here and talk to April."

She didn't look at me like I was crazy, instead her thin lips pulled up into a genuine smile, one that lifted her round cheeks high. "I think that's a good idea."

And then she was gone.

And then I felt the whisper of a touch on my check again, like a kiss of rose petals.

And then I had a good long talk with my dead wife.

I'VE BEEN THINKING ABOUT APRIL AND SCHRÖDINGER'S CAT lately. You know, the famous thought experiment about the cat in the box to explain quantum probabilities. How until you open the box, you don't know if the cat is alive or dead. Both possibilities exist simultaneously.

April is that to me now. I don't know if what I'm talking to and experiencing is a ghost or a soul or whatever... or just the April that is in me, part of me, my mind finding a way to assuage my grief.

And I don't really care and I don't really want to know. I'm not going to open that box.

I am an old man and I need April.

This was heavily on my mind three months after her death on one of my frequent pilgrimages to the graveyard.

The sky was shot with grey, high cirrus clouds thin and wispy, stealing away most of the blue, which was fine by me. The breeze was cold and the frosted grass crunched under my feet, the frigid air stinging my nose as I slowly walked.

I was still feeling like a ghost in my own life, but less so. I was starting to have moments when it wasn't just about her loss, when I laughed at something and was wholly there, when I forgot for a moment here and there that she was gone.

April isn't there by my side, not literally, but nearly all the time now I feel that slight warmth to my left that feels like her and it gives me comfort. Whether she is a ghost or delusion I keep safely locked in Schrödinger's box.

When I was young, I wanted to be cremated. I was very serious about this. I didn't want people hanging around and feeling sad whenever they went to the location of my carbon remains.

But Kyle, we buried his little body in a small plot with a granite plaque in the ground that said, "Kyle Struthers, 1975 - 1975". That's it. Nothing more.

The two years being the same always seemed so harsh to me. Not that we were being harsh by putting it there, it was the truth. It's that life had been harsh because our child hadn't escaped the year he was born to.

I stopped when I got to Kyle's granite marker and the one right next to it. "April Struthers, 1935 - 2018."

She has a lot of years on either side of that dash, but her loss still felt cruel to me. It still feels wrong even though I know that death is the most natural thing in the world.

The breeze stirred the oaks, their dried leaves rattling above me. I took a deep breath and caught a whiff of the dried leaves and the sharp scent of the nearby pines.

"I love you. I miss you," I said to them both.

I had gotten it wrong, the burying people thing. I do come here and cry, that is true, but it does me good to be close to their remains. I come here to feel close to them. To remember. To express my love.

Just because people die, doesn't mean that the love dies. I will love them both with all my heart until my own heart stops beating.

I'm kind of looking forward to that day, because that is the day when my Schrödinger's box will open and I just might get to know whether April still being by my side is just my imagination or her spirit.

Or maybe the atheists are right and I'll just be gone and I won't know anything. That's okay with me too.

Not that I think it really matters.

Love is what matters.

And that is what we have, still have, April and Kyle and I. Love.

BACKSTORY—APRIL AND ALAN

This story is, in many ways, the reason this collection exists. Despite the protagonist's "Schrödinger's" musings, it's entirely contemporary, rather long, out of my usual genres, and has a lot to say.

If you've read my writing before, you know a lot of it evolves around death and grief. Two things none of us humans get out of experiencing. Two things that I believe are essential to our humanity.

The irony here is that this story didn't start out as non-speculative and had a very different ending. It was going to be one of a series of interlocking stories that I am still working on that had a fantasy element.

I sent the original version to Dean Wesley Smith who praised the contemporary portion of it but called out the sudden veer to fantasy at the end. He challenged me to rewrite the ending and have Alan face this difficult reality.

I'm glad I did. Thanks, Dean.

PART 8
THE WRITER'S DILEMMA

THE WRITER'S DILEMMA

Evan knew it wasn't right. He knew Alice was sitting there fuming and dumbfounded, but he couldn't speak his feelings the same way he could write his character's feelings. So he told her, "I have to write," the words barely able to pass his lips, and walked away.

With his writing, he could be eloquent and precise, but speaking to Alice with her red-rimmed brown eyes looking so sad, rivulets of tears staining her cheeks, he could hardly breathe, much less talk.

The apartment was quiet, Evan could hear the hum of the electricity as it fed all the hungry appliances. He sat there in front of the glowing screen of his laptop, his fingers poised as he waited for something, for anything, that would start the story, that would let him express what he was feeling and then he could go read it to Alice—without ever looking at her, of course—and she would know how he felt.

He was a writer. He wrote.

Ed loved Anna, he typed on his keyboard, starting with the truth unvarnished, before deleting it all. Who was Ed? Who was Anna? How could he get some distance from Evan and Alice and write what he felt?

He began again.

Ed stood in front of the vast array of flowers under the cool lighting of the busy grocery store. He paused in front of the red roses, breathing in their sweet scent. But no. That was too on point. He wasn't normal, so he shouldn't get normal flowers.

Ed had screwed up. Royally. First a missed anniversary and then a slip of his tongue that had already been loosened by fatigue and one too many beers.

No. That wasn't it.

Well, it was. Evan had missed their anniversary, but it wasn't like it was a wedding anniversary—he hadn't yet had the courage to ask her to marry him and wouldn't mind at all if she did the asking. It had been their second "the day we met" anniversary.

And he had laughed when Alice told him about how embarrassed she had been at work today when she bumped into her boss in the hallway and spilled her Frappuccino all over her dress, the sweet smell and stains still on her when she had walked in all bedraggled like she had just lost her best friend.

Weren't these kinds of things funny, the little pratfalls of life?

No... no... he knew better. He held down the backspace key and deleted everything he had just written

Ed was stupid, and Anna was right. Period.

But was he stupid? He had ghosted five blog posts today that had all taken a lot of research. He was tired and she was late, and he had needed the beers to blunt it all. He still wrote fiction, but it had been shoved into a tiny corner by all the ghost writing he did to make a living.

"But that means you're a good writer," Alice had said last week when he was able to properly articulate his frustration.

"You're doing what you love, not working in a cubicle. Maybe you can celebrate that."

Evan shook his head and looked around at the narrow room he wrote in. It was a converted closet, a walk-in closet covered in movie posters with shelves for his Star Wars collectables, but it was still a closet. No windows. Poor lighting. A small desk and a wooden chair.

This was *not* living the dream.

He heard the glug-glug of wine being poured out in the living room and a sniff. They had fought, so wine was certainly called for.

Even turned back to his laptop.

Ed didn't understand Alice, not really. Isn't that the way it is for all couples? And isn't that beside the point?

Evan blinked when he realized he had written "Alice" instead of "Anna." He revised.

Ed didn't understand Anna, but that didn't keep him from loving her, from needing her. Isn't that the way it is for all couples? We understand our needs so well even if we don't fully understand our partner, much less their needs. And isn't that beside the point?

He leaned on the backspace key again. He didn't want to lecture. He wanted a story. A vehicle where he could inject his feelings into a character so that Alice would understand. And he needed that story now.

When Ed heard the snick of the dead bolt being thrown back on the door to their apartment, his heart beat a little harder and a smile brightened his face. He paused Netflix and put his beer down.

He realized the reaction was a bit Pavlovian, that he was acting kind of like a dog, but he didn't care. Anna was his partner, the one thing in this world that made his day worth living.

Evan leaned back, his eyes flicking over the words. The

Pavlov's dog reference might be a bit too much, but how else to express how glad he is to see her come home?

Anna's long blond hair was a bit disheveled and her flower-print summer dress had a muddy brown stain on it, the souring scent of old Frappuccino reaching Ed's nose.

"What happened?" he asked, standing but not going to her. Her shoulders were high and her brown eyes were darting away from his, searching their small apartment as if she was looking for something.

Something was wrong.

He chewed his lower lip. This wasn't fiction, this was what had happened, but maybe it would prove to be his way into the story. He heard more wine being poured and the sound of bare feet pacing the carpet. He didn't have much time, and that kind of pressure was just no good for the creative process. Nevertheless, he kept writing.

"Just a bad day," she said with a weak shrug.

Ed took a tentative step forward, his brain muddled from researching too many things in the past ten hours, his mind relaxed but sluggish from the three beers he'd consumed in the last hour. Should he go to her, embrace her, was that what she needed? It was clear she needed something, but he couldn't tell what.

"What happened?" he asked, pointing at the brown invading stains on her new dress.

"I ran into my boss," she said quietly. "This was my Frappuccino." She shrugged and smiled, but not in a happy way.

Ed saw the incident in his mind's eye clearly, the buzzing fluorescent lights, the tan industrial carpet, her boss in his expensive suit, and it seemed like the kind of scene you'd see in an old sitcom and he felt the laughter bubbling up.

"I had hoped this would be a good day," she said, her eyes

finally finding his and he saw the danger there, but the laughter was already on its way and couldn't be stopped. The pressure of his own day, his hopes of actually writing fiction unfulfilled again, the loosening of the alcohol, and he couldn't stop himself.

Evan stopped. This was pointless. She had needed him. He hadn't been there. And he had needed her and she hadn't been there either. Isn't this just the way of it, though? We know our own needs and struggles and they are often so overwhelming it's hard to see other's needs, especially for him.

This wasn't his fault. His laughter hadn't really been about her day, but about his.

He snapped down the lid to his laptop, his cheeks flushing red as he felt the rare rush of anger.

No one had gotten their needs met, and how could Alice help him when he hadn't given her even a single clue to his upset except for the three beer bottles on the coffee table.

He walked in and found Alice sipping wine on the couch, her shoulders slumped, her stained dress still on.

Evan took a deep breath and squeezed his eyes shut, seeing the words in his mind's eye as if he had already written them, his hands coming up as if he were typing on a ghostly typewriter right in front of him.

"I'm sorry I laughed at you. I am very frustrated with my writing. I hate ghosting, it leaves me nothing left for my own stories. And I'm such a lightweight and have had three beers. I am very sorry I missed our anniversary. The day we met was, and is, the best day of my life. I am just bad at remembering dates."

The words were fumbling. He wished he could go back and rewrite them, edit them, but then he heard her sniff and let out a big sigh. That encouraged him to forge on, his eyes closed, his fingers flicking in the air over an invisible keyboard.

"I love you, Alice, you are the best part of every day to me. Please forgive me."

Evan kept his eyes squeezed tightly shut. He heard her get up and pad over the carpet to him. He smelled the soured Frappuccino and her sweet perfume below it. He felt the warmth of her nearness.

"Open your eyes," she said softly.

He did and he saw the tears pooled in the brown orbs he loved so much. "You were back there writing about this?" she asked, her forehead furrowed.

Evan swallowed hard. "Yes."

"And you were writing in your head just now?"

He nodded slowly, his heart pounding so hard he was sure she must be able to hear it, the beer leaving him a bit unsteady on his feet.

She took him by the hand, her touch gentle, and pulled him to the couch and they sat down.

"Do it some more," she said.

"What?"

"Close your eyes, type it out, talk to me."

He nodded slowly and squeezed his eyes shut feeling so very self-conscious now that she knew what he was doing. "I laughed," he continued, "to release my own pent-up emotions. My own guilt. I should have been back there writing instead of vegging out and drinking. I..."

He opened his eyes and she was slowly nodding.

She licked her lips and said, "You feel like there's nothing left after you work for what you care about the most."

He nodded and watched a single tear run down her cheek. She got it, she finally got it. "And you feel the same way," he offered.

And then she was hugging him hard and Evan thought

maybe this was going to be a pretty good "the day we met" anniversary.

She pulled back, the smile on her face counterbalancing the tears staining her cheeks. "So, close your eyes, write for us the perfect thing for us to do tonight to celebrate."

He smiled, closed his eyes, and wrote the perfect night for them, and then they went out and lived it.

BACKSTORY—THE WRITER'S DILEMMA

This story came out of a very simple, and likely obvious, observation, which is this: as a writer, I often have a better grasp of my characters' emotions than my own. Actually, very often.

Something that stories do, and I think they are meant to do, is to take the complexity of life and boil it down some so it's easier to understand and digest. So while this observation may indeed be obvious, when I had it, it was striking and took me some time to process—thus this story.

If you are not a writer, maybe you can relate to this in consuming stories, whether it be books, movies, or TV. Are those characters' emotions sometimes easier for you to understand than your own?

PART 9
CAT CHASES MOUSE. DOG CHASES CAT

ONE

Edward the mouse launched himself off the wooden kitchen table. It was a leap like the little field mouse had never made before, and while Edward, being a mouse, wasn't particularly aware of his mortality, he knew the leap was dangerous, that he could be hurt, but he also knew it was a leap towards his destiny.

But Edward was no ordinary mouse. He had a mission and a purpose and a desperate need.

Time froze as he flew, his long tail twitching to keep him balanced, his chestnut-colored fur rippling in the air, his clawed feet outstretched hoping to be able to run when he hit the wooden floor.

The evil black cat, Oscar, was already in motion, leaping from the kitchen counter toward the mouse, his claws unfurled, his fangs bared. For there is nothing that will get a cat moving like a mouse moving.

And Theodore, the lazy hound dog, stirred, a growl rumbling out of his chest, for there was nothing that will get a dog moving like a cat running away from him.

Cat chases mouse. Dog chases cat.

Also in the cramped kitchen of the old house on the cliff above the ocean were two bipedal giants, two humans. A woman on the floor crying, her hands shaking as she placed a gun down on the floor. Even as he flew, Edward could hear her heart beating rapidly, too rapidly, and he could smell her terror.

Edward didn't know her name, he didn't even know his own name, the name she had given him, but his little mousy heart had come to adore her and his little mousey brain had been taken over by thoughts of her.

It was for her that Edward leaped, but he had no attention to spare. It was the even bigger bipedal giant, the male, that he focused on. He stank of fermented grains and was standing at the entrance of the kitchen, the source of her terror, like the cat was the source of Edward's terror.

He was playing with her like Edward knew the cat would play with him. Before eating him.

Edward had nightmares, of the cat finally closing his jaws around him or one of the seagulls swooping out of the sky and snatching him, dropping him from a great height before feasting on him. And the female giant had dreams too, dreams that made her toss and turn at night and cry out and Edward knew with his mousey instincts that this stinking male giant was the source of those nightmares and this was her nightmare come to life.

So while the evil cat had hidden and the lazy dog cowered, the little field mouse acted, flying through the air, causing the cat to stir and the dog to forget its pain, causing—

But wait. Perhaps this is the wrong place to start a story such as this. The place of heroics and death-defying leaps. For this story starts very simply several months earlier in a field with a little mouse whom no one had ever named staring at an old house with a longing he didn't understand.

TWO

A mouse is, if nothing else, brave. It exists in a world where most things are so much larger and it is but lowly prey. It lives in the cracks and eats the crumbs. It is hated and pursued and killed without a second thought or a moment of remorse.

Edward was very smart, for a field mouse, but otherwise quite normal. Until the day he explored farther than he ever had before, coming to the edge of his field, the one his family had been living in for many generations, and braved climbing a large rock to see better, and saw the house.

Well... he is a mouse, after all, so he didn't see the house clearly. He saw the straight lines of the structure which appeared massive to him. Climbing up and up into the sky ending in a point at the roof. But more, he smelled the sweet smell of baking pies. The scent he had been smelling all his young life now had a source. And it was close. Across another field and then past a swath of plain hard dirt near the cliff with the thunderous, crashing ocean below.

What was this wonderful place? What kinds of things would there be for him to eat?

His father squeaked at him from below, a scared, angry squeak. Edward was exposed to the hungry seagulls and to the evil cat that lived in the towering house.

Edward came down but kept sneaking back day after day. To look. To smell. To wonder what was there. He felt a pull he didn't understand. It was beyond the longing to taste those smells but something else. It was the quiet whisper of destiny.

And then the dream started. He dreamed of a leap through the air, a leap from a high place for a great purpose. He dreamed sounds that made his heart swell. And he dreamed of danger and constant vigilance.

Edward was but a mouse, so he didn't think as much as felt these things. He felt the pull of the house, and one night, he couldn't resist. He left his family behind and crossed the wide fields and the bare hard-packed dirt and made his way into the house.

For while Edward had no language and only a tiny brain, he understood destiny well. It was something you moved toward, not away from.

THREE

It was love at first scent and at first hearing.

Edward, who hadn't been named yet, was in the house a full two weeks before he dared look at her. The female bipedal giant that spent hours a day in her kitchen baking pies and other sweets.

And looking at her, when he did, was not the same as for you and I. Edward's vision was not great and better suited to scurrying around and finding crumbs. But his sense of smell and his ability to hear were marvelous.

She smelled amazing, a combination of the sugar and vanilla and chocolate she used in her baking along with a floral scent from her perfume and sweat from her labors. It was a foreign smell and so complex. It was the essence of the scent he had experienced wafting out over the field his entire life.

But it wasn't the smell that sank Edward but the sounds. She sang as she worked, her voice high and lilting. Sometimes humming, sometimes singing words Edward didn't understand, but he loved the sound. It filled his ears and made its way to his heart and filled it up.

She sang while she worked and when she was done there were plenty of sweet crumbs for Edward to eat. With great care, of course, given the evil cat that lived there, all sleek black fur and sharp claws.

The house was old with two stories and an attic. Edward had found many pathways to travel, through the walls, under the hardwood floors, through gaps in the baseboard or along wires that escaped the ceiling.

That day, the day he finally saw her, he found a crack in the wall, in a corner of the kitchen, just above the wainscoting. It wasn't a big crack, but it was larger than his tiny head and he peeked out.

The evil cat was in the big room off the kitchen, and the lazy dog was asleep under the large wooden table on an old blanket.

Edward stared as she sang at the kitchen counter, hunched over her work. She was huge. Massive. Towering even over the lazy hound dog. She was bipedal, standing on her hind legs with baffling ease. She had extraordinary long fur, a deep brown the color of Edward's eyes, but only on the top of her head, the rest of her skin exposed directly to the elements.

She was humming quietly as she worked, as she drizzled chocolate on a tray of cookies.

The cookies were massive, one would feed Edward for weeks, but it was the giant that attracted him, that drew him out of the hole and had him scurrying along the strip of trim at the top of the wainscoting, his sharp claws keeping him secure on the wood.

He listened carefully for sounds of the evil cat stirring in the next room or the lazy dog waking from under the table, but the cat was still and the dog was quietly snoring.

Although his sight was poor, he wanted to see her close up. She had massive eyes, the irises a golden brown and her hands were a marvel to Edward, the long agile fingers doing things the little mouse couldn't even imagine.

He inched closer and then closer, his little heart beating so fast, his sense of destiny drawing him forward, fighting through his instinct of survival. He was quick and clever, but the giant was so large she could crush him easily.

Her humming stopped and he froze, his heart beating so loudly she must surely hear it.

"Why, hello there," she said.

Edward, of course, didn't understand the words, and while it wasn't the same as her singing, he still liked it. Still it was too much. He turned and ran back to the hole, disappearing into the walls of the house.

And so it went, day after day. When the cat was away, Edward would sneak out and look at the giant, getting a tiny bit closer, fighting through his instincts that told him to run.

Soon he found tiny crumbs along the way, bits of sweet baked perfection for him to nibble on. She was the source of this, he knew that. The bipedal giant could put crumbs on the narrow strip of wood at the top of the wainscoting with ease.

But still he was cautious, crawling out, eating the crumbs, but stopping short of her very long reach as she worked at the counter humming or singing.

It was a sensory feast for Edward. The smells of her and the baking. The sound of her humming and singing. The taste of the treats in his mouth.

"I won't hurt you," she said, moving very slowly, her voice quieter than usual.

Edward, not understanding the words, just stared at her. The tone, though, did convey some meaning and it calmed Edward's hammering heart, just a bit.

Ever so slowly she took a crumb from the counter and placed it on the wood trim several body lengths in front of Edward. He backed up, but he didn't turn and run. It was a larger morsel and he could smell its warm sweetness.

She placed another crumb and it was clear she wanted him to come close. He listened, made sure the cat was not moving, and slowly crept forward and claimed the prize, chewing it slowly while he watched the giant.

She was so large, she was hard to watch. Should he look at those strangely dexterous hands and arms that moved so freely? Or the large face with the brown eyes where the sounds he loved so much emanated? Or the feet and legs or the vast torso?

She was a marvel, and each time he interacted with her, more of his little mousey brain became filled up with her. In another week he was eating out of her hand.

"I think I'll call you Edward," she said with a smile on her huge face. "What do you think?"

The increase in pitch at the end of the sentence caught Edward's attention and he looked up at her vast face and squeaked.

She laughed, the sound of it at first was so frightening that Edward froze, but then he sensed the joy in it and so he rejoiced and squeaked again, which only made her laugh harder.

"We shall be good friends, I think."

FOUR

The months passed and life was good for Edward. He had plenty to eat and a new friend in the form of the female bipedal giant that baked and sang.

Edward took to watching her while she was in the house. When she baked, spending most of her waking hours in the kitchen, when she sat in the large room at the front of the house watching the box of noise and color, petting the evil black cat or the dog. When she went for walks with the lazy brown hound dog out in the field, he would watch from the attic through old dirty windows. And when she would get in the roaring stinking contraption with her baked goods and drive away, he would restlessly wait for her return.

She became his world and it changed the little field mouse. It made him brave, he was so exposed to the evil cat whenever he came out to see her. It made him think in ways that mice don't usually think. And it made him content.

He was happy and she was happy. Except for at night when he watched over her from the attic through a little hole he had chewed in the ceiling. She had dreams, that kind that tossed you in your bed like a ship on stormy seas. The kind that caused sounds of fear to escape you. The kind that left you panting and sweating when you awoke.

At first, they were rare, now and again, and only brief, over before the mouse could think of anything to do. For what could a little mouse do to help a sleeping giant waken from her nightmares?

But then they got worse and more frequent. Almost every night she tossed and turned and cried out. And Edward had to act.

That lazy dog slept on the bed near her feet but seemed untroubled by her dreams. The evil cat slept on a carpeted perch near the draped window but seemed unconcerned, waking only briefly before going back to sleep.

The giant was moaning. Her heart beating much too fast. She was suffering and even the simple mouse understood that and he could not stand it.

He left his lookout and crawled down inside the wall behind the giant's bed to a crack in the baseboard. He stopped and he listened. The sounds of the giant's pain ripped at his little heart, but he could also hear the lazy dog and the evil cat sleeping. So with his own heart hammering hard, he crawled out of the wall, up the wooden post of the bed, and onto the vast soft sleeping surface.

He was so exposed. He was prey and the evil cat was predator. But she, his bipedal giant, was worth the risk. But how could he waken her? He had no conception of math or measured weight, but he understood that she was huge compared to him and she was moving in the bed and any action he took would mean danger.

But his heart demanded it and his mind changed. A brief spark, an idea, a novel thought.

He burrowed under the covers to hide from the evil cat and

made his way to one of her large hands as it clenched the sheet and a cry escaped her.

"No..." she moaned. "No... how did you find me? How?"

Edward did not understand the words but could hear the terror in her tone and he smelled her fear.

So he crawled up her hand onto her nightgown and made his way out from under the covers to perch on her shoulder. The cat was still and the dog was snoring as he listened.

What could he do to wake the giant? He thought of squeaking for that sound seemed to delight her, but that would just wake up the evil cat. If he bit her, that would awaken her, but also hurt her and he couldn't do that.

"No... No...!" she moaned.

Edward's brain changed then. The spark of a thought took hold, became a tiny fire in his brain, and he acted. He ran across her shoulder, over her neck to her enormous ear. It was a difficult journey for the giant was tossing and turning.

He gripped the edge of the giant's ear carefully with his claws. It was bigger than him and furless and with so many strange folds, but he recognized it for what it was.

He held on and put his little face into her ear, smelling the waxy substance there and gave a quiet squeak. Having such marvelous hearing Edward understood sound and ears and that the closer the sound is to the ear, the louder it seems to be.

Her thrashing stopped, but only for a moment and she moaned again.

It hadn't been enough.

So he did it again, a little bit louder. Again she stopped, but only for a few moments and this time he also heard the evil cat's breathing change.

As she moaned, Edward was faced with a choice. Leave his giant to suffer in her dream or try to wake her and wake the evil cat too?

A mouse is an instinctive creature, driven by the need for survival. But Edward had changed. He chose the giant.

He pressed his head into her ear and squeaked as loudly as he could. The kind of squeak he would make in the field to warn his fellow mice of a predator.

The cat stirred and so did the dog.

And the giant woke too, surging up.

"What... what is happening?" Edward fell from her ear into her blanket covered lap.

The evil cat sprung from his perch to the bed.

The dog growled, for the bed was his territory, his place to be with the giant, and he lunged for the cat.

Edward was beyond terrified and just froze there in the giant's lap as one of her enormous hands scratched at the ear Edward had just squeaked in.

And then the cat pounced and pressed a clawed paw down on Edward and the dog snapped, his jaws closing right next to the cat's tail, and the giant yelled.

"Theodore! Leave Oscar alone. And Oscar, what do you have there...? Oscar!"

The giant's yell made the cat back up and Edward was revealed there in the blankets.

"You did this, didn't you, Edward?" she asked the mouse. "You woke me up. That was the sound I heard, wasn't it?"

Edward didn't understand the words but he caught the rising pitch at the end of the sentence and squeaked in reply.

She laughed. It was a small thing but it brought joy to Edward. She brushed that cat away and held out her hand and he climbed onto it.

She brought him up so he was right in front of her vast face and he could see the moisture leaking out of her eyes. "You are my hero, Edward," she said softly. "I thought I saw him the other day, at the farmer's market. I don't know how he found me or... or if it was really him, but... you saved me, Edward."

Things changed after that. The cat was banished from the bedroom at night and Edward was free to waken his giant from her nightmares and she fussed over him more and fed him during the day.

It was a good life for the little mouse until her nightmare came true.

FIVE

AND THAT BRINGS US BACK TO EDWARD'S LEAP, THE ONE from his dreams when he was still a normal field mouse. The one that drove him across the field and across the strip of bare earth to the towering house.

About two weeks after Edward first woke his giant from her nightmare, that nightmare came true in the form of another bipedal giant coming to the house on the cliff above the ocean.

He drove one of the roaring stinking contraptions up the bare strip of earth and parked it in front of the house. It was dark and Edward was up in the attic peering out the dirty window to see what it was.

He had seen other giants. Some came from time to time in their roaring stinking vehicles. They came and took her baked goods away and left her with stinking pieces of dirty paper and sometimes bits of shiny metal. But this giant was strange. He was different. And the prey in Edward recognized the predator in him right away.

"Evy!" he screamed. "I know you are in there, Evy. I found

you, girl. Now get on out here. I'm your husband and it's time we go."

Edward, of course, did not understand the words, but he heard the threat. He heard the danger. And if a predator made this much noise before attacking, it must be very dangerous and very confident.

The little mouse scurried away down through the walls into the kitchen in the gap above the wainscoting and found his giant with her talking device, the little flat piece of glass and metal she held to her ear and talked into and voices came out of.

"What... What did he do?" she mumbled, sliding to the cold floor. "It... it's not working." Her hands shook and her voice broke and water leaked out of her eyes.

Edward heard the front door opening and the lazy dog growling and barking, followed quickly by a yelp from the dog. Theodore scurried into the kitchen and hid under the table, cowering in his blankets.

This worried Edward, for he had seen the hound dog chasing rabbits in the field and being quite the predator. It made the threat of the male giant that much more dire.

The evil black cat was there too, perched on top of the refrigerator seemingly indifferent to the proceedings, watching listlessly with his yellow eyes.

"So nice of you to pick a house here all by itself so you and I can have a nice long reunion," he said.

The male giant stopped at the entrance to the kitchen and Edward could smell him. He stank of fermented grains and old sweat. He was taller than his giant and much bigger. He was a predator, this much Edward was sure of, and she was his prey.

She didn't answer, her shaking hands fumbling in the cabinet next to the sink. She tossed out pans which clanged loudly and glass bowels which skittered across the wood floor.

"Where is it?" she whispered.

Edward smelled her terror, just like from the nightmares, and the little mouse realized that this was it. This was what she feared the most. The male giant was like the cat was to Edward. Predator and torturer.

She pulled something out of the cabinet. It was dark grey and metal and smelled of oil. Edward did not know the word gun, but he knew that these things barked the loudest noise and then rabbits fell over dead with holes ripped in their flesh.

Her hand shook as she pointed the gun at the male giant. "Leave," she gasped. "And never come back."

She sounded like a mouse cornered by a cat squeaking out a threat.

The male giant laughed. "Oh, Evy," he said. "I'd be real impressed if you had it in you to pull that trigger."

He took a step into the kitchen, his chest heaving, his hands balled into fists and the gun slipped out of her shaking hand.

Edward's brain worked furiously. The new giant was predator. She was prey. The mouse wanted to save her like from her nightmares, but Edward was a tiny mouse and he was a vast giant. The evil cat might be able to slow him down and the lazy dog was big enough to do some damage, but the cat seemed uninterested and the dog was cowering.

Edward's little brain sparked again, powered by his heart so filled with this female bipedal giant. There had to be something he could do. And then he remembered the first night he woke her. Cat chases mouse. Dog chases cat.

And then he remembered his dream, the one that brought him here. He felt his destiny calling, he felt the fire in his brain as he put it all together, as he could see something that had a tiny chance of working. He squeezed through the crack and he acted.

He ran along the wainscoting as fast as he could, making the kind of motion that the evil cat was sure to see. He got to the wooden table and jumped down on it, winding his way amongst the sweet-smelling pies.

The evil cat was watching, was up now, its tail switching as it jumped off the refrigerator and onto the kitchen counter, its yellow eyes trained on the little mouse.

Edward's heart beat so hard he didn't know how his body could possibly contain it. He was prey, just like his female bipedal giant was. But that does not mean that they were helpless.

As he approached the edge of the table, scurrying as fast as he could, Edward heard the hound dog growl below him. He had spotted the cat.

With a burst of speed, Edward hurled himself off the table towards the male giant, towards the stinking alpha predator.

Words were being said as the male giant puffed his chest and as tears leaked from her eyes and she whimpered, but Edward paid no attention.

Edward had that moment there in midair. The moment where time seemed to freeze, where he could see the cat hurtling towards him and hear the dog surging forth and see the male giant before him and hear the female giant behind him.

His heart thumped so loud and he felt fear like he had never felt before, but he also felt a fire in him. A desire to not be just prey. To fight back. To help the bipedal giant that meant so much to him.

He knew it was his destiny he was flying towards, for mice understand destiny. They are small creatures in a big world, but they know they have a place and a role to fill.

And then the moment ended and he was falling and he hit the floor hard, the wind knocked right out of him and he slid across the hardwood floor and smacked into the boot of the giant.

The cat landed just short of him, his paws sliding on the floor as he slid past the mouse.

The dog surged out from under the table snarling and barking.

"Edward!" the female giant yelled.

And the male giant took a step back.

It wasn't much, but Edward could feel his doubt. Something was happening that the mighty alpha predator didn't expect, didn't understand.

Edward was in pain and dizzy but he knew he only had moments. He ran, quite wobbly, and leapt onto the giant's boot and crawled up under his jeans and started climbing.

It was pure instinct. A need to hide. A need to help her, the giant he loved so much.

As he climbed up the hairy leg of the giant, the cat pounced onto the man trying to get to Edward and the dog lunged after the cat and ran into the man.

"What the...?" the man gasped as he fell backwards. As Edward continued to climb his leg. As the cat tried to pin the mouse under the denim while trying to avoid the dog. While the dog snapped and lunged at the cat.

Edward kept going until he found soft tender flesh, the acrid smell making clear where he was. He knew this was a tender area, even on the deadliest of predators. So he bit down. Hard.

The male giant screamed and thrust his huge hand down his pants and grabbed the little mouse. He pulled Edward out and raised his hand high getting ready to smash the little mouse against the hard floor.

"Drop him!" the female bipedal yelled, and Edward could hear something different in her voice. The fire that had propelled the little mouse had spread to her. "Drop the mouse, this instant."

"This thing bit me," the man spit.

"You're going to drop him," she said. Edward could still hear her fear, but he could also hear her growing strength. She was prey no more. "And then you're going to turn off your cell phone jammer and then you are going to go to jail."

"Come on now, Ev," he said as he opened his hand. Edward sniffed and looked around. The dog had the cat backed into a corner and was growling. "Surely this was just a big misunderstanding."

Edward scurried away, back to safety through a loose baseboard close by, into the wall, but he watched as it all unfolded.

As the man fiddled with a device from his pocket and then as she got on her talking device.

As she pointed the gun at him and he cowered in front of her.

As other bipedal giants came and took the man away.

As she dropped to the floor of the kitchen when the house was empty.

Edward then ventured out and went to her. He stood before her and squeaked.

She looked down at him and held out her hand. He crawled onto it and she brought him close.

"You saved me, Edward," she said.

Edward didn't understand the words, and if he had he would have disagreed. He didn't save her, he just gave her the time and the motivation to save herself. He squeaked again and she laughed. It was a small thing, but it was a laugh.

The little mouse was hurt and exhausted, but he was happy.

"Want some cheese, Edward?" she asked. "You deserve all the cheese you can eat."

He caught the rise in pitch and squeaked again.

She laughed, and as Edward ate his treat, he wondered what life was like after you fulfilled your destiny.

So far it was pretty good.

BACKSTORY—CAT CHASES MOUSE. DOG CHASES CAT

While this story, told from the point of view of a mouse, can be considered fanciful, I don't think it's quite fantasy.

Perhaps I am splitting hairs here—dog, cat, or mouse, take your choice—this story is about an ordinary mouse. Well... perhaps an extraordinary mouse, one that is just a touch psychic, and one that is fairly anthropomorphized, but a mouse, nonetheless.

I think what puts this one in the contemporary column for me is that this is not the kind of story a fantasy magazine would publish.

Animals may or may not experience love the way we do, but they certainly feed on attention and affection just like we do. Even a mouse that is chased by a cat, and a cat that is chased by a dog.

PART 10
BLUE

BLUE

I trust nothing but the color blue. Nothing.

The sky on a clear day is my greatest comfort, an endless expanse of glittering blue above and around me. It's why I can't stand to be indoors during a clear day—although the ocean-blue walls of my house did help... when I had a house. And I fear the night when the evil orange invades and the setting sun takes the blue sky with it. I don't go out at night if I can help it.

I don't know how I got this way. Perhaps it was the blue eyes of my mother, the only safe harbor in a troubled childhood where my father liked to hit things—namely us.

Maybe it's how the blues were the first music that reached my damaged heart. Not that music itself has a color, but it being named after such a fine color speaks very well of it.

Or maybe it's blueberries which I adore. And yes, in the store, I know they look more a deep purple, but they are quite blue when you pick them, they darken off the vine.

But really, it's my mother. I know that. It was her that I first trusted, and her eyes were what always comforted me when I was hurt and bruised, or sick, or confused, or crying.

The blue eyes of my mother were all that could comfort me. But my mother is gone. Now all I trust is the color blue.

THAT LAST TRIP TO THE ER WITH MY MOTHER, THEY DIDN'T put her in a blue gown, but a pink one. I pitched a fit, my father thinking I was drawing attention away from my dying mother and to myself, but he was wrong.

The pink meant something. It meant that she was going to die.

I yelled and cried. He dragged me into the bathroom and held his shaking fist in my face and told me, "Shut up, boy, or so help me!"

The "so help me's" was this disease my father had. "If you don't shut up, then so help me." "If that dog doesn't stop crapping in my yard, then so help me." "If your mother doesn't get well soon, then so help me."

It was a plague on his linguistic utterances and everything around him. "So help me" meant "Or I'm going to start hitting someone... everyone... until I feel the tiniest bit of control in this awful world."

In that bathroom, I stopped crying, I pleaded with him, told him that the pink was a bad sign, if they just changed her into blue then I knew that she would make it.

He didn't listen. I was an eleven-year-old boy, why would he listen to me?

She died.

In retrospect, I think he wanted her to die. He was tired of caring for her, although I did most of that. He was tired of watching her pain as she fought the cancer, dealing with the household chores that she could no longer do—although I did most of those.

After the funeral, I couldn't stop crying and my father and I had a long session of "so help me's."

I ran away from home that night with my face bruised and bloody.

Life without my mother felt wrong. Never mind the stealing of food and sleeping under cardboard boxes, or in kids' tree houses, it was my mother not being in the world that made the world seem foreign, unsafe, alien.

It felt so wrong it almost seemed like a dream I couldn't wake up from. Even the good days when I got enough food, got some sleep and stayed dry, stayed away from any of the world's "so help me's" it felt like I didn't belong. Like this existence was some kind of cruel trick, some plot by my father to punish me, that my mother must be alive, must be out there somewhere.

How can an eleven-year-old boy exist in a world without his mother?

I'm not dumb. I know the reality of the world. Even then. I read the headlines of the papers in the newsstands, I knew what a cruel place this is. How people like my father were everywhere. Some with real power that could do more than use their fists against their wife and child. Some with guns and weapons who threw their "so help me" tantrums at other countries. Some who used money as their weapon, separating themselves from the poor and the weak, keeping their money for trinkets instead of helping others live.

Others like me.

After six months on the street, I got caught stealing from a small deli. The big man with a shaved head and a grip of steel grabbed me.

"No!" I cried, not trusting his brown skin and brown eyes. I had a fist full of blueberries from the salad bar that I shoved in my mouth.

"You stealin' from me, boy?" he asked, and I thought for sure this was a "so help me" situation.

I went limp on the dirty linoleum and cried. I was terrified, yes, but sometimes it helped to cry, like the tears of a child could lubricate a situation.

He let go of my wrist. I was backed into a corner and couldn't get past his bulk.

"What's your name, boy?" he asked.

When I looked, he had blueberries in his big hand and was holding them out towards me.

This was different. I didn't trust him. He didn't have my mother's blue eyes. But then I saw his dark tie was actually navy blue, not black. It was a sharp contrast to his white shirt and white apron.

That made two blue things. I reached out, tentatively, and he let me take the blueberries from his hand. I ate them one by one, staring at him, waiting for the fist that didn't come.

***

"You don't have to go, Blue," the big man said, his hands on his hips. "You can sleep in the back."

Blue. That is what he started calling me after a few weeks when he noticed I would only eat blue things, like blueberries, red cabbage, blue cheese—although blue cheese is disgusting. He had asked my name many times, but I had never told him. After our first encounter, I started coming back for the blueberries. I always wore blue clothes. I had blue eyes like my mother. He noticed things, things my father would have never noticed.

I shook my head and left. Mr. Walters was not wearing his blue tie today and I didn't trust him when he wasn't wearing his blue tie. It was his red tie, which is a long way away from blue on the color wheel. Something green or purple, which both have blue in them, might have worked, but not red. Red is dangerous and right next to the terrible orange on the color wheel.

He wanted me to call him Hank, but I couldn't. It was Mr. Walters. I would come by and sweep for him, wipe down counters, clean the little bathroom, and he would give me blueberries or whatever else I would eat. If it was blue, purple, or very dark green, I would eat it. It had to be full of blue. A blue napkin or paper plate helped too.

I think about the color wheel a lot. About how the colors combine. And I knew that the color rules were different for pigments (blue and yellow = green) and light (blue and green = cyan) and this distracted my brain.

Outside, on the busy street, the horns honking, the smell of exhaust, the blue of the darkening sky still visible through the tall buildings, I stared at the stoplights. Green, when it is a light, has no blue, is not safe. Yellow and red don't have blue either. Blue is left out of it for traffic lights. Color is made by adding when it comes to light. So yellow is green light and red light combined.

The taillights are red and the only blue spectrum light is hidden in the white of the headlights.

I don't like cars. Well, blue ones are okay, but they are not safe. You can get trapped in a car with someone and their so-help-me's. You can get hit by a car. They are noisy and smelly and altogether not safe in the very least.

I shook it off, dark was coming and I needed to be safe before the blue was gone from the sky. I kept my head down and moved fast among the people on the sidewalk. There was blue in the moving mass of humanity, blue eyes, navy blue coats, blue jeans, but I didn't stop. I moved and turned off the busy street as soon as I could, followed alleyways and smaller streets, moving towards the river.

Water is blue, even dirty river water is blue deep down. It's full of blue even when it's hidden.

My mom was like that, the blue always there in her eyes, always safe, even when her eyes were closed or she had sunglasses on. I am starting to think that Mr. Walters has blue all the time too, even when he doesn't have a blue tie on. He's like the deep water, the blue not always visible, but still there.

SOMETIMES I DREAM IN COLORS. NOT THAT THE IMAGES are a particular color, but that the images are *only* color. With a good color dream, my mind is filled with undulating shades of blue, from the deepest of purples to the lightest of powder blues. Sweet moving forms of mixing colors.

A bad color dream is full of sharp reds and oranges, spikes of it trying to pierce me, hurt me.

The best of dreams start out blue, waves of it, and then a pinprick of black forms in the center and grows large and round, the blue coalescing until there are folds and striations in the blue with flecks of brown and gold as it surrounds the black. And then there is white around the blue, and then I can see that the image is an eye, and then I can see that the eye belongs to my mother and she is smiling sweetly at me.

I woke up from one of these dreams, a smile on my face, and then the cold hit me, my bladder complaining and my stomach clenching in hunger and I felt the hard ground below me and cardboard above me providing scant warmth. My beautiful dream twisted into a bitter reminder of what was lost.

Tears stung my check and I harshly wiped them away. I

didn't have any "so help me's" for the tears, but I didn't want them. I didn't have room for them.

I needed food and water. I needed to go to the bathroom, preferably not in an alley. I needed to stay dry and warm.

All things I never thought about before my mother died.

I shut my eyes against the dirty grey light of dawn and wished my dream back. My mother's kind blue eyes.

A voice intruded on my quest. It was too loud and awkward, as if the person speaking was ashamed of what he was doing. "You seen a boy around here? Eleven, about yay high, blue eyes and black hair with bangs starting to get in his eyes."

I knew that voice. It was a voice filled with "so help me's". It was my father.

"Wadda ya wanna know for?" I heard Vinnie ask, a nice guy, used to be in the army.

"He... I..." I heard my father sniff, like he was crying or something. My father didn't cry. "He's my boy. I... I'm looking for my boy."

He spoke more, his voice shaking with emotions, but I quietly got out from underneath the cardboard, ignored the rotting garbage scent of the alleyway, ignoring my about to burst bladder, and I ran. I ran as fast as I could.

"WELL, YOU'RE HERE EARLY, BLUE," MR. WALTERS SAID AS he unlocked the door and opened it up. A puff of warm air hit me and the smell of baking pizza made my mouth water.

This is where my legs had carried me. I had run straight, hadn't even stopped to pee or anything. Today he had on his blue tie, I smiled, and asked, "Can I please use your bathroom?"

His forehead wrinkled, and he was old enough for that to be quite the show. For a moment I thought I had made a mistake, that he wasn't trustworthy, that my early arrival would bring on a "so help me."

And then his face formed a big smile and he opened the door wide. "Of course, Blue. Of course."

After I got out of the bathroom I found him sitting at one of the little Formica tables—dark purple, old, and scarred. He had a plate in front of him and he pushed it towards me. On it was a slice of pizza. The crust was normal, but that was it. No red sauce, but something green, and the melted white cheese had flecks of blue in it.

"I've been experimenting," he said with a chuckle that rumbled through the small deli. "It's a pesto pizza with blue cheese."

I stopped and swallowed, my stomach clenching. It had been a long time since I had eaten something substantial like this. "For me?" I asked.

His chuckle turned into a big laugh and he said, "Who else would want a pizza like this? You know, blue cheese is not a normal pizza thing."

I licked my lip and nodded. The pizza was on a blue plate and Mr. Walters pulled out a blue napkin and a blue plastic fork.

I sat down warily and looked back up at him.

"I trust you washed your hands in there, young man," he said.

I nodded.

"Well then... eat!"

And I did. And it was so good despite the moldy note of the blue cheese. I almost forgot that my father was searching for me.

"More?" he asked when I was done.

I nodded my head enthusiastically.

It was so early still that the deli was closed, I hadn't been in here with it closed before. And that felt... I don't know. In one way it seemed safer with only Mr. Walters to worry about, but on the other hand it was just too quiet.

Where was he? What was taking so long. He had fussed with a pizza, started it in the pizza oven with its little conveyor belt, and told me he forgot about something and then gone up the stairs to the apartment that sat above the deli.

I would have left, but for all the blue and how good that pizza felt in my stomach.

So I sat there, kicking the leg of the table, looking around, biting on my thumbnail. Breathing in the scent of the baking pizza, my stomach growling.

The minutes ticked past. The blue cheese pizza rolled out the far end of the oven and still no Mr. Walters. And still I sat.

Outside on the street, the light was warming up, the grey of predawn chased away by the sun. People were starting to rush past. The salad bar was set up, the coffee brewed, the refrigerated cases stocked with drinks and breakfast burritos. Shouldn't Mr. Walters be opening up by now?

Was something wrong with him? Did he fall or hurt himself? I thought of going through the door marked private and going upstairs to check on him, but no, that wouldn't be right. That wouldn't be safe.

And then he came through the door and I was so relieved, but his face made me want to throw up what I had eaten. He looked scared. He looked guilty. He wouldn't meet my eyes.

I swear he whispered, "I'm sorry" as he shuffled by.

He opened the front door and two men and a woman walked in. Of the three of them, I could only see one. Tall with black hair buzzed short, hollow grey eyes, sunken cheeks.

My father.

I was trapped. My father, who had to be so full of "so help me's" by now, was here. Mr. Walters with his tantalizing blue had called him, told him where I was, that must have been what he was doing upstairs. He called him and waited for him to get here.

I couldn't trust Mr. Walters and that meant... I could barely think it, but that meant I couldn't trust the color blue anymore.

"It's okay, son," my father said, his hands out and his palms open, pretending that he didn't want to make those hands into fists and take out his rage on me.

"No!" I cried, standing up, the chair clattering to the linoleum. I backed up until I was pressed against the metal side of the salad bar at the back of the deli. "He hits me. He hurts me."

I hated myself for saying it. It was true, he was my father and he hurt me, but it was also true that he was my father and I loved him.

My father's face fell, and I could see something I hadn't expected. Shame. He stopped moving and the other two people moved in front of him and I could finally see them. One was a police officer dressed in blue, the second was a woman with kind brown eyes and a haggard-looking face.

"No one is going to hurt you," she said. She stopped three feet from me and squatted down. "My name is Dawn," she said and extended her hand. "I'm with Child Protective Services. I'm here to help you, Wyatt."

I shook my head, tears flowing down my cheeks. I sank to the floor and hugged my legs.

"You better leave, Mr. Issacs," she said to my father. "Thank you for helping us find him."

The bell on the door rang and I heard it softly shut. I peeked out and my father was gone. Mr. Walters was there and the woman Dawn, both sitting on the linoleum in front of me. The police officer stood behind them both.

"He hurt me," I said.

Dawn nodded. "And he's not going to hurt you anymore."

"I miss him," I added and Dawn had a strange, twisted look on her face. She wasn't wearing blue, but that look was, without a doubt, a "blue" look.

I like sweeping. It's simple, mundane, satisfying. The swish-swish of the broom, the feel of the handle in my hand, the simple result of a cleaner floor. All very admirable.

B.B. King was playing low on the old CD player Mr. Walters had in the back, his rumbling voice singing a song called "How Blue Can You Get" that made me feel very happy and safe.

"I think that's clean enough," Mr. Walters said, a smile playing on his old face, his hands on his hips.

I looked up, smiled, and nodded. I didn't want to go. My foster family was fine. They got angry—like everyone does—and that made me worry about the "so help me's," but they remained calm, they dealt with their anger in ways that didn't involve fists.

I put the broom away, but still wished I had it in my hands, had something simple that I could do, that I could finish. I wanted to hear more blues. I wanted to keep looking at Mr. Walters's kind old face and his blue tie—he never wears the red anymore.

My foster family, they let me come help Mr. Walters after school. It actually helps them because I am here and safe until it is time for them to come home from work. It's a short bus ride from here and Mr. Walters made sure all the bus drivers knew me. He rode with me the first few times.

My foster mom and dad call me "Wyatt" and I don't like that. I mean, it is my name, my mother gave it to me, but I don't feel like Wyatt anymore.

I am Blue.

"See you tomorrow, Blue?" Mr. Walters asked.

I nodded. "Can we listen to B.B. some more?"

He smiled and chuckled and nodded his head. "God knows this world could use a little more blues, couldn't it?"

I smiled and left and walked out into the honking, growling noise of the street, the blue of the sky darkening. There are so many "so help me's" in this world, I know that. There are more than any single person can handle.

But there are the blue people, too. Like my mother and Mr. Walters and my new foster parents. If kindness had a color, surely it's blue.

BACKSTORY—BLUE

It may not look like it, but this is one of those very personal stories.

Someone in my family was obsessed with the color blue. It wasn't just a "favorite" color for them, it wasn't just the predominant hue of things they surrounded themselves with and loved, but it seemed to be something more to them.

After this person's death, I was pondering their love of the color blue when this story popped out. Other things, obviously, mixed in with that observation, but it is the center the story revolves around.

The world is hard and messy, but there are people, and things, and perhaps colors, that make this world a better place.

PART 11
UNCLE LARRY'S INFAMOUS TOILET GARDENS

UNCLE LARRY'S INFAMOUS TOILET GARDENS

My uncle Larry loved his toilet gardens. Not that the neighbors did or my mother or anyone else but me. At first, at least.

Larry wasn't really my uncle, not by blood. He was my mother's best friend from college, the one she never lost touch with, and when we moved to the Oregon coast, he was there to help us.

This was in 1974 and my father's "little problem" with heroin had ended up killing him and bankrupting us. We moved from Austin to get a new start. "Little problem" was my mother's preferred euphemism. I was fourteen at the time and found such euphemistic turns of phrase to be cowardly and repugnant, but we weren't the kind of family that talked about such things, so I kept my mouth shut.

I was a teenager and thought I knew everything. It was probably for the best that I kept my mouth shut about that particular topic, anyway.

Our new home was a converted garage that sat six feet away from an aging ranch-style house with the gurgling sound of a creek nearby, a big yard that I was already committed to taking care of, and more trees than you could count. The trees were all dense and leafy and just a little bit too smug about how much rain they got here. Texas trees were properly grateful for the water they got.

I wasn't happy. I pictured going to school and introducing myself. "Hi, I'm Brian. Just moved here and I live in a garage. Yeah, and my Dad OD'd on heroin and died a junkie's death. And I used to be a Texas spelling bee champion. Want to be friends?"

Yeah, that wasn't going to go well.

After he had helped us unload our small U-Haul, Uncle Larry got this weird grin on his lean, pockmarked face and said, "I've got a gift for you. I'll be right back."

Uncle Larry was built like a stork, all thin limbs that seemed to be eminently foldable and a long neck. His Adam's apple was almost the size of a real apple and bobbed distractingly when he talked. He had an unruly mop of thick brown hair with shards of silver beginning their invasion.

I was young enough to think that such things would never happen to me. I wouldn't get old. I wouldn't go grey. I wouldn't give in to life and settle.

My mother's lips quirked into a smile watching him run to his old faded blue F-150 and drive off. But she didn't say anything.

Mom was in her late thirties and still pretty. Well... okay, my mom is still pretty to this day. Big blue eyes and silky black hair with just a bit of wave and enough chemicals to hold off the grey invasion. She was short but thin, all coiled energy and sharp wit.

She looked tired in her old jeans and ragged blue sweater, oversized gardening gloves on her hands. She was paranoid about breaking a nail.

"I don't like this," she said, but there was a smile dancing on her thin lips. She took off her gloves, fished in her jeans pocket, and pulled out lipstick, applying a fresh coat. The color was reddish but not garish, matte not shiny.

I did my best to not wrinkle my nose at the perfumey waxy smell, but I was fourteen. Mom didn't seem to notice.

"We just going to stand here?" I asked, my hands shoved into my jeans pockets as I kicked the eroding cement of the old driveway.

She looked at me, those blue eyes of her going into full-on boring mode as they drilled into me. "Larry lives two minutes away. The man doesn't have a good back and he just hauled our crap for two hours. Yes, we are just going to stand here."

She ended in a lopsided quirky smile that dared me to question her logic.

Mom could never control Dad, couldn't save him from his addiction, but she was dedicated to keeping me safe and raising me right. Whatever the hell that meant.

Truth was I didn't want to be here. I had friends in Austin. Trisha Montoya and I had kissed under the bleachers and I didn't mind the smell of her lipstick one tiny bit.

I sighed and kicked at the driveway. My mother marched over to our car, an older Jeep Cherokee, grabbed some trash from our journey and shoved it into my hands. "If you can't just stand there and wait, make yourself useful, Brian."

So I did. Slowly. Using that teenage skill of looking like you are busy but getting precious little done. Not that it was wholly conscious. I'm not so old that I've completely forgotten what it was like to be young. It was like my resistance to more activity was a palpable force slowing me down, making it hard for me to move to the steel trash cans stationed on the side of our converted-garage apartment, open them, dump the trash in, and go get another load from my mother.

But I did move and "make myself useful" and we did clean

out the old red Cherokee. It was off-gassing, the smell of coffee and sweat and oil and that stupid tree-shaped air freshener dangling from the rearview. That sped me up, at least as I walked away from it. I was tired of that old car smell.

Soon enough Uncle Larry came back, towing a trailer behind the F-150, a toothy grin on his face.

In the back of it was a white porcelain toilet with green things sticking up from the bowl and the tank. Not just green, but colors. Red, blue, and purple decorated the bowl, a forest of pale green erupting from the tank.

My mother pursed her mouth so completely that you couldn't see her lips anymore. I think she might have been biting on her lips in there keeping herself from speaking.

Me, I was fourteen, so I said, "That is so cool, Uncle Larry."

And I meant it. It was clearly going to drive my mother crazy and that right there was the definition of "cool" in my teenager's dictionary.

"Thanks, Brian," he said beaming.

The toilet garden was strapped in the low trailer. Uncle Larry dropped the gate, undid the strapping, and slipped a dolly under it and rolled it off the trailer.

It truly was a garden. The bowl had a variety of flowers. Pansies, snapdragons, and daisies. Colorful and happy. The tank had a thick forest of wispy greens.

"Carrots?" I asked, pointing at the tank as he rolled the toilet garden to the driveway and stopped in front of my mother.

"You bet," he said swallowing, his Adam's apple bobbing like a bird pecking the ground for food. "All ready to eat."

A slight groan escaped my mother. It was a toilet. You don't grow a garden in a toilet and you don't eat food grown in a toilet. But she didn't say anything. That wouldn't be polite.

"Where do you want it?" Uncle Larry asked, his brown eyes bright as he looked at my mother.

I CHEWED ON THE CARROT LOUDLY AND SLOWLY HOPING THE sound carried to my busy mother. She was bustling around the small kitchen, not much more than a short counter, a refrigerator, and a two-burner stove. There was a microwave on the counter but no oven. Which meant no meatloaf or apple pie which made this a rather grim place to live.

I mean, the kitchen was nice enough with new-ish laminate countertops in a swirling brown, but it was so small. Our kitchen in Austin was at least twice this big.

The carrot I was eating like a gleeful Bugs Bunny had been pulled from the toilet garden and hastily washed in the sink. I crunched down loudly again and her blue eyes flickered over me, all sharp and icy. I'm not known for my love of fresh vegetables.

"How is your snack, dear?" she asked with a smile sharp enough to draw blood.

"Delicious," I replied, smiling around the very orange root vegetable.

"Why don't you go take it and set up your room." She sighed, her fists finding her hips, and she stared at me. She looked tired and drawn. She had lost weight, more than she needed to, in the last few months. Her blue eyes weren't as vivid as I remembered, and her long black hair had mostly fallen out of the impromptu bun she had put it in, giving her appearance this frayed look.

The toilet garden was right next to the door to our apartment, right there for anyone to see. She hadn't answered Uncle Larry about where to put it, so I had.

A new thought wormed its way into my brain—quite a feat considering my hormone-filled age. Mom looked old. Mom was getting old. The last couple of years had taken so much out of her.

I blinked, a stab of guilt piercing through my teenage schadenfreude moment.

Our new home, the converted garage, had three rooms. The kitchen / living room, a bathroom, and a bedroom. My mother was going to sleep on the couch. She was giving me the bedroom.

"You know..." I began, the carrot forgotten for the moment. "Why don't you take the bedroom. I can sleep anywhere."

And I could. It was like a superpower, one of the only things I miss about being a teenager.

Mom blinked and then stared at me, her blue eyes searching mine. Her eyebrows flickered above her tired eyes and something passed over her face.

Regret, probably. Fatigue, certainly. Fear of the future, without a doubt. We were starting over. Dad was dead. Suddenly that toilet garden carrot didn't taste so good.

"How about you set up the room," she said as she watched me carefully. "Put your stuff in it, and whoever has to get up first sleeps on the couch. Sound good?"

She took a tentative step toward me and then stopped, her arms folded awkwardly in front of her, her upper lip quivering just a bit.

Mom had taken a job at Fred Meyer working checkout and her shifts started early. I opened my mouth to object, but that quiver stopped me. She was giving me a way out of my offer without refusing it. It would keep her on the couch most nights, but I dedicated myself to letting her have the bed on her days off.

"Sure, Mom. That makes sense," I said, remembering my carrot and raising it up like a microphone as I took a step towards her. "But tell us, Veronica, what does it feel like to have one of Uncle Larry's famous toilet bowl gardens in your yard?"

Her eyes widened and flashed dangerously, but I persisted, stepping closer. "Fresh carrots, right out your front door. What do you have to say about that?"

I shoved the carrot in her face like some annoying reporter. Her eyes widened and her lips pursed, but then her head bobbed forward and she bit a chunk off the carrot.

"Now go get busy, young man," she said, the carrot in her mouth garbling her words a bit.

I took a step through the maze of boxes towards the small bedroom.

"You know," she said around her crunching. "That is a good carrot."

I REMEMBER GOING TO SEE MY GRANDMOTHER, MY FATHER'S mother, when she was dying.

It was this surreal experience. It wasn't her there anymore, not really. She was so thin lying there, the extra weight having melted off of her during her last few weeks when she hardly ate. Her skin was wrinkled and flaccid, flaps of pale flesh almost inert lying against the worn white sheets. She was pale in a way that just scared me and there were strange bruises here and there, dark blue splotches under her paper-thin skin.

We were in Grandma's old house, the spare bedroom having been cleared. It was just the narrow hospital bed, a few chairs, and family pictures crowding the wall in her line of sight.

Mom was standing behind me, hugging herself and "giving me a moment with Gran."

I didn't want a moment. I was thirteen and hadn't confronted death, not even a little bit. Death wasn't even real to me yet.

I stood there, my nose filling with this cloying smell that I couldn't identify. Something rotting, maybe blood, with the sharp smell of cleaner mixed in. My nose told me to run from such smells, but it was my grandmother.

The kind old lady that always kissed me on the cheek and slipped me a piece of hard candy when my parents weren't looking. She drank wine in fancy glasses and was obsessed with watching boring science shows on PBS.

She was emaciated. That was the word that flickered through my mind. The word finally made sense. I still think of her in her dying bed when I hear that word.

Her eyes flicked open, her brown irises faded to almost grey, and they widened. Her wrinkled mouth opened and then her lips pressed together as if trying to form a "B," trying to say my name.

"Hi, Grandma," I said. "I'm glad to see you."

My mother had coached me. She had said, "Don't under any circumstance ask her how she's doing. She's dying."

My grandmother didn't get my name out, her warm breath expelling and her eyes closing again, the dark fetid smell flowing out of her like she was a rotting piece of meat.

I looked back to my mother, my eyes way too wide.

Her brow furrowed and she whispered, "Sit. Hold her hand so she's not alone."

My father wasn't there. He was off getting high leaving Mom to try to deal with the creditors and keep food on the table and dealing with his dying mother.

I think that was the moment, right there, when my mother gave up on my father. If his addiction was strong enough to keep him away from his dying mother, it was more than anything she could overcome.

I was terrified, probably more terrified than I had ever been in my life. But I sat. I took her hand, which was all bony and warm with paper-thin skin. Her eyes had fluttered closed, but her hand tightened, just a touch, with less strength than a newborn baby.

"Just sit with her," my mother said from behind me. I didn't dare turn around. I knew I would bolt if I saw fear in my mother's eyes or even compassion. "She doesn't have long."

I didn't know what that meant. Was "not long" minutes or days or weeks or months?

Months seemed like "not long" to me when it comes to dying. Hell, years seemed like "not long" at that age. Was I to sit on this hard wooden chair next to my dying grandmother in her narrow hospital bed and stare at the powder blue walls until she died?

How would I know? What would it feel like? Would it even be much different than this, because this wasn't my grandmother anymore with her round form and booming laugh.

Even then, I suspected it wasn't like in the movies with some dramatic speech followed by the eyes fluttering closed and the last breath being dramatically exhaled. Just looking at the wasted form of my grandmother, I knew it was a hell of a lot messier than that.

"I don't know if I can," I said, my voice just a whisper.

My mother didn't reply. Her still silence behind me was disconcerting. And then she sighed and I heard the scrape of a chair over the worn brown linoleum and she was sitting beside me. She took my other hand.

I held my grandmother's hand and my mother held mine.

I looked at her and tried to smile, but I think it came out strange and probably looked terrifying, but my mother just smiled back.

"What do we do now?" I asked.

"We just sit here and be with her," she said.

I nodded and looked at my grandmother, her short grey hair dirty and unkempt, her eyes closed and her thin form still.

I almost asked her why we needed to do this, just looking for any excuse to escape, but I didn't need to. I knew. My grandmother loved to be with people, it wouldn't be right for her to die alone, and my father wasn't here.

My father was never here.

As the minutes ticked by, a thought creeped into my mind, dark and cold. It would be better if it was my father dying, not my grandmother.

My father had chosen heroin over us where my grandmother had always chosen her family.

NEW KID NAMED BRIAN. NEW SCHOOL. DEAD DAD. EATS carrots grown in a toilet.

That was me. The first two were unavoidable, the second two needed to be kept secret. Well... if some kid couldn't handle that I happily ate root vegetables grown in a toilet tank (not the bowl, mind you) they could go jump. The part about my dad... I wasn't ready to talk about it.

I didn't think I'd ever be ready to talk about it.

My mother looked me over, her blue eyes roaming with deadly efficiency, like she was a cyborg designed to locate my flaws and point them out. Her eyes lingered at the rip in my jeans at the right knee, and at my old concert T-shirt and the dollop of a bleach stain on the black fabric. My blue hoodie was frayed a bit at the cuffs and her eyes found that too.

"Don't you have better clothing than this?" she asked, her lips pursed.

I did. Of course I did and she knew it. But this outfit was carefully chosen, each piece communicating something important. From the band on the T-shirt, the Cure, to the clean but older clothing. The shirt said I cared about the band more than I cared about the bleach spot. The hoodie and jeans, both expensive when new, said that I was not poor but I wasn't rich either.

We were standing in our now settled living room / kitchen in our converted garage apartment. The couch was the same over-stuffed brown one from Austin and the oak bookshelf that had pictures of our family, including Dad.

The wooden kitchen table had cereal and orange juice ready to go, but the thought of food just kinda made me want to puke.

"This is what I am wearing," I said. It wasn't worth the discussion. She would reject the very basis upon which my logic was built.

She sighed. Heavily. And nodded her assent. Thankfully this wasn't a battle worth fighting for her.

"Well, have a good day, son," she said, standing there biting her lower lip. She was dressed in jeans and the shapeless baggy top she wears to the grocery store. It was short-sleeved and black with the red Fred Meyer logo. Underneath it, she had on a blue long-sleeved shirt. It was the size she used to wear, but it hung on her making it clear that she had lost some weight. Too much.

She wanted to kiss me, I know she did. Part of her wanted me to still be her "peanut." Not my choice of a nickname. I was a small baby.

"Yeah. Thanks," I said, shoving my hands into my pockets, not knowing what else to do with them. What could I say? This wasn't Austin. I had precisely zero point zero friends and going to a new school would be epically awkward and colossally dangerous socially.

We stood there, my eyes roaming the small space. There was no TV. My mother didn't "believe" in them. As if belief has anything whatsoever to do with it. She didn't like television, but that is not the way she put it.

There was a Georgia O'Keefe print on the wall. She loved that thing, but it just looked like a couple of big blobs of red, not a flower or anything.

Under the O'Keefe was a small desk made out of two

banged-up metal filing cabinets and a piece of plywood. It was very neat with an inbox, an old coffee mug holding pencils and pens, and a stapler.

My mother's desk where she sat on one of the old folding chairs we got from Goodwill and worried about "making ends meet."

Another euphemism. I didn't like those. Especially not when it came to my father and people telling me "he's in a better place." That little phrase made me want to put my fist into their mouth and say, "Here's a 'knuckle sandwich.'"

The truth was we didn't have enough money, that an unexpected trip to the doctor could mean not enough food to eat or ramen for a week.

And that is what Mom didn't like about my clothing. I knew that in her eyes it made it look like we were poor, that there had been better days, that those days were gone for good.

We were poor. Best that we get used to it.

"I gotta go walk to the bus stop," I finally said, breaking the thick silence.

Mom nodded and pursed her lips, her blue eyes darkening. Neither of us moved.

She needed something from me. Even in my teenage fog I could tell that, but I didn't know what it was and I was quite sure that I couldn't provide it.

She needed to roll back time and stop my father from sticking a needle in his arm for the first time. Or maybe even further back and avoid getting pregnant with me when they were dating in college. Or even refusing my father's awkward frat-boy advances when he was just a few years older than me.

That thought sent a shiver down my spine and I bolted for the door.

I sure didn't understand it then, but all Mom needed from me was to tell her I loved her and that I was okay. She needed a hell of a lot more from the world, but from her only child that was all she ever really needed.

<hr>

I CAME HOME THAT EVENING AND PAUSED IN FRONT OF OUR toilet garden. I felt like a shell-shocked veteran.

Now I know that might seem like hyperbole and all, but the key word is "felt." It *felt* like I was a shell-shocked veteran, my hormones a thick confusing soup. My nerves were raw and jangled. I had spent all day trying to blend in enough to avoid trouble, but not so much that I couldn't be seen.

And then everything changed. I saw a girl that shined so brightly it seemed like she had a spotlight on her or the world went dim around her as she strode down the locker-filled hallway on her long, athletic legs.

I had just finished algebra and was heading for history when I saw her. Dark hair almost down to her waist, porcelain skin, glasses, and hazel eyes. She walked with her eyes straight ahead like she owned the place and wasn't an insecure teenager like the rest of us. My head swiveled to follow her, as if of its own voli- tion, and I walked straight into the muscular form of the school's alpha jock. He was staring at her too.

We tumbled to the floor ungracefully and in front of enough teenagers to make sure the whole school knew about it in three seconds. Down on the dirty linoleum, he shoved me off and sat up and stared at the retreating form of the girl, as did I.

Alpha-jock was mad, his cheeks reddening under his now mussed blond hair. We started to get up at the same time and bumped shoulders. He shoved me down hard with a curse and a sneer. I stayed down. Not only was I visible, I had just clearly created an enemy.

It was fine for new-guy-dweeb to lose himself watching shining-girl, but not alpha-jock. This was his school. His to lord over and his right to choose his desired mate. Except he had been as lost as I was looking at her.

Back home, I stared at the petunias and the snapdragons in the porcelain toilet bowl and at the carrot tops sticking out of the tank. What would shining-girl or alpha-jock think if they saw this sitting in front of my house?

My teenage brain leapt to what it thought must be, had to be, the truth of it. Shining-girl would react somewhere along the lines of my mother—in other words, she would be repulsed. And alpha-jock would tease me mercilessly, use it as a way to denigrate me over and over making sure I was shoved down as far as possible socially... and stayed there.

Uncle Larry did us no favors with this damn thing. Mom knew it from the moment she saw it. We were brand new here. Appearances did matter. The damn toilet garden had to go. Now.

I crouched down and put my arms around the cool porcelain and tried to move it. I grunted. Sweat popped out on my forehead. My lower back almost groaned. And... nothing. It didn't budge. Not one bit. Not even a little.

I remembered Uncle Larry with his dolly, so I shifted to the side and pushed. Hard. And the whole assemblage rocked up a little.

The damp air seemed to close in around me and I felt hot. What if shining-girl lived in the neighborhood? What if she saw this and never looked at me again? Not that she had looked at me as her long legs carried her down the locker-filled hallway earlier. But you couldn't tell my hormones that.

I wasn't muscle-bound like alpha-football-jock-boy. I was short and skinny and not very strong. Rocking up the toilet was hard. But I did it. So I gave it a twisting shove, the porcelain scraping against the aged concrete of the driveway in a way that sent a chill down my spine. The toilet rocked back down with a clink as the porcelain banged onto the concrete.

The front of the damn thing moved maybe three inches. Big whoop. It felt like it would take me weeks to move it out of view. But I summoned shining-girl into my mind. Long limbs and silky black hair. Glasses in front of her hazel eyes. Cute up-turned nose and a slightly pointed chin. She had curves in all the right places and I had smelled roses as she passed by. She had worn a blue-green sweater and a skirt that stopped right above her knees showing slim, strong legs.

I didn't even know her name, just shining-girl. So I shoved and I twisted and I grunted and I labored.

This thing was an abomination. It had to be moved. It had to be moved now. This was all of my world. This was the only thing I cared about. Rock it up, twist it, ease it down. Up, twist, down. Up, twist, down.

My muscles complained, I sweated, my nose full of the loamy scent of the soil the plants were thriving in. Up. Twist. Down.

I was careful—I didn't want to break it—and I was desperate, summoning strength I didn't know I had.

By the time Mom got home, the toilet garden was moved just around the side of the house, our trash can moved to sit in front of it. I was sprawled on our old brown couch, my muscles feeling like they were made out of overstretched rubber bands.

When my mother entered our small home with an exhausted sigh, I looked up, trying to keep my expression neutral knowing she would ask about it. But she didn't say a word about it.

"How was your day, dear?" she asked, trying to put some energy in her voice, but I could tell she was exhausted.

"Fine," I lied.

The next day, Friday, I walked home from school. Alpha-jock was on my bus. There must have been something going on my first day because he wasn't on the bus. On Friday as I avoided getting on until the last minute, I saw him hop on, his shoulders back and his spine straight, just like he owned the place.

His name was Frank Ingram. Didn't take long to find that out. And he was a junior and the quarterback of the football team. Which meant there would be ample time for him to exercise his dislike of me in the most embarrassing ways.

So I didn't get on the bus. I needed to. I thought I had to. But I just paced in front of the grey cinderblock building in which the state was providing us an education. It was an outdated education, mind you, designed to make us good factory workers, not prepare us for our rapidly changing world, but it was my dutiful obligation as an adolescent American.

After the bus left, I walked. There was nothing else to do. Three long miles along a route, fortunately, that I knew.

At first I hated it. Exercise was not something I had embraced. I was most definitely not a jock. My grades weren't great, so I wasn't an egghead either. I had done a little drama at my last school, but that had its share of social consequences, the type of which I didn't want to take on as the new kid halfway through the school year.

My legs protested, but not for long. After they warmed up it felt okay—not that I would have admitted to it. My legs were fairly long—I was taller than alpha-jock Frank, after all—so I chewed up the distance.

When I got home, the toilet garden was back, just to the right of our door. Sitting there all cheery flowers and soft green carrot tops.

My breathing was coming fast from the walk and I looked around. My mother wasn't due back yet and I didn't see anyone else in the bland suburban neighborhood, older houses with attached garages, tall trees, mowed grass, a garden gnome here and there.

My mother wouldn't have done this. No way. Was this Uncle Larry, driving by and seeing his offering had been relegated to hiding behind the trash can?

It made no sense.

I looked around again. This had to be alpha-jock Frank. He did this. He had somehow known about this, gotten off the bus early, and done it. He wanted *her* to see it, shining-girl.

I still didn't know her name. I hadn't asked. My voice would undoubtedly break and whomever I asked would know I've got a whopping crush. That would instantly spread around school and I would never be able to look anyone at school in the eye again.

So I squatted down, rocked the stupid toilet garden up, heard that porcelain on concrete scrape, and set it down, moving the front of it a few inches. My muscles complained, but not as much as I expected. I was still warmed up from the walk.

Slowly, I rocked it back and forth and got it out of sight. Frank "Super-jock" Ingram was not going to get the best of me.

The weekend passed in a haze of helping Mom clean, trying to get my homework done for classes very different than the ones I was used to, mowing the lawn, and thinking about shining-girl.

No mention of toilet gardens. No munching on fresh carrots. It was like it never happened. Every time I went outside, I felt a tiny stab of guilt, the toilet garden hunkered behind the stainless-steel trash can like some refugee. I snuck out and watered the plants when my mom was in the shower.

On Sunday, Uncle Larry came over for dinner. Nothing fancy, meatloaf cooked in our new toaster oven, and green beans with store-bought apple pie for dessert.

I watched Uncle Larry as he watched Mom. He smiled, he was talkative and animated, his long limbs jabbing out as he emphasized a point, his prominent Adam's apple bobbing as he talked, his brown eyes bright when he made a joke, his eyes even brighter when one of the jokes hit home and Mom laughed.

Things looked good in our small space now that we were moved in. The air perfumed with the sweet scent of the pie warming in the toaster oven.

At first I thought the lack of a real oven was disaster, but my mom had been cheerful about it and found the toaster oven at the Goodwill. It took up a lot of our limited counter space, but meatloaf and apple pie made it feel more like a home.

The wooden kitchen table was small, so we were pretty close even though there were only three of us. I could smell the meatloaf and Mom's flowery perfume and she even put the good tablecloth on the table, a lacy white doily thingy handed down to her from her mother.

And then it hit me as I watched Uncle Larry watch Mom. She was his shining-girl. My stomach tightened around all the food and their laughter seemed too loud and a little bit forced.

Uncle Larry helped her get the job at Fred Meyer. He helped us move in. He proudly brought the toilet garden with beautiful fresh flowers and ready to eat carrots. They met in college, where Mom met Dad. Mom has always been his shining-girl.

This sent my emotions into a nosedive. I mean, it had been a pleasant enough evening. Food. Laughter. Not one mention of the hidden toilet garden—which was admittedly weird.

But Uncle Larry wanted to be with Mom. Which was… horrifying. Dad hadn't been dead that long even. Forgetting the fact that he had stopped being a father years ago when he started using. Forgetting the fact that Mom had been taking care of him like one might care for a child for the last year of his life.

It just felt wrong to me. Too soon. Too damn soon.

And it was clear that Uncle Larry had wanted to be with Mom since they were, like, twenty. Which was… terrifying. What if it was like that with me and my shining-girl? What if it was worse, what if she never knew who I was?

The air felt hot and I couldn't get a breath. The walls of our converted garage apartment were closing in. Uncle Larry had been Mom's best friend for nearly twenty years always wanting more. How could he live with that?

Is that why we moved here, because Mom wanted to be with him too? Would Uncle Larry become my stepfather? Would I be expected to call him "Dad"? Would he fall into an addiction like my own father did and leave us?

"Brian, are you okay?" Mom asked, her forehead furrowed and her lips pursed. Those lips had fresh lipstick on and in a brighter shade than normal. She was wearing a nice blue dress and Uncle Larry was wearing slacks and a button-down shirt.

"No," I said, my lips feeling strangely numb. It was so hot in here. I looked around at the small space and it felt so empty. My father was gone. No, he was dead. He had killed himself. Everyone said it was an overdose, that he was an addict, that he couldn't help himself, but in that moment I knew different. He killed himself. He hadn't wanted to live anymore.

Uncle Larry was staring at me and he swallowed, his Adam's apple bobbing. How could Mom even like someone with an Adam's apple like that? He had been married once, I remembered that, and divorced. No kids.

"Are you okay, son?" he asked, his voice gentle.

"I'm not your son," I said, my voice leaping out in a shout I hadn't really meant.

I stood up, the old plastic chair clattering to the floor behind me. He's my "uncle" and that meant Mom always thought of him as a brother. But had she? Had she just been waiting for Dad to die so she could go be with him?

I stumbled into the bedroom and slammed the door behind me.

***

THE TEARS WERE BITTER AND STUNG AS THEY RAN DOWN MY cheeks, but I was silent as I lay on the bed. I heard noises in the other room and then a door opening and closing, but I didn't care.

My mind wasn't right. I wasn't right. I thought I understood this move. We had to leave Austin after Dad died. We had to have a new start, but if this was all about Mom finding her next husband, well that felt... wrong.

And none of this would have been happening if Dad had been strong enough to not collapse into his addiction time after time. Then we wouldn't have lost the house and we wouldn't have moved and I wouldn't have seen shining-girl and I wouldn't have had to wrestle with that stupid toilet garden.

The bedroom was small and narrow, the twin bed seeming large in the cramped space. You had to be careful when you walked in here with the narrow desk and dresser and the bed shoved against a wall leaving just enough room to walk around.

It was a terrible bedroom with fake flowers on the dresser—Mom's contribution—next to my spelling bee trophies. I hated them.

I was that nerdy little boy that loved words. When my dad was okay, when he was with us, he would spend hours and hours drilling me, taking me to the competitions, driving me everywhere so I could go compete. I won the Texas state championship when I was eleven.

It was us, it was our thing, until he started using and then nothing was as important to him as his high.

The off-white walls were unadorned—we hadn't hung any art yet. We had too much for the little wall space we had. I hated this room, this tiny life, this state, and I really hated how "Uncle" Larry looked at Mom.

"Honey?" Mom said quietly from the door. I had been so in my own head that I hadn't heard her open it.

I rubbed at my tears and said, "What?" It came out too loud. I was on the bed facing away from her, but I couldn't look at the trophies anymore so I stared at the worn grey quilt covering the bed.

"Uncle Larry is gone," she said. "Do you want to come out and talk about it?"

I swallowed hard. "What is there to talk about?"

She was silent for a few breaths and I knew what was going through her mind. Was I just being a teenager or was I grieving my dead father and lost home?

"You need to talk about it," she finally said. "Either you come out here or I'm coming in there."

Her voice was gentle, but it was clear there was no wiggling out of this one. I sighed and got up and nodded, my back still to her. I wiped the sticky tears off my face and heard her close the door.

I went to the dresser, took my spelling bee trophies, and shoved them in the top drawer.

Mothers can be terrifying. It's part of their nature, part of their job. Sometimes nurturing you is giving you a big fat shove out of the nest so you can fly.

My mom wasn't one to hover, she gave me plenty of room and let me follow my own interests to a certain degree, but when it was time for her to shove, she was all in.

When I came out of the bedroom, she was at the small kitchen table. It had been cleared and the lacy tablecloth put away. A steaming cup of tea was in front of her and I smelled a whiff of chamomile.

I slumped into the chair across from her and folded my arms across my chest. Mom was still wearing her nice blue dress and her redder lipstick. And I noticed she had on eyeliner and a bit of rouge.

She was pretty, even I could see that. The wrinkles lying in around her eyes and mouth weren't deep yet and her long black hair was well past her shoulders. But those blue eyes of hers were in full-on deep drilling mode, boring right into me. They were so intense I couldn't hold her gaze.

"What's going on, Brian?" she asked. Her voice wasn't harsh, but it wasn't gentle. It was as direct as her gaze.

I shrugged, not because I didn't know, for once I did, but because I didn't know what to say or how to express it. I have often found it strange that adults expect teenagers to know their own minds, as if that is possible with the stew of hormones floating through their veins.

"You can talk to me," she said. What was implied was that I *have* to talk to her.

These were the opening salvos, her way of giving me a chance to spill before she pulled out the big guns. But I had played this game before, so I fired back. "Uncle Larry likes you," I said, my voice surprisingly calm.

Mom blinked and then her stare wavered and her cheeks

flushed red. She took a breath and pursed her lips. "Is that so?" she asked.

"Yes," I said. "And you like him."

She blinked more and her jaw moved, but nothing came out. I got up and walked back into the bedroom. It was an epic victory in the mother and son "having a talk" department, but it didn't feel that way. I just felt lost.

It sometimes seems like pretending is the default mode for middle-class America in the seventies. You get in a fight with a loved one, just pretend it never happened. Your father makes one stupid mistake and gets addicted to a powerful opioid, pretend it didn't happen, and then when you can't do that, pretend that he somehow has it under control by sheer force of will.

Figuratively slap your mother in the face with the fact that she's playing metaphorical footsie with the man she always said was an "uncle," pretend that you didn't do it and it isn't happening.

This was the way of my family.

I spent the rest of the night in the bedroom and didn't speak to my mother. I didn't brush my teeth or go to the bathroom until my bladder was about to burst at 3 a.m. Not until it was an emergency.

I snuck out of the room like a thief, opening the door as quietly as possible, slowly padding over the short carpet. But I wasn't quiet enough.

"He's a good man, you know," Mom said from the couch, the bed folded out from it. In the dim light I couldn't see her at all—she must have been lying down.

I stopped and held still like a scared rabbit in the presence of a predator. We weren't going to pretend that none of this happened? If that was true, I didn't know what kind of family I lived in.

"I'm the one moving the toilet garden," I said, the secret slipping out of me much to my chagrin, my cheeks flashing hot. Maybe it was the pressure of my bladder making me offload another kind of waste, maybe it was my mother's honesty.

"He is one of the reasons we moved here," she said. "I need a friend, and if..." she trailed off and I was glad there was a limit to the honesty.

"There's this girl at school," I said, my voice barely above a whisper. "With all that is going on, I feel bad about it, but I can't stop thinking about her and I don't even know her name."

The silence of the night descended and I think maybe she had gone back to sleep and I took a step towards the bathroom to relieve my bursting bladder.

"Is that why you moved Uncle Larry's garden?" she asked.

"Yeah," I answered. "I don't want to be too much of a freak."

She was silent again and I felt this strange sensation like I wasn't in our little converted garage apartment but somewhere sacred, somewhere holy, like on the top of a mountain or in a church. For the first time in years I felt safe.

"Did you move the garden back?" I asked.

She didn't hesitate. "Yes."

"And you knew I had moved it?" I asked.

"Yes."

We hadn't talked about it. We had been in that default mode, pretending the things that happened that should be talked about just hadn't happened.

"Why?" I asked, surprised at my directness. It was freeing in a way that I had never imagined.

Darkness and silence again, the air still smelling faintly of dinner. She sighed and finally said, "Because Uncle... No, because Larry is a good man and even though the hideous thing is so strange it has a peculiar kind of beauty."

"I'm going to get teased about it," I said.

She laughed—it was an aborted little snort. "If that's all they have to tease you about, you'll be doing well."

"What... what if *she* sees it?" I ask, the words slipping out. "And then when she looks at me all she can see is the toilet garden?"

"Then she's not worth your time, Brian."

With her dark hair, hazel eyes, and trim athletic body, how could my shining-girl not be worth my time? My hormone-infused brain told me it was quite impossible, but my mind, remembering stork-like Uncle Larry and his prominent Adam's apple and how my mom seemed to like him, told me otherwise.

"Do you like him?" I asked.

The silence was heavy this time and I was listening so closely that I forgot my straining bladder for a moment.

"I do," she finally said, "but it is complicated."

We were living in a tiny garage apartment, not in Uncle Larry's rambling old house on the hill. They were both interested, that was clear, but Mom wasn't sure. He was. I saw it in his eyes when I realized that Mom was his shining-girl.

"Dad," I said, and the silence was the thickest of all. I was only fourteen, in many ways my mom had lost a whole lot more than I had in all of this. I was old enough to think I really understood it, but not nearly old enough to know that you never fully understand these kinds of things.

She sniffed and shakily said, "Yes. Your father."

My mouth was dry and tasted like old socks and my bladder made itself known again, but I didn't move. I think it was only the hour and the darkness that let us throw off our pretending ways and have a real conversation, and I didn't want to break the spell.

"Uncle Larry is a good man," I finally said. "I am sorry for the way I acted."

I heard her blankets rustle and saw her dim silhouette as she sat up. "Thank you, Brian." She paused, but only briefly. "You know, you owe him an apology too."

I nodded my head and then realized she probably couldn't see me. "I know. I'm... I... I still miss Dad. The way it was... you know, when we were doing the spelling bees and he was still really with us."

My words were fumbling and I didn't know if she understood what I was saying. That I was telling her that it would be hard for me to trust anyone that acted like a father to me. That I would expect his betrayal at any moment, any time he wasn't where he said he was going to be exactly when he said it.

"I miss him too," she said. She was crying. Not deep sobs but tears had to be flowing.

Of course she understood that worry. She was the one that did all the terrible, hard things with my father, the one that picked him up and dragged him to rehab more than once.

But it wasn't enough.

And how could we know that Uncle Larry wouldn't be that way someday?

"I'll move the garden back in the morning," I finally said. I couldn't think of anything else to say.

"That would be nice," Mom said, her dark silhouette disappearing as she lay back down.

Her name is Abigale. I wouldn't say she looks like an "Abigale" with her silky black hair, pale skin, and piercing hazel eyes. Maybe Brooke or even Alice, not Abigale.

She still shines in my eyes, but not quite as brightly. She has a nasally voice and a laugh that sounds a little bit like a goose.

"I'll be damned," she said looking at our toilet gardens, her mouth open showing off her straight white teeth. Her athletic legs were encased in tight jeans and she had a blue sweater on that hugged her lovely curves.

Uncle Larry brought over another one of his infamous toilet gardens and it sat on the other side of our door. Mom liked that there was a symmetrical balance to the hideous things. The new one had flowers growing in the bowl and lettuce in the tank.

It was two weeks later and Abigale was my friend. I wanted more, of course I wanted more, but she was a year and a half older than me and that was huge at this point in our lives. She'll be a senior next year and then off to college. There was no way she's going to date a freshman.

But she was flunking English and that was my thing. I have always loved words and my obsession with them goes far beyond knowing how to spell them correctly.

"Want a carrot?" I asked with a smile that I knew was way beyond goofy. "They are delicious."

Her delicate nose wrinkled up and she looked like she just sucked on a lemon and I laughed.

I didn't charge for my tutoring and our time together was strictly in the friend-zone, but she was my friend and it had made my life in school as the new kid a lot easier.

"But... I..." she stammered.

I walked over and pulled one out and shook the dirt off. "It's perfectly fine, not radioactive or anything, but you should wash it first."

I handed it to her and she took it, holding it like it was a stick of dynamite and gave me the strangest look. "You are so weird, Brian," she said, her smooth forehead furrowed.

"And you like me anyway," I said, laughing again.

She nodded. "Can we study now?"

I smiled and opened the door for her. It was just a one-room garage apartment, but it was becoming home. I stood there for a moment after Abigale walked in.

The other night when I got up for an early morning pee, Mom and I had another conversation. We seem to be getting better at talking, but it's still only in the darkness when we are both still barely awake.

Uncle Larry asked her out on a formal date and she wanted to have my permission before saying yes.

My chest had tightened and the room felt so very small, but only for a moment before I said, "Sure, Mom. You two should go out on a date."

She didn't reply, not right away. I heard her sniff and then she said, "Thank you, Brian."

It feels dangerous, honestly, to trust him to not be like my father. But it feels good too.

I shook the memory off and went into our little garage apartment to help my friend Abigale, my shining-girl, with English.

BACKSTORY—UNCLE LARRY'S INFAMOUS TOILET GARDENS

The origins of this story are so clear.

I was installing a new toilet at our house and told my wife that I thought we should keep the old one and use it as a planter.

I was joking, but I'm pretty good with the dry delivery and her reaction was—how shall I put it?—rather strong and rather clear.

Honestly, it's one of those quirky things that I rather wished I had the guts to do. Who cares what the world thinks? Toilets make great planters. Why throw them out when you can create beauty with them?

But my wife is not the world, and while I might get a chuckle looking at it every day, she wouldn't.

In this story, I got to create a character that was just quirky enough to go ahead and do it. And like "Little Greeny," I got to write another coming of age story.

PART 12
DANCING KITE

DANCING KITE

T̲HE KITE DANCED IN THE WIND, A MAGICAL CREATURE WITH no real magic at all. It could be a dragon with a long streaming tale of red and purple. Or a jet airplane with gouts of fire propelling it forth. Even a spaceship driven by mysterious forces dancing and turning in the hazy blue sky. The only magic it took was a bit of imagination.

Billy was at the controls of his stunt kite, two white strings running from the handles clenched in his chubby fists, connecting him to the dancing creature made of fabric and carbon fiber rods. Two hands. Two lines. Pull the right line and the kite turns to the right. Pull to the left and it turns to the left, the salty air of the Pacific keeping it in the air.

Magic of a kind.

Billy was eleven and today he needed magic. Any magic.

He focused, feeling the pull of the wind through the taut strings, feeling the wind speed and direction change, ever vigilant for a lull where he would need to run to create the wind to keep the kite up in the air. A kite on the ground is an extremely unmagical thing. A bit of ripstop polyester formed into a triangular wing by the rods, streamers trailing off the end.

The wind was strong coming off the ocean, so he pulled hard on the right handle and the kite dove and curved around in a circle, the streamers chasing it and making a corkscrew pattern. Once. Twice. Three times. Four times around. It neared the ground and the picnickers below, and he could hear his father admonish him for putting others at risk. But his father wasn't there.

Billy breathed deeply of the tangy sea air and sucked on his cinnamon candy wishing it was stronger, wishing it burned more. If it hurt enough maybe it would drive his other pain away. He wanted the wind to come up hard, a hurricane, strong enough so that the kite lifted him off the ground and carried him away. Up into the sky and out of this strange life.

His father had left, stormed off after his parents had fought and yelled for a long time. They said mean things, hurtful things. Dad had met another woman. He loved her and not Mom. He wanted a divorce.

The word "divorce" scared Billy down to his core. Who was he without his parents? What would happen to him? When he thought of his dad he could almost feel his scratchy beard and smell his sharp cologne. He didn't like the cologne, it made his nose hurt, but he loved his father. Funny, strong, with a deep, calm voice. It was his father that had taught him to fly a kite and ride a bike and how to mow the yard.

His father traveled a lot, all over the country, so he didn't get to see him enough. This time when he had come home, he had poured himself a drink, pacing over their tiled floor, and asked Billy to go to his room. His father's eyes were hooded, his mother's scared.

They talked in low voices and then the shouting and then the crying. Billy didn't come out of his room until after the door had slammed and his father had left, after he couldn't hear the sobs of his mother anymore. He had his folded-up kite in his hand and had asked his mother, "What happens to me now?"

Her eyes were red rimmed and her mascara had run down her face making her look scary. Her lips twisted and Billy realized that she wanted him to ask her how she was, but he couldn't. She was the adult. He was the kid. "What happens to me now?" he asked again.

She sniffed, blowing her nose and shoving the tissue in the pocket of her sweats. "You'll stay with me, of course." She had reached for him, but Billy had mumbled, "Going to the beach," and left thinking that maybe if she made herself pretty more often, Dad would still love her.

He pulled the kite out of the spinning dive, its two strings now twisted around each other making the controls sluggish. He pulled hard on the left string briefly and it shot up. After it had altitude, he kept pulling on the left string and it did its corkscrew pattern in the other direction, four times, until the strings were untangled.

He smiled, a bitter little thing, and crunched on the candy, wanting the flavor and the burn.

"Good one," a deep voice said and Billy turned to see his father. His eyes were red rimmed and he looked haunted.

"I... Ummm... Thanks."

They were silent as Billy pulled right, evened out the strings briefly, then left, even, and right, the kite dancing in a horizontal figure eight, making an infinity symbol. He didn't want forever from his parents, he just wanted more than this.

"You've gotten good," his father said.

Billy nodded and licked his lips. "You okay?" he asked.

"No. That didn't come out right today. I shouldn't have told Grace like that."

They were silent as Billy kept the kite fairly still, bobbing to the left and the right, dancing in the wind like a magical guardian watching over them from the sky.

"It was nice of you to ask, though," his father added.

Billy nodded and bit on his lip. The fact that he hadn't asked his mother was implied in the statement. He should have. "Is... is she pretty?" Billy asked, referring to the new woman.

His father took a deep breath, letting it out slowly.

"Because, Mom doesn't seem to try anymore," Billy said. "She's sad. Dresses in those sweats when she's at home, saving the good clothes for work." He tried to stop himself, knowing that this wasn't his place, but couldn't. "Maybe if she tried more. Was nicer to you. Then... then.... this wouldn't have happened."

"Let's go down the beach a bit, get away from the people." He put his hand on Billy's shoulder and guided the boy down the beach, the kite following them until it was dancing above empty sand. "Now give me the right handle."

Billy glanced at his father, a puzzled look on his face, but let him slowly take the control away.

"Now, let's do those figure eights."

"Dad... I... this won't work. You have to work both hands so closely."

"Relax, Billy. Let's just try. I'll call out my pulls and you yours. We'll go slow, make it a big, wide eight. Ready."

Billy bit his lip and nodded.

"Right, okay... even," his father said, and then Billy said "left, even," and then his father "right, even." The first figure eight was awkward but they kept at it until they got good at it. Right, even. Left, even. Right, even. Left even... The kite danced in the sky, the streamers flew behind it etching a colorful infinity symbol against the blue.

Billy beamed. Here was magic, simple magic, real magic, magic with his father.

"That's good," his father said. "Let's hold it steady now."

They stabilized the kite and Billy said, "That was amazing!"

His father nodded, meeting his smile, but then it disappeared. "Son, I want you to hear me now. This is kind of like what marriage is like. Each one holding on to one of the strings, working closely together, always communicating."

"Okay..." Billy said, his face puzzled.

"Now stay there. Don't move."

Billy nodded and his father walked forward three feet, which jerked the kite hard to the left in Billy's direction and it spiraled down over and over and crashed into the sand.

"Dad!" he said, letting go of the handle and running to the kite, inspecting it, making sure it wasn't damaged. The strings were horribly tangled and it would take time to sort them out. Dealing with the strings was the worst part a lot of times. "Why did you do that?"

His father was there squatting next to him. "Your mother didn't do anything wrong. It was me. I handled this badly. I stepped forward a few feet and..." he shrugged and pointed at the kite. "And your mother is beautiful, even in sweats."

Billy blinked, his cheeks flushed, his heart pounding in his ears. His parents had been a team and now they weren't. Was Billy the kite? Was he going to crash with them splitting up?

"You were very selfish back there with your mother. I expect more of you. Your mom and I just changed. That's all."

Billy swallowed and nodded.

"Do you understand?"

The tears he had been holding back came as he nodded his head again.

"This is going to be hard on you. I am sorry for that."

Billy's crying turned to sobs and his father held him tight. He could feel his strong arms and smell his aftershave and that just made him cry harder. "Billy, listen to me," his father said, his voice thick. "We're not going to let go of you, either of us. We'll get through this."

Billy pulled away, wiped his face, and nodded.

"Now let's untangle this string," his father said with a smile. "And then we'll go home and discuss this as a family."

BACKSTORY—DANCING KITE

Dealing with a divorce as a child will change you. It has to. The arrangement of your family is core on a level that is hard to describe.

I was young when my parents divorced and it was an entirely unmooring experience. It seemed that the world I was living in changed fundamentally and permanently in a moment.

This story attempts to capture some of those feelings clothed in an insulating cover of fiction.

This is another one of the stories I wrote from my 2017 Short Story Marathon. You can find more about the process at *RobertJMcCarter.com/category/story-marathon*.

PART 13

THE DOUR MR. M.

THE DOUR MR. M

"She's going to die," Mr. M. said, his lean, middle-aged face serious as he stared at the old woman who had a grimace ruining her once lovely face. She was on a narrow bed, the sheets tucked in around her neck.

"No shit," I answered. Mr. M. had a habit of stating the radically obvious like he was conveying the mysteries of the ages. Like, "Well, you know, the sun will be rising in the morning." Or, "You've got to pay your taxes, no real choice there." Not that he said either of those things, not his area. His prognosis concerning my mother was his area.

"When?" I asked. She was suffering, the tears slowly leaking out her eyes, her quivering jaw, darting eyes, and clenched expression made that clear. Her damaged brain brought her nothing but fear now. Her breath was sour and caustic, the scent would linger in my nose long after I left. Death would be a relief —for me and I do believe for her—if nothing else.

Mr. M. shrugged his thin, bare shoulders, his washed-out blue eyes briefly connecting with mine. "'But of that day and hour no one knows, not even the angels of heaven,'" he said, his voice dry as he quoted the Bible. Something else I didn't like about him. The Bible seemed unequipped to explain the breadth of human suffering, especially what this disease was doing to her.

Lately, I've been referring to my mother by her first name—Olivia—because the Alzheimer's took my mother away long ago. Her grey hair was short and plastered to her head from too long in that bed.

The room was nice enough. A twin bed, a nice blue recliner, pictures on the wall of tropical locations my parents had visited after retirement. It was most of her world at this point, which made the room seem small and mean.

"It won't be soon enough," I said, regarding how long to Olivia's death. This wasn't life. This was suffering.

Mr. M. raised an eyebrow and stared at me. I sat on the bed, holding my mother's hands. Her joints were large and arthritic, but her skin still so smooth. He stood on the other side of the bed, nude. Mr. M. didn't believe in clothing, calling it "a useless shield against the vagaries of living."

"Are you planning something?" he asked, a small spark in those dull blue eyes.

I shook my head and looked back at my mother. "It's okay, Mom. I'm here. I won't let anyone hurt you."

But the truth was I was desperate to end her suffering, and the suffering of those that loved her—especially mine.

I met Mr. M. about three years ago, just after we had moved my mother into the memory care unit. I was lying in the snow, staring up at the startling blue sky and snow-covered pine trees, disoriented and confused.

"You fell," he said, his middle-aged, dour face floating into view surrounded by that blue. Without that expression, he might have been handsome, his face gently wrinkled, crowned with short salt-and-pepper hair.

I nodded. I had fallen. I was up on the roof trying to remove two feet of snow that my old house couldn't handle. At first I thought he was a neighbor.

"You're dying," he said. His face was passive as he delivered his prognosis, kind of like he was telling me it had just snowed, or that spring was still ten weeks away.

A shiver ran through my body, the cold snow that pressed against my back was sucking the warmth out of me. I tried to move and an electric spike of pain stabbed at my gut.

"It's a tree branch," he said, like he was reading the telephone book. "It has run you through. You are bleeding quite a lot."

I sucked in a breath and could smell the clean, cold air, tinged with iron. I couldn't see it, but I imagined a red stain seeping into the perfect white snow.

"Help me," I said, my breath gushing out in a cloud of condensate.

"Everyone dies."

I blinked, noticing for the first time that this man was nude, in the snow, early in the morning, with the temperature well below freezing. He didn't seem cold, and I didn't notice any condensation as he exhaled.

"Who are you?" I asked as I started to fumble for my phone. It was in my jacket pocket, wasn't it? My arms were clumsy and my hands stiff in their gloves.

"You can call me Mr. M."

"You... you're not real, are you?" My teeth chattered as blood flowed out of me and the cold creeped in. My wife and daughter were still asleep. I heard shoveling close by, but my house was set down from the road and no one could see me. I pulled a glove off and got my phone out of my pocket, but it slipped.

Mr. M. shrugged his bare shoulders. "What's 'real' anyway?"

"Help!" I tried to shout, but it came out thin and weak, barely a croak. "Help me!"

"They can't hear you," my naked companion said. "It's just you and me. Don't worry, though, I won't leave you."

I panicked, my bare right hand fishing in the snow for the phone. Where was it? I had to find it. It seemed like hours passed, my hand numb when I finally found the glass and plastic rectangle. I pulled it up in front of me; it was covered in pink and red snow.

"It's best to just relax," Mr. M. said as I fumbled to unlock the phone. I pulled the glove off my left hand with my teeth, drawing my password pattern, once, twice, three times... I couldn't get it. My hands were not working right.

"Tap where it says 'emergency,'" Mr. M. said.

I did and the dialer came up, but I couldn't manage to get 911 dialed properly, my hands shaking, my teeth chattering.

"Here, let me," he said, his pale finger stabbing down on the three digits. "Not sure if it will help."

"Nine-one-one, what is the nature of your emergency," a female voice said from my phone. I could barely hear it; the phone wasn't in speaker mode.

"Fell," I croaked. "Bleeding. Help me."

"Sir," the tinny voice said, "I can't hear you. What is the nature of your emergency?"

"Dying," I tried to shout, but it was a croak. "Help!"

The phone slipped from my hand back into the snow. I could barely hear indistinct mumbling.

I looked back up at the sky and the passive face of Mr. M. I couldn't struggle anymore; I didn't have it in me. The sky was so blue, so beautiful. I love mornings like this after the storm has broken, when the air is crisp and fresh, the snow clinging to the pine trees like puffy cumulonimbus clouds. The world is so beautiful.

My vision began to tunnel in and the last thing I saw before the darkness came were the pale blue eyes of Mr. M.

MR. M.'S EYES ARE WATERED DOWN, AS IF AT ONE POINT THE blue had been vibrant, like the winter sky on a mountain, but he lost something and the intensity bled out, like a slow tire leak you don't notice until it becomes dangerous. Some mornings, my eyes look a little like that too. Not that they were ever very intense—passion is something I long for in my life, but I don't fully understand.

After that visit at my mom's bedside, I kept thinking about the tiny spark in Mr. M.'s eyes when he thought I might do something to end my mother's suffering. As if that, and only that, could breathe life into his tired soul. And I would do it—end her suffering—if I could. That's what I told myself at first, that I would do it, but there wasn't really a way. The truth was there were many ways, just not any that were without significant risk. To my mother and to me. Well... mostly to me. She's barely there, her brain finally approaching the end of its long, slow digression. One of these months she'll forget how to breathe, or better yet, contract pneumonia and pass from that. But any action I could take would risk jail, and that puts my family at risk.

That's what I told myself, but a little niggling voice inside of me told me that if I was a passionate person, I would figure out a way. I could end her suffering humanely and not get caught.

These thoughts flitted through my mind on my next visit. Her hand was so warm, the skin smooth like expensive leather.

The tendons stuck out and the skin clung to the bone as she had lost a lot of weight. She was dying, there was no hope for improvement, and yet every day, three times a day, the caregivers shoveled food into her mouth. And she ate, mostly from reflex, I think. I wanted to yell at them, to tell them to stop, that we all just needed to let her go. But I didn't even have the courage for that.

She moaned and her eyes flickered open, their glassy brown depths unfocused and then, for a moment, her eyes snapped onto mine like she recognized me. Her lips moved, pursing, and then breath puffing out in a weak "p" sound.

"I'm here, Mom. It's Peter."

She continued the p-puff and I had to pull back, the scent of her breath rotten, cloying, and slightly metallic.

Mr. M. sauntered in, his hands behind his back, his naked form gaunt and pale.

"I'll be your lookout," he said with a thin, toothless smile. I had never seen him smile before.

I shook my head and looked back at my mother.

"Your work is suffering. Your marriage is stretched to the breaking point. Your daughter misses you. These people will do everything they can to preserve her 'life.' They can't help themselves." He actually used air quotes when he said "life."

I shrugged. It was all true, but what could I do? Leave her here to die alone? Take a pillow and smother her?

"It's wrong," I said.

"Ending suffering is never wrong."

I didn't look away from my mother's drawn face until I heard him shuffle away.

Is Mr. M. a hallucination? I've tested him many times, the first was on the slopes in Aspen, Colorado. My recovery from my fall had left me, if not passionate, then more energetic than my stable and steady norm. The ambulance had gotten to me just in time, and it was strange to know I had Mr. M. to thank for that. After I recovered, I took my wife and daughter for a nearly spontaneous skiing trip. I was enjoying a brief moment of solitude looking down a route much steeper than I was comfortable with, when Mr. M. showed up walking through the snow.

"I want to show you something," he said, his voice dull like an old kitchen knife.

I looked around, and since no one was near, I followed him to a nearby fir tree. Under it was the half-frozen remains of a rabbit, its back end torn, a garish, ragged red. "He didn't run fast enough," he said, his pale eyes finding mine. "You never know when you won't be fast enough."

I sighed and dug my poles into the snow, ready to push off down the slope, the terrifying grade be damned.

"Test me," he said, suddenly right in front of me.

"What?"

"You don't believe I'm real, so test me."

I shrugged and thought for a moment. "Describe the next person I will see."

He nodded and smiled. "Hot pink down jacket with blue ski poles."

I shook my head but waited the two minutes it took and there she was, a teenage girl dressed just as he promised.

He did it three more times and would have done it more, but I couldn't take it. I shoved off and started making my way down the slope, slowly cutting from side to side to regulate my speed. About halfway down, some kid slammed into me and sent me sprawling.

Mr. M.'s pale face appeared above mine as I sucked in cold air, my lower back feeling as if someone had chopped it with an axe. "You never know when you won't be fast enough. But don't worry, my friend, you aren't dying... this time."

MOM WAS ASLEEP IN HER BED, HER BROW FURROWED EVEN in slumber. I sat there next to her in a hard, wooden chair staring at a piece of paper in my hand. On it was a list of times with a few words scrawled next to it. Like "4:15 p.m. 'Yes, you do live here, Margaret,'" or "4:33 p.m. 'You're not George! Where's George!'"

My hands looked older than they used to. Boney with prominent veins on the back and spots you might prefix the word "age" to. They didn't look like they were mine anymore. They were shaking a little, like fall leaves in a slight breeze. You see, I never did believe that Mr. M. was real. Despite the predictions in Aspen and the many other times, I was convinced that fall I took off the roof, the stick running me through, and facing my own mortality had jarred something loose in my psyche. I was sure that the predictions were a trick of memory. Even though I remember seeing him, remember him making predictions, there was still no objective proof.

But this piece of paper and the picture on my cell phone were that objective proof. I had written the note the last time I had seen him, yesterday morning when I was home sick in bed. He told me that I wasn't dying and I would be fine in the morning. He told me to write down the times and phrases. He had me take a picture of it with my phone so it would have a time/date stamp, and when I began to doubt, I could know it wasn't just a trick of memory.

He made me promise something before he did it, though. He

said, "Peter, you promise me you'll end your mother's suffering and I'll prove I'm real beyond any shadow of a doubt." That little spark danced in his watery blue eyes.

So I promised, sure I was promising myself, and that nothing would come of it.

And like clockwork, each of the eight phrases were said at the exact time predicted. The last one was my mother. George was my father's name and he's been gone five years now. The picture of the piece of paper is on my phone.

Mr. M. is real. Real. And I promised to kill my mother.

"WHAT ARE YOU?" I ASKED MR. M. AS THE DISTANT, warbling cry of an ambulance got slowly closer. I could barely hear it over the ringing in my ears. My mouth tasted funny, like talc or something, undoubtedly from the airbag deploying. My front right tire had blown, my car ramming into an ancient oak tree. Blood dripped down my face into my mouth, the taste of iron overwhelming the talc.

This was six months after that Aspen ski vacation.

Mr. M. shrugged from the passenger's seat, nude as always. I don't know why, but "naked" seems wrong to describe his state. Naked implies a vulnerability that was completely lacking.

"You don't know?" I asked, struggling to focus my eyes so the two Mr. M.'s turned into one.

He ignored my question. "You might die, chances aren't very good, a brain aneurysm is highly unlikely from the blow to your head, but..." He ended in a hopeful tone with a small shrug.

"What are you?" I said, gritting my teeth.

"It's not a simple question," he said. "What are *you*?"

I wasn't sure I heard him right. It was the simplest of questions. "I'm Peter Maan. I'm a middle-aged white man that teaches high school history and lives on planet earth."

"Are you sure?"

I closed one eye and wiped the blood from my forehead, it was flowing at an alarming rate, but at least there was only one Mr. M. now. "Yes. I'm sure."

He harrumphed, as if my assurance held no weight with him. "Well, I'm not sure that's what you are, and I have no idea what I am."

"Are you real?"

He sighed. "We've been over this. From your rather unimaginative perspective, yes, I am real."

"What are you?" I asked again. The ambulance was close and I didn't think I had long with him. My stomach was roiling, the smell and taste of blood mixing with what must be a nasty concussion. The world began to spin, darkness creeping along the edges of what I could see through my one eye.

"I am Mr. M.," he said with the saddest of smiles as I passed out.

To the small matter of killing one's mother in a humane and undetectable way, I say, no!

First off, killing is wrong. In all cases. Even to reduce a suffering you know will never abate. The suffering of a brain slowly eating itself on its way to forgetting how to breathe.

Secondly, it's against the law. Even if it wasn't morally wrong, risking my family's future is just stupid.

I was pacing outside the facility that housed the body of the woman that once was my mother, the summer sun beating down, bright and unrelenting in a washed-out blue sky. Sweat trickled down my back, and my mouth was dry.

I had a plan. It would work. The chances of getting caught were slim. I hadn't done one google search, checked out one book, talked to one person—save Mr. M.—about this. There was no evidence of planning, no clear motive, just a few trips to the library and a couple cash purchases while I was out of town.

But, first off, killing is wrong, and second off, there was a chance I could get caught.

I kicked at the cracked blacktop—it too was sweltering in the heat.

"You would put down a pet, in fact you have." This was Mr. M.'s counter to my "first off." And "I will watch" was his response to my second. But I didn't trust him, the way his watery, washed-out blue eyes sparked at the thought of this act meant there was something in this for him. Something dark.

I fingered the pill container in my pocket. It was stainless steel and slightly cool to the touch. I just had to slip the two pills into her mouth, let them melt, and bye-bye, Olivia.

Bye-bye, Olivia.

She doesn't know me. When she is aware, she's afraid. She doesn't have a life anymore. What was left of her was suffering. I wouldn't put a dog through this, but I would put my mother through it?

So, my "first off" was bullshit. Nothing in life is that black and white. And my "second off" was a bit out there too. Slipping two pills in her mouth, not very high odds I'd get caught. Was I hiding from something here? Something going on beyond the normal and appropriate compunctions of humans to preserve life even when it's not appropriate?

My brain raced as my steps took me to my car. Mr. M. was there waiting. "I'll do it," he said, his voice sounding so very disappointed. He held his pale hand out. I slapped the metal container in his hand and got in my car and drove away.

At my mother's funeral, Mr. M. smiled. "It was a gentle passing," he said, showing his teeth. I had never seen him smile like that before.

My wife held my hand and my daughter looked to be in cell phone withdrawal as we watched Olivia's—my mother's—casket lowered into the ground. After everyone had thrown a bit of dirt in, they shuffled off towards the wake. It was a small gathering, just us, a few of my mother's old friends, and a cousin. I heard "relief" filter through the hot summer air a few times.

And relief was part of it, but only one of many. Oliva was back to being my mother and she was finally gone.

"I need a few minutes," I told my wife and daughter, and they scurried away, their relief obvious.

I stared into the hole, a deep, unnaturally straight cut into the earth, the cheap wood casket at the bottom.

"Why are you so happy?" I hissed at Mr. M., that smile still on his face.

"You did it," he said, nodding down into the hole, his nudity looking sensible as sweat soaked through my suit.

"I did not."

His eyes stabbed at my pocket where I gripped the stainless-steel pill container. I had given it to him in the parking lot. How had it gotten in there? I took it out and slowly shook it. Not a sound. I unscrewed the cap, the pills were gone.

"But... No!"

His eyes were bluer than the washed-out summer sky. "I'm proud of you, Peter."

"No. You did it. I never went in."

"Who do you think I am, Peter?"

My mind reeled and I remembered back when I had first met him after falling off my roof. Had he dialed 911, or had I?

On the ski slope in Aspen, had I found that rabbit on my own, and when I was on my back in the snow, had my mind made those predictions up? And the note and the picture, the incontrovertible truth? I pulled my phone out and searched for the picture—it wasn't there. Had there even been a note?

My heart beat hard and my suit clung to me like a wet blanket. I couldn't breathe. I remembered the grainy feel of the pills as I pulled them out of the stainless-steel container. I remembered being surprised at how dry Olivia's mouth was as I tucked the pills in. After the pills had melted and the drugs taken effect, I remembered her eyes flying open, dull and brown; she was clearly not there. And then she sighed.

I had done it. Mr. M. was real, but he was me.

Mr. M. smiled, it was a childish smile, his frown lines pulled into an impossible configuration, like he had just woken up on Christmas morning and gotten every present he had ever wished for. He nodded to me like we were two old friends and words weren't necessary anymore. He slowly turned and walked away.

BACKSTORY—THE DOUR MR. M

Despite first appearances, this story is a contemporary one. There is no fantasy element beyond the fantasies our minds can create for us, sometimes out of great need. "Laura's Magic Clock" is a lighter survey of this same phenomenon.

This story is extremely personal, cathartic, an outlet, and very dark. It's so personal, in fact, I really shouldn't say anything in terms of a back story, but here we go.

The idea of Mr. M., which to me means "Mr. Mortality," was spawned in some very difficult times and this dark little tale was my subconscious dealing with some of the trauma of it.

It's a bleak story, so the backstory is rather bleak, I'm afraid. Suffice it to say I've seen suffering with a loved one similar to this story.

There are some questions worth asking in this story, questions I've had cause to ask myself.

When would death be a kindness, be the "right" thing to do despite our culture's tendency to value the length of life over the quality of life?

When would the crime of taking a life be justifiable when weighed against the suffering it would end?

What would it take for a "normal" person to break through their training and take such an action?

This story isn't about answering those questions, but about asking them.

This story originally appeared in *Anomalous Readings: Thirteen Curious and Confounding Tales.*

PART 14
A GAME OF KAT AND MOUSE

A GAME OF KAT AND MOUSE

I was at that point in the heist where the odds had tipped decisively in my favor and the outcome was almost assured. I have done this enough to know that now was not the time to let my guard down, but my body was buzzing with the thrill of it all.

I was standing on the beautiful black and tan marble of the eighty-ninth floor of the Empire State Building in front of the lovely art deco elevator doors dressed in full Santa Claus regalia ready to make my escape when I heard her.

"Don't move," she said, her voice pitched low but clear.

It was December 20, 1969, and the Christmas party I had slipped away from was going on two floors below where I had been posing as their rent-a-Santa. Outside, New York City had on its best face for the season, all bright colors with a fresh sugar coating of snow on the ground and Christmas carols competing with the honking cars. The city was more energized than usual as we got ready to say goodbye to the tumultuous decade that the sixties had been.

While the black and pewter pattern on the elevator door was

true to the time and spirit of when this magnificent building was erected, it was not the best reflective surface. Nevertheless, I looked at the polished shine of the metal and saw an imperfect reflection of who was behind me.

I recognized her instantly. The Kat.

She was dressed in form-fitting black clothing, her hands gloved and much of her face covered by a soft black mask, her long dark hair pulled back, her form slim and lithe but most definitely feminine. She had a gun pointed at me, one of those little black ones that fit nicely in a clutch purse. My heart beat faster than if the police had found me.

I should take a moment to point out that her modus operandi certainly hearkened to the fictional comic book character Catwoman, and entirely on purpose, I might add, but she was real and, no, there were no silly cat ears in sight.

"My darling," I said in my suave (and fake) British accent. "We meet at last."

The jewels I had just stolen were the ostensible goal of this night's work, but in truth, it was her that I sought. The Kat.

Our paths had nearly crossed in Paris, and then in London, but each of us tended to stay in our own lane. She focused on precious gems and I focused on art and antiquities.

I took a deep breath and caught the scent of perfume, expensive and floral, and hoped that it was hers, hoped it was a clue.

I could not see much of her face, but the skin I could see through the imperfect mirror of the elevator doors was olive toned, and from what I knew of her and with how she looked she must have been in her mid-thirties, a few years younger than me.

"I am not your darling," she said, taking a sinuous step forward. "And you have something of mine."

There were several security cameras on this floor but it was clear she had done her homework, staying in a blind spot.

I smiled, but I'm sure it was lost with my back turned and

the fake, white beard I was wearing. "It would take a rather loose definition of the word to call these yours," I said. "Besides, I left your lovely little calling card, so you will get credit."

The Kat had a flair for the dramatic and left a calling card at each of her crimes. A square of the highest quality linen paper with a red heart drawn above her chosen moniker, "The Kat." On my last heist in London, I had found her calling card stuck to the bottom of the golden statue of Bast that I had stolen and I had not been able to stop thinking about her since.

I, on the other hand, left no calling card and preferred jobs where my theft would not be discovered immediately. I liked to get in and out unnoticed and undetected and was usually referred to as "The Mouse." Not all that flattering, but accurate enough. I was not the tallest of men and I was known for coming and going unseen and unnoticed, so it fit well enough.

"Yes, but I have the gun," she said. "So they are now mine. Just toss them back, but don't turn around."

She had no trace of an accent, her speech Standard American having no more character to it than a television news anchor. I was disappointed at that. And I was disappointed by the gun, such heavy-handed measures, I have found, are usually the result of a lack of planning and imagination.

I felt my heart sink. I had been so excited to meet her, a kindred soul in this odd world I operated in and an intriguing woman. But I had no interest in guns or crimes that required them.

The light above the elevator lit with a green down arrow. She was out of time.

"I *will* shoot you," she said with enough calm to make me believe her. "Now, toss them back."

I sighed and pulled a velvet bag out of the left pocket of my Santa suit and tossed it back. After I did, I spun around.

Foolish? Yes, of course, but I had to get a better look at her. I just had to. Just like those that pursued her, trying to bring her to justice, I had built up this image of her and had to know more than I could determine from the poor reflection I had been looking at.

She snatched the bag out of the air with an impressive level of agility, saw me spinning around, and fired.

AFTER THE KAT FIRED HER GUN, I MUST SAY, I WAS MORE than a little delighted to still be alive and whole. The gun was not what I thought it was and that meant that the Kat just might be.

I laughed as she ran off with the bag of gems down the lovely art deco hallway of the Empire State Building. I laughed out of joy and because I was more than a little smitten. And I laughed because that gun of hers had turned out to be a squirt gun and the contents of that squirt gun had been Champagne, very expensive Champagne, and my face was covered with it.

The Kat did not disappoint.

The elevator opened, the small space full of dour-faced businessmen who badly needed a little Christmas spirit. I turned the laugh into a ho-ho-ho and got onto the elevator.

I reached into my right pocket and smiled wide behind my white beard. I had two sets of fakes made for this job. One was in the safe I had just broken into and the second set I had just given to her. The real gems were still there.

I had a feeling I would be running into the Kat again soon.

I LIKED MY DAY JOB AND IT SUITED ME. I WORKED FOR A Wall Street consulting firm and traveled the world evaluating the worth of companies that were being considered for mergers and acquisitions.

It let me travel and aligned with my detail-oriented nature.

And I believed in having a day job, one that met my basic needs easily so that any "extracurricular" activities could be evaluated with clear, unemotional eyes.

The Kat changed all of that.

I was not clear or unemotional.

I kept thinking about that tantalizing glimpse I had of her, the smell of what I believed was her perfume, and the taste of the Champagne she squirted me in the face with—a good vintage of Dom Pérignon, if I'm not mistaken.

"Call her," my friend Silvo said. Not his real name, which he had never told me and I of course knew. He was a big man of Middle Eastern descent with a full black beard shot with grey and a turban the same color as his dark suit. He was a Sikh and did not cut his hair and he always carried a knife, his "kirpan."

"It is not that easy," I said, standing in front of Renoir's glorious *Luncheon of the Boating Party*, the canvas nearly six feet across and four feet high feeling like you could walk into the gentle scene of wine and friends with the boats sailing on the placid river in the background. The texture of the oil paints gave the image a dimension and feel that a photograph or other reproduction could never match.

This is why I liked art more than gems. The mastery of form. The understanding of humanity. The utter beauty.

"It's not like she gave me her number," I added.

I was in disguise, of course. To my knowledge, Silvo had yet to see my real face. He was an extracurricular friend, a good one. One does not pull off a graceful heist without help and his had been useful on many occasions.

"I did not mean that literally, my friend," he said. "But this obsession is not like you, so perhaps a more direct approach would suit your goals."

I was "The Mouse" and the direct approach was not my way, but he had a point.

We were at the Metropolitan Museum of Art on Fifth Avenue right on the edge of Central Park. It was Christmas Eve, the museum having pulled out all the stops for the beginning of its centennial celebration and the season.

The two of us were safely tucked away deep in the huge building on the second floor. With its stone walls, columns, and many additions covering multiple centuries and multiple styles of architecture, the building was a work of art in its own right. Footfalls echoed quietly and mixed with the hushed whispers of the patrons as we stood in the gallery admiring the Renoir.

"Don't take her next conquest from her," he added. "Leave her a calling card instead, like she did."

I nodded and stared at the woman in the foreground of the painting, her lips pursed like she meant to kiss the terrier she was holding on the white linen-draped table. The painting spoke of a time of leisure where one would linger over food and friendship.

I was opening my mouth to speak to my old friend when a high-pitched cry rang out from another gallery. And then several. We stared at each other and then looked towards the growing disturbance. And then louder, a male voice shouted, "It is gone! It is gone! The Mouse has struck again."

I looked at my friend and he looked at me. "Or perhaps she will call you first," he said with an arching of his bushy eyebrow.

IF ONE IS TO HAVE AN ILLEGAL VICE IT IS BEST IF YOU HAVE alternate ways to scratch that itch. If there is only one way for you to be satisfied, that way can easily land you in jail... well, *will* land you in jail, eventually.

I had other things that made me feel truly alive. Drinking fine wine or viewing master works of art did nicely, thus my time with Silvo. But because of my attempts to get the attention of the Kat, I had been working more than I intended to, gaining much more visibility than I liked. Which is what I thought was going on when the voice rang out and echoed through the Met gallery that day.

I feared that I had elevated my profile high enough so that if a painting went missing then I would be blamed.

With Silvo by my side, we rushed towards the next gallery, but it was not easy. Everyone else was exiting the gallery, a sea of nuns fleeing as we tried to wade through.

It was then that I collided with one of the nuns. I did not get a close look at her, her head was turned away, but she was about my height and slim.

"I'm so very sorry, Sister," I said, this time I was using my French accent and wore a grey beret that went nicely with my three-piece suit. I also had on a blonde wig, a fake nose, glasses, and thin blond beard.

"Think nothing of it," the nun said and then was gone. But her scent lingered. Her perfume was decidedly floral and very expensive, but nuns don't wear perfume.

I checked the inside pocket of my suit and found that my wallet was gone and I had to smile. The wallet went with my disguise so there was nothing important in there, but the fact that she had pulled it off was a delight.

"That was her," I whispered to Silvo. "I am going after her. Find out what happened in there. Let's meet at our usual place in three hours."

THE MET WAS A WARREN OF GALLERIES SMALL AND LARGE, halls, and atrium spaces, the building nearly a quarter of a mile long. The space was beautiful to a fault with elegantly tiled floors, beautiful wooden parquet, and soft neutral-colored carpets. The ceilings were high and the rooms well lit, the larger halls containing statues and other artifacts, the smaller paintings. Some galleries containing circular couches for patrons to relax on while they viewed the art.

And there were plenty of viewers today, the city full for the holiday season and the Kat used that to her advantage, sliding behind a group of tourists before backtracking and going into a different room than the one she was headed towards.

But I knew the Met well and followed her at a discrete distance. Her path was circuitous, almost as if she were taking me for a tour of the great place first across the second floor and then down to the first, but I finally lost her when she merged with a group of nuns in an elegantly carpeted hall with Egyptian artifacts safely displayed behind glass.

Was she trying to tell me something?

As the chase went on, a few things became clear. She knew the Met and she was very confident she could keep ahead of me, never looking back. And this game of chase was of her choosing and I knew my odds of catching her were low, but still I played. I could do nothing else.

Once I had followed the nuns outside, past the columns and the ornate front of the building and onto the broad stone steps, one of them broke away. She was the right height and moved with agility and grace.

This was a beautiful part of Manhattan where Fifth Avenue cut a path between Central Park and the old stone buildings of the city. Trees were plentiful, and the scene was decorated with a light coating of snow clinging to the bare trees and the rooftops, lining the sidewalks.

I stopped for a moment and watched. This could easily be a diversion, but once it was clear no other nuns were going to separate from the group. I rushed across Fifth Avenue, the crosswalk favoring me with a green light, and followed the nun on to 82nd Street.

It was a narrow street with mature trees and old stone buildings that hugged the sidewalk on either side, a mixture of limestone facades and exposed red bricks. Buildings from the turn of the century and on. My pause had given her enough time to get away if she wanted to, but something told me that she didn't.

Once I got across the street I did spot her, at least I thought I did. Just past an apartment building with a cheery burgundy awning and a doorman out front was a woman dressed in a long dark coat with a pile of black clothing in front of her, a white splash on top, which had to be her discarded habit.

The street was not empty, there were people walking, cars driving, but this was New York. No one paid her much mind.

She was too far away for me to see her clearly, but it had to be her. I did not shout, but I walked quickly down the sidewalk.

She saw me and turned, and in a set of athletic jumps and pulls, scaled the grooved limestone façade of the building, and dropped behind a ten-foot-tall iron fence blocking the alleyway between the apartment building and the turn-of-the-century mansion next door.

When I got there, much to my surprise, she wasn't gone. She was standing still six feet down the alley her back turned to me.

"Those diamonds were fakes," she said.

"Indeed," I said, reverting back to my English accent. The gate to the fence was securely padlocked and it was tipped with pointed iron prongs. I had neither the agility nor the experience to scale the wall of the building like she did. "Such an operation does not come cheap," I said. "I had expenses."

She shrugged and said, "I had plans for the money. Important plans. So I took something you wanted."

It was an interesting moment. The eternal honking of the city faded and the cold December air was exhilarating after our chase and I thought I caught a whiff of her expensive perfume. "Jules Dupré's *The Old Oak*, I presume," I said. My visit with Silvo was to scout security and I loved the moody look of the stormy sky, the rich earth tones, and the small figure staring up at the magnificent tree.

The painting was quite small, just over 12 inches by 16 inches, and not incredibly valuable, making it an easy target.

"Of course," she said.

"And you surely do not have it on you," I said.

"No."

"Well then, I am flattered to find you know me so well," I said.

Her head turned, but only a fraction before she turned it back. "Your tastes are quite obvious," she said, her tone clipped.

"But you know them," I said, "and this pleases me."

Her shoulders stiffened. "And why would that please you?"

I chuckled. "Surely you don't think my stealing of those gems you were after was an accident."

My life on Wall Street, the one I lived in the open, was full of friends, but I felt that they didn't really know me, that there was a large part of me that I had to keep hidden. And I had friends like Silvo on the other side, but I had to hide from them too, always covering my tracks, always in disguise.

She did not speak right away and a simple realization hit me in the silence: I was lonely.

"Of course not," she finally said and there was something different in her voice. It was slightly softer, or maybe I was just fooling myself.

"Perhaps a trade then," I said.

She nodded but was silent. The only thing I had a good look at was the back of her head, her dark hair falling like a sheet across her coat, glistening in the sun. Behind me a car drove by playing "O Holy Night" loudly accompanied by the hiss of its tires on the wet pavement.

"Then we shall meet in one week," she said, her words slow and careful. "At a New Year's Eve Masquerade Ball, the one that is a benefit for the city's orphanages. I trust that is enough information for you to find it. The tickets are very expensive, but I know you can afford it."

A masquerade ball was intriguIng. The Kat liked her anonymity, which was something I could relate to.

"Very well," I said, pausing a moment to think. "I will be dressed as the most famous of Montagues with a silver mask," I said, smiling. It was the most basic test of English literature but being completely direct did not seem warranted in this little game of ours.

"And I as the most famous Capulet with a mask of gold," she replied, and I could not help but smile wider.

With that, she walked away but left me with hope in my heart that I would get to see her again. And hope that choosing Romeo and Juliet for our disguises was not prophetic of a coming tragedy.

"It was cleverly done," Silvo said from across the small table, both us perched on tall stools next to the exposed red brick of the hole-in-the-wall coffee shop not far from the Met. The sun had gone down and the little place was crowded, Christmas lights were strung along the ceiling, garlands of tinsel taped to the tables, and the air was heady with the scent of coffee and sweet baklava. Christmas carols were playing quietly in the background.

He sipped from a steaming cup of espresso and watched me, his eyes intense. I did not have any coffee, I felt enough energy coursing through me as it was. "Well?" I asked.

He smiled, his cheeks rising and turning his warm brown eyes into narrow slits. "I've never seen you like this," he said.

I sighed and nodded. I hadn't either. "She is one of us," I said quietly. "And very good at what she does. It's..." I trailed off with a shrug, I could not find the words.

The bell on the door rang as more people came in, a rush of cold air blowing around us. It was damp and felt like more snow was going to arrive soon, promising a white Christmas.

"Very good is right," he said. "I have not seen the security video but my source is reliable."

I nodded. This was Silvo's forte. He knew everyone and what would inspire them to give him the information he sought. And I would pay him well for the information he had gathered.

"Seven of the nuns gathered in front of the Dupré you love so, the other two were across the gallery," he said and then took another sip. "The first shouts we heard were because of the mice."

"Mice?" I asked.

He nodded. "Mice, my friend. I believe your desired paramour has a sense of humor. The video is not clear but I suspect one of them had something rigged under their robes and let the mice out."

"So not nuns," I said.

He shook his head. "No. The detectives on the case have called around, there was no large group of nuns out at the Met today."

I smiled. It was the rodents that led them to think that I had done the robbery. My heart sped up and I didn't think I would need caffeine ever again.

"The rest were crowded around the painting," Silvo said, "and while everyone else's attention was on the mice, one of them took it, stripped the frame and, presumably, hid it in their habit."

The door opened again with another gentle ring and a blast of cold air and I felt my elation drain away just as quickly as it came.

"What am I going to do, Silvo?" I asked.

He chuckled and said, "You are going to go to the masquerade ball and you are going to tell her what is in your heart."

"But I don't even know her," I said

He smiled and his eyes crinkled into slits again. "But don't you? Perhaps not the little things but you know how she thinks because you think the exact same way."

I WAS MORE NERVOUS THAN A TEENAGER AT PROM, MY palms sweaty and I couldn't stay still. I had had a full week to think about this night, and think about it again, and then think about it some more.

On any night, the Victorian-style Grand Ballroom of this century-old club was breathtaking. The expansive oval room lined with ornately arched windows on one side that overlooked the East River, a domed ceiling thirty feet above the wooden floor with a long skylight letting in the starlight, the warm wood panels on the walls decorated with iron sconces, the ceiling hung with chandeliers. All of it with the rounded edges and ornate touches you would expect.

But for this night the ceiling had been strung with glittering lights and there was a raised stage with a chamber orchestra playing. The ballroom was for dancing, but there was a silent auction close by and another ballroom for dining. But I didn't care for any of it. I walked among the masked guests, all of them dressed in elaborate costumes and draped in expensive jewels, looking for my Juliet.

It was, admittedly, not the most recognizable costume, but I knew her height and build. I knew the color of her hair. I knew she would be wearing a golden mask. And if I knew the Kat at all, she would be dressed in an exquisite fourteenth-century costume.

I wore stockings and knee breeches, a puffy long-sleeved white poet shirt with ruffles along the laced closure at the neck, a rich blue velvet sleeveless doublet, and an ornate silver mask. The event had started an hour ago and the band was warming up, but I had not found her yet.

I feared that she was not going to show and then chided myself for such fear. This was a woman I did not know and I had not even seen clearly—why did I feel this way?

"O Romeo, Romeo," a voice said from behind me. "Wherefore art thou, Romeo? Deny thy father and refuse your name... or something like that."

I turned and couldn't help but smile. She was here and dressed in a magnificent floor-length gown of green and white satin that highlighted her athletic build. The dress had a low neckline and a laced bodice, an ornate golden mask edged in feathers covered her face. Her luxurious black hair was gathered in a pile on her head with ringlets framing her face.

I smiled widely but could find no words.

The band started playing and she curtsied and said, "This may be presumptuous for me to ask, but shall we dance?"

And we did, we were the first two to take to the center of the ballroom under the skylight with the stars above and dance out there, a simple ballroom-style dance. She was a graceful dance partner, easily turning my more awkward moves into something elegant.

I loved the feel of her hand in mine as we glided across the wooden floor. I drank in her scent and stared into her lovely brown eyes. They practically glowed, the color of polished mahogany.

We didn't speak, we just danced and soon my stomach tightened as I realized something was wrong but I didn't know what it was. My dancing faltered and she did a graceful twirl under my arm to cover and pulled me back into the dance. She was now leading. She was so good at it that it didn't feel awkward at all.

"What troubles you, my lord?" she asked, leaning close so I could hear her clearly over the orchestra. "Am I not all that you expected?"

"And more," I said, but I did not feel it. The next time the dance moved us close I breathed her scent in and realized what it was. She wore the same expensive perfume as the woman I had been dealing with, but on her it didn't smell quite the same. "But you are not her," I added. "You are not the Kat I seek."

She shrugged and a smile showed off her dazzling teeth. "Does not a cat have nine lives?" she asked, a playful lilt in her voice.

It took me a moment as I thought back to what Silvo told me about the robbery. Seven nuns at the painting. Two nuns letting the mice loose. Nine nuns. The Kat was not a single person but a group of women. My smile matched hers as I realized that this was a test.

"But you are right, my fair Romeo," she said. "I am not the one you seek. Meet your Juliet up above." She looked up at the skylight and then back at me. "But not until after eleven bells, then all will be ready."

The song was over and I was turning to go but she said, "A word of advice, if I may, my lord."

"Please," I said.

"Be gentle with my sister," she said, "or you will have to answer to all of us."

———

THE WAIT WAS INTERMINABLE. THERE WAS DANCING AND food and a silent auction. I met many intriguing people, saw the Juliet I had danced with circulating through the crowd, relieving them of some jewelry here and there, I suspected. I even danced with a few other revelers, all of them happy and a little drunk, and on any other night delightful enough, but my heart was not in it.

I had never been in this club before since I wasn't a member and the only opportunity for nonmembers were events like this. But I did my homework. I knew the layout of the place. I knew the security. And I knew how to get to the roof and had the tools I needed on me.

This was just a normal precaution for me. The Kat's motives were intriguing but certainly not clear, so I made sure I knew where I was going.

I slipped out of the festivities and made my way to the roof shortly after eleven. I paused at the door, the words of the Juliet I had danced with echoing in my head, *Be gentle with my sister.*

I was having trouble imagining anything this woman would have difficulties with and it worried me. What didn't I know?

But I did not pause long, opening the door and stepping out onto the roof. The night was clear and cold, a recent storm cleansing the air, so the stars were a glittering field above me.

The roof was flat with a low wall around it, the triangular edge of the grand ballroom skylight sticking up. The building wasn't right on the water but it was tall enough so the East River was visible and beyond it were the glittering high-rises of downtown Manhattan adding their own lights to accompany the stars above.

But that is not what I looked at. I looked at the masked woman waiting for me dressed in the same green and white gown as the Juliet I had danced with, including the golden feathered mask, with a dark wool coat on top. She was standing beside a small table on the rough tar roof that held a bottle of Champagne and two crystal flutes, a candle flickering in a jar, and a leather wallet. A small square wrapped in plain brown paper sat under the table which had to be the painting.

"It's cold," she said, handing me a wool coat that was similar to hers but cut for a man.

"Thank you," I said, using my real voice, sounding like the lifelong New Yorker I was. I put on the coat—it fit me perfectly. I fished the velvet bag containing the diamonds she sought out of a hidden pocket in my costume and put them on the table and took back the wallet she had stolen.

I suddenly felt shy and did not know what to say. I ignored the warm light coming out of the skylight along with the sounds of the orchestra, and I ignored the skyline and the stars and focused on the most remarkable thing. The Kat. Or, one of the women that was part of the Kat, as I had just learned.

Her eyes were the same warm mahogany color as the other Juliet and I was beginning to think that this was another test.

"After deducting some expenses, of course, the sale of the diamonds will benefit the orphanages," she said, nodding to the revelers below. Another fascinating detail about her that I'm sure spoke volumes, but I had no words so I nodded my head.

"And I trust the painting will end up back at a museum soon," she said.

This was something I often did, especially with a work like

this that was not all that valuable and I mostly wanted for personal reasons. And for the fun of the heist. Like I said, my regular job supported me just fine.

I nodded again and my brain finally clicked into gear. "Excuse me if this sounds rude, but may I smell you?"

A brief smile played on her lovely, full lips, and she nodded.

I leaned closer and breathed in deeply, the scent right this time. It was her.

"You approve?" she asked when I leaned back.

"Wholeheartedly," I said.

"Shall we have a drink then, or will it be all business?" she asked.

I smiled. "There is nothing about this that is business to me," I said and was delighted to see both her eyebrows rise above her mask briefly.

"Do the honors then," she said, nodding towards the bottle.

It was Dom Pérignon, a very expensive bottle of it. I managed to uncork it without spilling any and poured, handing her one of the crystal flutes and taking one myself.

"What shall we toast to?" she asked.

You would think I would have planned multiple clever things to say in case this meeting went well. But I had not been myself, the carefully prepared Mouse. I was in awe and feeling things I did not really understand.

"To the Kat and the Mouse meeting at last," I said because I could not think of anything else.

The glasses sounded like a small bell when they touched and the Champagne was cold, dry, effervescent, and exquisite.

"I hope there is not too much to read into your choice of costumes," she said with a laugh, but the stress in her voice was clear.

I took another sip of the Champagne. "That choice was based on my hope that we can experience the degree of passion they experienced and be as sure as they both were of it, not the ending."

She nodded and I could not be sure, but I suspected she was blushing under her mask. We both sipped but didn't speak. I was struggling with what to say and the alcohol did nothing to calm my nerves.

I took a deep breath, cleared my throat, and said, "May I speak frankly? I have no words like Romeo had for Juliet and I want to spend this time wisely."

She nodded cautiously.

"I am fascinated by the Kat... by you. I have been for years," I said. "Both the daring nature of your exploits and the apparent impossibility of them. All with not a drop of blood shed."

"You say you have no words," she said with a smile, "but these are fine words. Please continue."

"And I know that you must be fascinated with me on some level. That calling card of yours you left me in London under the Bast statue."

She nodded, but I couldn't tell if she was telling me to continue or agreeing with me. My stomach tightened around what little food I had eaten.

"All this time I thought it was the Mouse chasing the Kat," I said. "Stealing gems to get your attention, in hopes of running into you. But as I waited for you down there, as I considered it all, I realized it has been the Kat playing with the Mouse all along starting with that calling card you left me."

She rewarded me with a smile big enough to narrow her lovely almond-shaped eyes. "This much is true."

"May I ask you why?"

She shrugged. "You first, please. Why did you play my game?"

I matched her shrug. "It is lonely not being able to fully be yourself. I have found lies to be a terrible thing to build a relationship on. Things work for a while, but then they always crumble." I took another sip of the fine beverage. "And you?"

"I have my sisters," she said, and I had to wonder at that. Surely the one I danced with was her actual sister, but all of them could not be. "And that is enough for some," she continued, "but not me. And..." She paused and looked out across the skylight to the glittering view of Manhattan. "There is precision and thoughtfulness to your work that I admire and thought it might be worth seeing if..." She trailed off again, put her glass down on the table, and walked away.

"What is it?" I said, following her, my shoes crunching loudly on the asphalt and gravel roof.

"Perhaps I slurp my soup," she began, not looking at me but gazing out over the water at the skyline, "or sleep on the wrong side of the bed. Or perhaps I am not beautiful, perhaps I—"

"I care for none of that," I said, cutting her off. "You are clearly intelligent and capable and ever so clever, and you understand this life I live. How could I ask for more?"

There was silence, thick and uncomfortable, the muffled sounds of the orchestra below no longer soothing. There was something stopping her, something causing her to hesitate, but I did not know what it was.

"Perhaps I chew with my mouth open," I offered. "Perhaps I am exceedingly plain and not nearly handsome enough for a woman like you." I felt my stomach tighten again and could hear it in my voice. I feared that that last part was true.

She turned quickly and stared at me. "Will you take off your mask and let me be the judge of that?"

I swallowed hard. I had no disguise today, the mask my only shield. My heart beat hard and my mouth was suddenly very dry. But I slowly pulled off my mask and let her see me in the dim light.

To call me handsome would be an exaggeration. My face has

served me well, but one of the reasons is that it is very forgettable and entirely average. I have short brown hair that could be described as mousey without one bit of irony, thin lips, and a large nose.

I could see her eyes taking me in from behind her mask. She stepped forward and put her hand on my chest and my heart beat even harder. I had never shown my true face to anyone on the "extracurricular" side of my life and I felt like I was standing before her naked.

She reached up her hand and her cold fingers touched my cheek. "I like this face," she said. "I am honored that you have shown it to me."

I put my hand against hers as she touched my cheek and put my other hand behind her neck. She did not resist, so I pulled her forward, and even though I didn't think it was possible, my heart beat even faster. She still did not resist so I pulled her slowly closer until our lips finally met.

Her lips were cool and soft, drenched in Dom Pérignon, and the kiss was... It was a slow, patient kiss that spoke of a spark that had ignited that could easily turn into a blaze. It was deep, like the ocean, and I felt something move within me.

Although the kiss lasted a good long time, it was over much too quickly. I wanted more and at the same time knew I could never have enough.

My breath was coming fast and we just stared at each other. At first, I feared she had not felt it, but then I noticed she was breathing fast too.

"Will you take off your mask for me?" I asked.

She took a small step backwards. "Whatever you think is under this mask," she said very quietly, "you are wrong."

I was puzzled. Had she not seen my face? The beauty I sought in her I had already found. "Please," I said.

She nodded, but walked back to the table and quickly

drained her glass of champagne. It was a shame to drink the Dom so quickly, but I understood.

I could not see her face clearly, but I could see emotions running through it by the movement of her lips and her forehead. She was afraid.

"It's okay," I said. "Please."

She pursed her lips and nodded. She took off her mask. It was not what I expected and it must have shown on my face because she turned and ran.

THIS WOMAN HAD ONCE BEEN EXTRAORDINARILY beautiful. She had the kind of symmetrically gorgeous face that Helen of Troy was fabled to have had. Olive-toned skin, high cheek bones, full lips, almond-shaped eyes, and elegantly expressive eyebrows. The kind of face that could launch a thousand ships.

But something had happened to her. Someone had done something to her. Something terrible.

A deep cut ran from the middle of her nose across her right cheek, the scar pulling at her face deforming her nose, her cheek, and her right eye. She had not been born this way. Someone had done this to her.

I felt many things. Shock. Anger. And, yes, a measure of revulsion. The twisting of her beauty by such a cruelty twisted my stomach in kind.

That was what she saw on my face, and I could not blame her for running.

"Wait!" I shouted. She had reached the door and had her hand on the handle. "Please."

I ran after her as she stood there frozen. "You are beautiful," I said when I reached her.

"But..." she prompted, her back to me.

The orchestra had stopped below us and I could hear a muffled voice saying something but I cared nothing for the revelers or for the diamonds or the painting or for the wine or the view.

"Not a 'but,'" I said. "Just an 'and.' You are beautiful *and* something terrible has happened to you *and* I need a few moments to process it."

She turned around, her eyes barely meeting mine. "Really?" she asked like some shy little girl.

I smiled and nodded. "Really." I slowly reached my hand forward and touched her right cheek like she had touched mine but below the deep scar.

I wanted to ask her what had happened. I wanted to ask her why she didn't take some of her earnings and get plastic surgery. But I had not earned the answers to those questions so I spoke the words of Shakespeare to her softly, gently, and just slightly altered

"But, soft... what light through yonder window breaks? It is the east, and you are the sun. Arise, fair sun, and kill the envious moon, who is already sick and pale with grief, that thou her maid art far more fair than she."

I paused and she did not say anything, her eyes searching mine. So I dropped the Shakespeare and used my own words. "I am the plainest of men," I said. "And you are the most beautiful of women. This will take some time to become accustomed to, but I would beg you to give me that opportunity."

Tears sprang into her eyes as they sprang into mine.

"I want someone that can know and accept all of me," I said. "And I want to know and accept all of them."

She nodded and put her hand against mine and pressed it into her cheek just as I had, sliding my hand up so my finger just touched the hard edge of that cruel scar.

Below me I heard voices rising and counting. "Ten... Nine... Eight..." It was nearly midnight.

She took her other hand and placed it behind my neck and pulled me forward, just as I had pulled her forward. I did not resist.

As the revelers counted down below us our lips came closer and when "Zero!" was shouted and people started blowing on their noisemakers, our lips met again.

As the revelers shouted, in the distance I could hear the sound of fireworks going off across the river, flashes of light reaching my closed eyes, but I did not care. All there was for me was the kiss.

This time the kiss was different. It was neither slow nor patient, but full of fire and need. My need to be fully known. Her need to be fully accepted just as she was. She pulled me close and held me fiercely and I felt tears on my cheeks and neither knew nor cared whose they were.

When our lips finally parted, we laughed, silly laughs, like two teenagers. I took her hand as we turned to watch the rainbow color of fireworks illuminate the Manhattan skyline and reflecting in the East River.

I had never seen them from this vantage point and I think I had been missing out all this time.

"I think the seventies are getting off to a good start," I said, squeezing her hand.

She squeezed my hand back and said, "Me too."

I did not know what this new year and this new decade would bring, but I knew that my passion was no longer fine wines or exquisitely executed heists, but the amazing woman next me.

After the fireworks ended, we went back to the table and spent hours drinking the Champagne and talking as the

Manhattan skyline glittered across the water and the stars spun above us.

She did not put her mask back on and I smiled so much my cheeks hurt. We got to know each other slowly, carefully in an elegantly shy dance. When the sun finally started to lighten the horizon, we left together hand in hand and I had hope of a future where I could be truly known and I could truly know another.

BACKSTORY—A GAME OF KAT AND MOUSE

While many of these stories are rather personal, this one is only personal in that I love stories of clever thieves that have a moral compass (think the Ocean's movies or the *Leverage* TV show) and I love romantic stories, people overcoming their obstacles and finding each other.

This one is just about having fun and telling a story that combines both elements in the classic backdrop of New York City.

I was once in the presence of Renoir's *Luncheon of the Boating Party*. That time made me understand the power of seeing art in person. It was very much like the difference between seeing a picture of the Grand Canyon and standing on the rim. The two experiences are related, but only distantly.

PART 15
LAURA'S MAGIC CLOCK

LAURA'S MAGIC CLOCK

THE TICK-TICK-TICK OF THE OLD CLOCK GREETED ME AS I slowly emerged from unconsciousness, my bladder full, my head thick, wisps of dreams circling my mind. I wanted to go back to sleep. I *needed* to go back to sleep, but the tick-tick-tick wouldn't let me submerge into the darkness I craved.

I rolled over on the smooth, silk sheets and pulled the pillow under my chest. I hate silk sheets, how my body slips around on them, but she had loved them, so I keep them. Just like she had been so excited when she found that damn old tick-tock clock at the flea market. The old man that sold it to us told her it was magic, that it had a gypsy spell and would "grant a great boon to its owner at their darkest hour."

It's an odd thing. A rearing unicorn about a foot tall made of polished redwood with a brass horn and hooves, a round clock under the creature's belly.

"It's hideous," I told her, the old man giving me the stink eye.

"I love it, and I love you." Her face lit up like an eight-year-old on Christmas morning. I bought it for her—if you had seen her smile, you would have bought it too. She smiled with her whole face, her cheeks full, her blue eyes scrunching like upside-down crescent moons. She hugged me hard, my nose filling with her delicious scent, my heart overflowing with love. I didn't say a word when she put it in our bedroom, despite the fact that I hated the sound of it.

Tick-tick-tick. It was the same every morning. That damn clock brought me back to the world, made me think of her.

She's a pronoun now. It's always "her" or "she" these days. I don't speak her name. I don't think her name. Pronoun she may be, but I can't let go of her. I can't even move that damn clock into the living room.

The cold air on my skin woke me up a bit more as I got out from under the covers, my bare feet taking me to that damn clock as if of their own volition—and it's "damn clock" in my mind now. It wakes me up. It reminds me of her. Her smile, her scent, those crescent-moon eyes, come flooding back to me.

I laid one hand on the back of the unicorn, feeling the raised grain of the wood, smelling the pungent polish she had lavished it with when we got home. With my other hand I turned the cool brass fob on the back and wound up the clock, a clickity-click-clack sound briefly overwhelming the tick-tick.

I can't let it wind down either. This used to be her ritual, winding the clock first thing in the morning before doing the bladder's or the stomach's bidding. "Gotta wind it to keep the magic going," she would say. But she's not here to do it, so I do it.

It's almost like the clock is talking to me. Tick-tick. It's time to wake up. Tick-tick. Don't forget to wind me. Tick-tick. She's gone, but I can help you remember her. Tick-tick. You know you want to remember her. Tick-tick. She's dead because of you. Tick-tick. The guilt is tearing you apart.

I wish the clock had really been magic. Maybe then she would have lived.

OUT OF THE BEDROOM AND AWAY FROM THE DAMN UNICORN clock, my life seemed almost normal. I showered, dressed, grabbed coffee and a bagel on the way to the subway, and sat in the rhythmically bouncing car as it took me to Wall Street.

The subway is all about smells. Dirt tracked in from the last rainstorm. Bodies and their sweat and perfume concentrated by proximity. And something else—it smells old. As if the decades have permeated the worn steel poles and drab plastic seats with its own scent. As if time itself has a smell—not a very pleasant one, I might add.

All the other senses get tuned out there. Everyone's got head-phones on, their heads down, fiddling with their phones, trying to pretend they're not in a little metal car zipping along under the towering skyscrapers above. Everyone's bodies are closed in tight, although you can feel the touch of your neighbor's hip if you're sitting, or an elbow swaying into yours if you're standing.

But you tune all of that out. Scroll through Facebook. Tap on your laptop. Blast your ears with music. Then, all that's left is that smell. Dirt, sweat, perfume, time, desperation.

That morning, I was standing and wasting time on Facebook. I didn't want to waste time on Facebook, with its endless pictures of food and self-congratulatory posts from people I barely knew. I should have been reading a book, for God's sake. But I didn't have the will.

I was flicking past one of those annoying link-bait articles a girl I had dated briefly in high school had liked—and being glad I had only dated her briefly—the clack-clack of the subway sounding like the tick-tick of that clock, and I smelled her.

Maybe my nose was just overloaded with the subway. Maybe my mind was playing tricks on me. But it was *her*. I was sure of it. Perfume in the bottle is not the same as perfume on the skin. A good perfume changes with each person, transforms into something unique.

This scent was sweet, like roses, with something distinctly sharp, like aged Parmesan cheese, plus something a little sour and lemony. Her scent.

My heart started thump-thump-thumping in my chest and prickly sweat formed on the small of my back. I didn't move fast. I was hoping she was there, but knowing it was impossible. I wanted so desperately to see her face, but not wanting the inevitable disappointment.

The subway slowed down for the Fulton Station stop. I looked up from my phone and saw a woman with long brown hair and a dark coat stepping out of the car. I couldn't see her face, but the hair, with its chestnut hue and gentle wave at the tips, was hers. The scent was hers.

I felt her name form on my tongue. No longer a pronoun, I mumbled, "Laura?"

My hand, still gripping the steel rail, shook. I let go, reflexively rubbing my sweaty palm on my pants before stepping off the subway car into the cavelike station.

I couldn't see her anymore. She was lost in the crowd. The train whooshed away behind me and the crowd departed, and I just stood there.

It smelled like Laura. What I saw of her looked like Laura. But it couldn't be her. Laura's dead.

***

SOME PEOPLE BELIEVE IN GHOSTS, THINK ANY LITTLE oddity—like the flickering of a light—is their loved one communicating with them. I don't buy it. I don't believe in ghosts, but I do believe that most of us are haunted. Not by some literal, ethereal spirit but by our pasts and our regrets and our guilt.

She has been haunting me since her death. And it's no surprise. I'm to blame. How could I not be haunted by it?

My nose was still full of her as my feet carried me up out of the claustrophobia of the subway into a crisp New York morning. The sounds of the city descended on me. Honking cars, a distant ambulance—its siren bouncing off the high-rises of Broadway—the shuffling of pedestrians, the murmur of conversation.

I pulled my leather jacket tight around me and looked for her. But it was no use. If it had been her—even though it couldn't have been her—she would be lost in the crowd by now.

I joined the throng and headed south towards Rector Street and my job at Larry's Downtown Deli. I'd gotten off the subway too soon, but I didn't feel like going back down. I breathed deeply of the smell of New York City hoping to get another whiff of her, but all I smelled was exhaust, old grease, coffee from a street vendor, and odor de Dumpster. If you live in a big city, you know what I'm talking about. The scent is not pleasant, but familiar. It's so strong you can actually taste it.

At work, I tick-ticked through my day with a rhythm almost as regular as that redwood clock. Running frozen pizzas through the little oven, stocking the salad bar, checking people out, my feet always moving across the worn linoleum.

After her death, I quit my job as a claims adjuster. The pressure was too much. I've been running one of those little ubiquitous Big Apple delis for the last six months. Not that there isn't any pressure at the deli, there's plenty, but because I'm always dealing with customers and I'm always moving, my mind has a harder time wandering back. Back to when Laura became a pronoun in my vocabulary.

There is surprisingly little to the story of her death. A Wednesday night out in the city. Too much to drink—way too much—she more than I. Distraction. Tragedy.

She was also a claims adjuster and had just received a "stern talking to" from her supervisor over some of the claims she had handled. She was, honestly, too kind for the job.

It wasn't much, really. Not in the long view, but that night it was a big deal—thus the excessive drinking after work.

We had decided to walk home. Thirty blocks didn't seem that far in our inebriated state. Besides, I think going home right away would have felt like a return to reality, the last thing she wanted.

It was the end of summer, an almost full moon throwing silvery light down the high-rise canyons as we walked, a little unsteadily, and talked. She smiled a lot, widely and with her teeth showing, but her eyes never did that upside-down crescent moon thing, so even in my altered state I knew it wasn't a real smile.

We held hands. I kept squeezing hers, trying to let her know it was okay, that I loved her. I wore a gray suit, she a brown skirt with heels and a sweater. It was our work clothing; we had decided to drink our dinner as soon as we got off work.

"Oh," she said, her speech less slurred than it had been. "*This* is why you wanted to walk."

I didn't recall being the one wanting to walk. "What?"

We were on Columbus Circle, almost to Time Warner Center. She let go of my hand and pointed. A Tesla Model S was parked in front of the towering, glass-walled entrance. It was Batmobile-black and beautifully lit, looking like Bruce Wayne was about to step out wearing a tux with a supermodel in a red evening dress on his arm.

I'm not from New York. I grew up in California where

everyone drives all the time, and truth be told, I miss owning a car and driving.

I stared, gape jawed. I smelled the city, dirt and exhaust and rotting trash. I heard the cars honking, tires humming, brakes squealing. I felt the warmth that had once been her hand in mine. But none of that mattered. It was just me and the beautifully designed electric car.

"I'm tired of... of..." she said, moving away from me, but I didn't turn. "Walking!" she added with a laugh once she had finally pulled the word out of her sodden consciousness.

I heard her heels scraping over the sidewalk. "Cabby!" she yelled.

Then horns blared, brakes screeched, and there was a sickening crunch, a scream, and a thud.

———

DEAD IS DEAD. THE DEAD STAY DEAD, EXCEPT IN MY dreams.

I dream of that night in front of Time Warner Center, the broken body of my Laura in my arms. After her last rattling breath and the last beat of her heart, she suddenly seemed light, somehow insubstantial. It was no longer Laura, just a body that looked like Laura. The demarcation was so sudden, so final.

In my dreams it's worse.

Sometimes she struggles to get up, but her broken limbs won't support her and she collapses with a wet thump. Other times I pull her into my arms and her blue eyes open, except they're not blue, they're all bloody and she says, "You did this," as coagulating blood pours out her mouth.

I did do wrong by her in the past. A brief moment of drunken infidelity cost us most of six months. The time I forgot her birthday. When she opened up to me about problems she was having with a coworker and I accidentally laughed.

Each time we would talk it out—much longer than I ever wanted—with the tick-tick of her clock in the background. I just wanted to apologize and move on, but she needed to talk about things. A lot.

But this we couldn't talk out. I couldn't tell her how sorry I was for getting so drunk. It was her bad day; I should have been taking care of her. I couldn't tell her how awful I felt for letting go of her hand. How horrified I was that a stupid car distracted me at the single moment in our history together when she needed me the most. If only I could apologize.

After the funeral, I quit my job and started working at the deli. I almost left New York, but it was all I had left of her. She is New York to me. We met the day I got to the city, after all, and we spent nearly every day after that together.

She was on the subway with me again today. That sweet, sharp, sour smell again alerted me to her presence. I glimpsed a woman from behind that could be her. Long brown hair with a bit of curl at the bottom. Tall and willowy. A purposeful stride.

I got out a stop early and tried to follow her. I pushed through the crowd as fast as I could, but when I came up into the bright sunlight of an April day, I couldn't find her. People everywhere, but not her.

My heart thumped in my chest the whole time, my mouth sour from the adrenaline playing in my veins. My head didn't believe it could be her, but my body did.

The Fulton Station subway stop comes out near Zuccotti Park. It's not very big, just a paved area with cement benches and lots of trees. I found myself standing on the Broadway side, my legs shaky, watching, hoping, praying.

I felt like I was a boy again, the time I broke the delicate porcelain vase my mother had loved. I held the sharp shards in my hands wishing I could take it back, praying that it hadn't really happened. But I couldn't do anything about the broken vase, just like I couldn't do anything about my broken Laura.

Broken is broken. Dead is dead.

The rhythmic honking on Broadway, for a moment, sounded like the tick-tick of the unicorn clock.

"Are you okay?" a woman asked.

I was slumped against a streetlight, my head in my hands.

The woman's voice sounded young and sweet. It had a melodic lilt to it and a trace of a New England accent. My heart started pounding again. *She* had a voice like that.

I looked up but couldn't see much, the morning sun haloed behind her hair.

"Do you need me to call somebody?"

I blinked against the sunlight, her name dancing on my lips, when I saw the woman clearly—a ragged homeless lady with a grocery cart full of junk behind her.

She thought I needed help. All the people in this park and she thought I was so bad off that she could help me.

"No. No, thank you," I mumbled, getting up and walking toward the deli.

———

Laura and I never got married, officially. She had issues with her family and couldn't bear the thought of them all coming together—and the drama that would ensue—for her wedding.

I remember the night I asked her. We sat on the floor of our little apartment playing Scrabble.

"We should get married, you know," I said as I tried to figure out a word with two *T*s, an *S*, and an *I* that wasn't a dirty word.

I wasn't looking at her, but I heard her suck in air through her nose and hold it. I could feel her eyes on me, the tick-tick of that unicorn clock in our bedroom counting down the seconds.

Tick-tick. No answer yet.

Tick-tick. I couldn't look at her. What if she hated the idea? What if she was just staying with me until she found someone better? Although, after five years, I should have given up that irrational insecurity.

Tick-tick. Did she just sniff?

I finally looked up, and she was crying, but there was a smile on her face and her blue eyes were squished into those upside-down crescent moons. The tears freaked me out. Asking her freaked me out. I had thought about it for a long time, but didn't plan the asking.

"Are you okay?" I finally asked.

She nodded, swept the Scrabble board out of the way, the tiles clattering everywhere, and then she was in my arms. I tasted the salt of her tears and the perfumed waxiness of her lipstick. She was warm and so alive that night.

Later, after we made love, she told me she couldn't stand inviting her family to her wedding, and she couldn't get married without inviting her family. I mean, Vegas would have been fine with me, but she couldn't do it. She was caught in this familial paradox.

Hours later we were still on the floor, our backs up against the couch, drinking wine. I was frustrated that I couldn't figure out a way to meet her needs. Excited that she had said yes—although not directly in words. And tired from the glorious physical expression of her "yes."

I shrugged and smiled. "What do we do?"

She was quiet for a long time. The tick-tick of the clock and the honking of horns twenty floors below the only sounds. "I got it!" she said, her smile wide. She pulled a blanket around her nude body and sat right in front of me. "We don't need a priest, and we certainly don't need my family. Right here, right now, we are married. I am your wife, and you are my husband."

I studied her face, her beautiful face. High cheekbones, sparkling blue eyes, lovely full lips. She was always too good for me. Not just in terms of beauty, but the kind of person she was. She would carry granola bars in her purse and give them to homeless people. "They'll just drink any money," she told me once. "This way they can at least eat something." She always thought of others more than herself.

The declaration wasn't exactly what I wanted, but I wanted her even more. "Umm... I do," I said.

She was on me again, her lips brushing at my ear. "I do, too. And I expect a ring."

I HATED THE SALAD BAR MOST OF ALL. PEOPLE SLOPPED food all over, and I had to clean it up. Constantly. Bacon bits in the beets, hard-boiled eggs in the carrots, lettuce absolutely everywhere. It's disgusting.

It felt a little bit like my own version of hell. A menial task that I kept doing—wiping, picking, refilling from the bins in the back. It went on and on. It never ended. It seemed like I could never catch up. Sometimes, though, I considered it my penance for what happened to her. Then I don't really mind it.

The deli was on the ground floor of an old high-rise on Rector, just off Broadway. The walls were white and the fluorescent lights whiter. It wasn't very big, just enough room for the little salad bar, the deli case, the baked goods, a small pizza oven, and the checkout area. One long counter with tables on the other side.

I was on the night shift and actually making progress on the damn salad bar. I didn't usually work nights—I was the manager, after all—but some recent personnel turnover had me working doubles. During the day we've got at least two people. At night it's just one person from 10:00 p.m. to 2:00 a.m.

And then I smelled her. Sweet like a flower, sharp like cheese, sour like citrus. That smell is in my soul. All our years together she used the same perfume. No one else ever smelled that way.

I was wiping between the round containers of the salad bar, my heart suddenly thumping in my head like a two-year-old with his first drum. I didn't look up. I didn't want to look up. What if I didn't see anything? What if it was a woman walking away from me again or a homeless lady?

I read once that the sense of smell is hardwired directly into the brain. It's not like the eyes and the ears where you can see and hear things that aren't real. If you are smelling something, it's because those nerves are stimulated. There is a cause. There has to be.

I froze, gripping the white rag as hard as I could. That smell didn't go away. It got stronger. It came from the person standing on the other side of the salad bar. I stared at the sliced cucumbers, but out of my peripheral vision I could see a dark skirt and a white blouse. The same thing she wore that night I failed her, the night she died.

"I'm sorry," I whispered as I closed my eyes tight against the tears. "I'm so sorry."

That night came back, like it always did. I let go of her hand, just for a moment. The squeal of tires. A sickening crash. A scream. Holding her in my arms, the metallic smell of blood mixing with her normal flowery scent. Feeling her life ebb away.

"Are you okay?" she asked.

"I'm sorry. I'm sorry. I'm sorry." I slid down to the floor, sitting among discarded bacon bits and shredded carrots.

I heard the clicking of high heels on linoleum, reminding me of the tick-tick of the clock in my bedroom. My arms around my knees, I rocked back and forth chanting, "I'm sorry. I'm sorry. I'm sorry."

"Mister, are you okay?"

I heard her voice, but it was distant. That smell, sweet and sharp and sour, filled my nose. Images of that night filled my eyes as tears leaked out.

I didn't look. I couldn't look. It couldn't be her. But while my eyes were closed there was still the tiniest chance that it was.

The beeps of a dialing phone. "Yes, I'm at Larry's Downtown Deli on Rector, right off Broadway. Send an ambulance. Someone here needs help."

I felt a hand on my shoulder as I continued to rock. "It's going to be okay. You're going to be okay."

I didn't believe her. I couldn't believe her. I kept my eyes closed.

LAURA WAS SMART, MUCH SMARTER THAN ME. I WAS A little better with numbers, but she was a lot better with people. She understood people in a way that always baffled me. She quickly seemed to "get" them and could say just the right thing.

That woman in the deli seemed more and more like Laura.

"I'm right here," she said after I had been loaded into the ambulance. My eyes were still shut tight. She slipped her warm hand into mine and squeezed. "I'm not going anywhere."

It was the kind of thing Laura would have done.

Who was she, this late-night salad bar patron? She smelled like Laura. Her voice was a lot like Laura's. She acted like Laura.

"I'm sorry," I whispered, probably for the hundredth time. The ambulance was on the move, the siren loud, the rumble of tires on pavement and the ever-present honking of cars making it hard to hear. I didn't expect her to hear me.

"It's okay," she whispered back, her face close to mine, her Laura-smell filling my senses. "I forgive you."

There was a paramedic in the ambulance with us. I could smell his sweat and hear him move, but I didn't care. It was like it was just me and Laura and no one else.

I held my breath. Did she say that she forgave me? "You do?"

"Of course," she said with the smallest of chuckles. "You didn't mean to."

I squeezed her hand, and she squeezed back. It was her. It had to be her. Somehow she had come back to me. Somehow she was here. I thought of the redwood unicorn clock and the gypsy spell. Could it be?

"I was so careless," I said. "I shouldn't have let go."

She gently squeezed my hand again. "It's okay, really it is."

My eyes were still closed. I hadn't dared to look. I didn't want to take the chance that the illusion, or spell, or whatever it was, would shatter.

"But how are you here?" I asked. "You can't be here."

"I'm... I'm here for you," she said, and I could hear something in her voice. It sounded thicker than it had and was tinged with sadness. Was she crying?

"I miss you, Laura," I said. "God, how I miss you."

We didn't speak the rest of the trip, we just held hands. It took everything I had, but I kept my eyes closed. If this was a spell, if this was magic, I wasn't willing to do anything that might disturb it.

When they opened the ambulance doors and pulled out the gurney, she said, "Give us a moment, will you?" She must have been talking to the paramedics.

"I have to go," she said to me.

I took a deep breath of her scent. "I miss you already."

She sniffed, and I felt a single tear fall onto my cheek. "I forgive you. You know that, don't you?"

I nodded. I hadn't cried much since Laura died, and I felt a tsunami of tears coming. "Yes. Thank you."

She squeezed my hand one last time. "I love you," she said.

"I love you too."

She left and I so missed the warmth of her hand. I heard her heels as they click-clicked on the pavement as she walked away.

I SAT AND STARED AT THAT GARISH OLD UNICORN CLOCK AS it did its tick-tick thing on the dresser of our bedroom. No, of *my* bedroom. I had decided. It was time. But still I waited.

It's been three months since my breakdown in the deli, since the woman that smelled and sounded and acted like Laura said she forgave me. I've thought a lot about what happened that night and what happened afterwards. A few days in the hospital getting a psych evaluation, then into daily counseling for a while, now down to once a week.

I'm doing better, much better. I still miss Laura, I still feel guilty about what happened, but it is no longer tearing me apart and defining my every moment.

Tick-tick, the clock tells me. One step at a time is the way through this. One day at a time. One hour at a time. One tick at a time.

I never went back to the deli. I just couldn't return. I took some real time off and have tried to get my life together. I started back at the firm, staring at insurance claims all day.

Tick-tick. I still wish I hadn't let go of her hand, but I'm not perfect. I'm human. I make mistakes.

It was late, 11:00 p.m., and I should have been sleeping, but I stared at the clock just a little longer.

Maybe that woman was just a Good Samaritan somehow playing the part of Laura. Maybe the clock was magic and it was really Laura coming back from the dead to help me. Maybe it doesn't matter.

I carefully picked up the clock and carried it out to the living room and placed it on the mantel over the little gas fireplace. The unicorn looked good there. It didn't seem so garish to me anymore.

This was Laura's magic clock, and I loved it because of that, but I was ready to sleep without that tick-tick in my ear.

BACKSTORY—LAURA'S MAGIC CLOCK

Grief is a tricky thing. It can play with your mind. Especially when it's combined with guilt. Ticking clocks can mess with your mind, too. It was a ticking clock and my annoyance of it that got me writing this story and then it took on a life of its own.

Once again this story strays into the fantastical but isn't fantasy. The human psyche is complex enough to easily explain the events of this story, no visitations from the afterlife required.

This story was originally published in *A Game of Horns: A Red Unicorn Anthology*. If you like stories that examine grief, you might be interested in my short story collection *Life After: Stories of Life, Death, and the Places In Between*.

PART 16

HAUNTED BY THE PAST

HAUNTED BY THE PAST

The guy letting me into the now defunct Metrocenter Mall in Phoenix, Arizona, looked me up and down. All six-foot-five and 170 pounds of me. It's not that I look like a scarecrow that makes people gawk, it's the unmistakable Crocodile Dundee outfit complete with alligator-skin boots, a wide-brimmed bush hat, a crocodile claw hanging from my neck, and an eleven-inch bowie knife on my belt.

I won't call it a costume because this is my everyday wardrobe. And I want people to gawk—it keeps them from remembering my history which was big news in Arizona twenty-five years ago. Alcohol. Teenage jealousy and rage. Death. That will get people talking for a good long time.

"G'day, mate," I said with as much energy as my sleep-deprived brain could manage, complete with my well-practiced B-movie-quality Australian accent. "My name is Conner Bright and I believe I am expected." I stuck out my hand but he just stared at that too.

This guy wasn't much to look at. Mid-fifties with a face that reminded me of a weasel, his short brown hair most of the way to grey. Faded jeans, and an oversized Clint Black concert T-shirt that wasn't big enough to hide his bulging belly, glasses, and a sloppy goatee. A forgettable face except for his oversized nose and prominent mole which was hard not to look at. His breath smelled like stale cigarettes and his eyes kept flicking around like he didn't know what to look at.

"I'm the private investigator," I offered, trying to get his brain in gear. It took five minutes of pounding to get him to answer the door and, frankly, the empty parking lot of this 1.4 million-square-foot mall on Christmas Eve was kinda freaking me out. Where were all the guys doing their last-minute shopping? Where were the teenagers gossiping? "Detective Tricia Sanchez sent me over. Hear you folks got a bit of an odd situation here."

His eyes widened and he gave a lazy nod looking kind of like a bobblehead that had been barely touched. I had no idea what the case was at this recently closed mall. Sanchez was still pissed at me and didn't tell me, but I wanted to get this over with.

I fingered the three-month AA recovery chip in my jeans pocket to settle my nerves. It was the reason I was so tired. I was either a drunk or an insomniac and on days like this I wondered which was better.

"We got ghosts," he said, his voice hushed like someone might hear us at the entrance to this abandoned husk that was once a monument to American consumerism.

I swallowed a string of swear words. Sanchez always gave me the weird cases and I could almost hear her gleeful cackle. Purple unicorns. Alien abductions. Chupacabra attacks. So far it had only been creative criminals, and I expected this one to be the same, but Jesus-H, couldn't I just get a nice "I think my husband is cheating on me" case? A nice boring stakeout where I could charge more per hour than I get working as a bouncer?

But this one was different. They had called the cops, talked to Sanchez, but they had asked for me by name.

"Then I'm your man," I said as cheerfully as I could manage. "Let's get started, eh?"

To a kid like me that grew up in the small town of Globe, Arizona, coming to Metrocenter was pretty much like going to Disneyland. There was so much to see and so much to do and so many other kids your age running around. Even if you didn't have more than a buck in your pocket it could be fun.

At twelve, I kissed a girl for the first time in front of the Orange Julius. Her name was Amy. She had curly red hair and wore overalls. I met her in B. Dalton and impressed her with my knowledge of Piers Anthony's Xanth books series. We giggled at some of the more adult items in Spencer's Gifts. And we kissed in the food court, her mouth all cold and orangey.

I had memories from Metrocenter, important memories, so when I saw the empty husk of it, our footfalls echoing loudly, you will understand that I felt a little freaked out, maybe even freaked out enough to believe it was haunted. There was just something wrong with it being so empty and so very quiet.

I looked around as I followed the odd man with the mole on his nose and felt my happy memories of this place eroding by what I saw. A manikin arm lying here, a head over there; the dark shadows of signs taken down above some of the barred shops; an antique chaise lounge under the expansive skylights that ran the length of the main concourses all by itself; a lonely pile of dirt where a potted plant must have stood; shopping carts all over the place full of odds and ends getting ready for auction; parts of cabinets just lying on the floor; turned over signs; and escalators that would never run again.

The magic was gone and my stomach tightened on the long walk under those skylights and then down some narrow hallways in the bowels of the structure into a cramped office with a metal cabinet, two beat-to-hell office chairs, a broad metal desk, and lots of LCD screens with black and white views of this empty place.

I never got the man's name who let me in, but the guy in the office was different. He had a big steel-grey mustache, a firm handshake, and a round face that squeezed his green eyes into slits when he smiled. He even had on a clean button-down shirt and looked like he shaved regularly.

"Glad you could make it, Mr. Bright," he said.

"Happy to help if I can," I said. My guide was already gone, scurrying away like some scared mouse. "But call me Conner, please."

"Conner it is," he said. "I'm Mitch, Mitch Jones, and I'm overseeing operations here." He paused and looked me over and chuckled, his eyes lingering on the bowie knife. "I will say that your reputation precedes you but... you are even more than I expected. And I mean that in a good way."

I didn't know how to take that. My Conner Bright persona was not meant to be impressive, just so overwhelming that my past stayed hidden. But I didn't want to explore it either. I wanted to get out of here. "I hear you've got a little ghost problem," I said.

His smile evaporated and he bit his lower lip. "That we do. There's a lot of work to be done here. Auction what we can. Get rid of what we can't. Keep the lookie-loos out. But I can't keep people." He paused, looking around. The door to the office was open but there was no one else back here. "At least not the kind of people you want to keep."

He was referring to my guide.

"These aren't ghosts, mate," I said. "I can assure you of that. Just someone tryin' to slow ya down, stop this process for some reason."

He blinked and looked away. He thought there were ghosts too. He sat down at the desk, tapped at the keyboard, and pointed at one of the screens. It was timestamped "DEC 21 02:02" and showed a long view of the mall from a camera on the ceiling. A man was running and looking behind him. "I didn't mean to hurt her," he yelled. "I didn't mean to. I swear. I swear!"

The footage was grainy black and white but clearly shot in low light with an infrared camera, the man glowing on the screen like some kind of ghost. His running was erratic and he kept looking behind him. He soon tripped over a sign and went sliding down the tiled floor and bumped into a column and didn't move.

Mitch paused the video and swung around to face me, his cheap office chair creaking as he leaned back. "This kind of thing happened to two other people and now I can't get anyone to stay the night."

"What was he hearing?" I asked.

"He told me he heard his dead mother," he said, rubbing at his mustache, "but he wouldn't tell me what she said."

"I'll need his name and address, then," I said. "And that of the other two that had themselves an 'experience.'"

He nodded but didn't move to write anything down. "So... you don't believe in ghosts," he said, his voice hushed again.

"No, sir," I said. "I do not."

"Then you won't mind being the security guard here tonight," he said, his green eyes locked with mine. "And maybe if you happen to have an 'experience,' *you* can get to the bottom of it."

I didn't bother to tell him it was Christmas Eve, that I had somewhere to be tomorrow and I really, really needed some sleep, and that without a stupid amount of beer I only sleep every third night and this was the night. I didn't tell him there was a reason I had made it past three months and earned that AA chip, and that her name was Irene and she was nine years old, and I had saved her from what appeared to be a rampaging purple unicorn, and that little girl's trust had turned my life around, and I wanted to be there for her on Christmas, sober and awake.

That was none of his business and the two hundred dollars in cash he offered right then and there, enough to keep my utilities going for another month and fill my gas tank and get Irene a nice present, was all I needed to take the job.

But I didn't want it. That mall felt haunted. And, sure, there was probably no literal ghosts, just some enterprising criminals, but a lot of us are haunted by our past. Some more than most. And this derelict mall was a literal part of my past.

It felt like the setup of some lighting-laden, B-horror movie where the protagonist enters the obviously dangerous cobweb-filled mansion on the hill on the flimsiest of pretexts.

But I was going to enter that "haunted" mall and my pretext didn't feel flimsy at all.

I only had a couple of hours before the night shift started, and instead of spending most of that time driving home and back, I went to the Walmart Supercenter just south of the mall, bought a cheap thermos, filled it with cheaper coffee, and found Irene a nice stuffed unicorn and a unicorn jigsaw puzzle. She's still unicorn crazed even after the madness we went through. I then drove back to the mall, parked in the middle of the empty parking lot, lay down on the bench seat of my vintage 1976 El Camino, and tried to sleep.

Tried being the operative word. I didn't sleep at all, just hoped for a quiet night so I could go be with Irene.

―――――――

My boots clicked against the tiled floor of the empty Metrocenter Mall and the keys to the place jangled at my side. It was past midnight and officially Christmas and it felt like I had been at this for days already.

The moon was up, casting a ghostly light through the arched skylight that ran the length of all the main concourse. Each was two stories tall with the upper floor extending out a bit but leaving a wide airy pathway down the middle. There were bridges on the second floor here and there and dead escalators every fifty yards or so.

The mall opened in 1973 and it showed in the style of the place. The ceiling was gently arched and a lot of the surfaces were slightly rounded, most noticeably the cantilevered edges of the second floor.

My flashlight beat the darkness back some, but it seemed like not enough in the big space, every sound I made echoing in strange ways.

Mitch Jones had given me the tour at the beginning of my shift, showed me how to log my passes through the mall on the computer, given me a taser, and told me to call 911 if something happened.

When I asked him about that, he had said, "It's Christmas Eve, Conner. I'm going to be with my family." I decided then and there that I didn't like the guy. Did he assume I didn't have a family to spend time with or did he just not care?

He gave me a bottle of Jim Beam to sweeten the deal. It was the cheap stuff with a beat-to-shit red and green bow stuck to the top. I didn't bother to tell him I was an alcoholic in recovery. Hell, it had been a major accomplishment to admit that in a room full of alcoholics, and I hadn't built up to telling a stranger yet. After he left, I stowed the booze away in the metal cabinet in the cramped office so I wouldn't have to look at it all night.

This looked like a simple case to me. Maybe not easy, but simple. Someone was "haunting" the mall to slow operations down. An investigation would have two prongs, interview those that had an "experience"—one or more of them was likely involved—and follow the money, someone was benefiting from this delay.

But if being a security guard on Christmas Eve was what it took to audition for the work, so be it. This was a big case and could turn things around for me.

This was my fourth pass through, one an hour, and I had my route laid out and went the same way every time. My main job was to check all the doors and make sure they were still locked. Every door. That meant walking through the debris filled bowels of the big department stores as well as the little shops. Every single one of them that had an external door.

At its height, the mall had 175 shops, not all of them were on the ground floor with an external door, but plenty were. Most were chained and padlocked from the outside and were easier to check, but it was still a lot of doors.

My secondary job was to have an "experience," which was just a timid euphemism for being haunted. Which I wasn't worried about because I was already plenty haunted and going past the empty cavities that used to contain Spencer's Gifts and B. Dalton Booksellers, walking past the counter that was once Orange Julius, wondering whatever happened to Amy was haunting enough.

It was on that fourth pass that something happened. Well... I think something happened. I had just exited, and locked behind me, the cavernous remains of Dillard's, glad to leave behind the pile of manikin parts piled just inside the doorway when I noticed something different.

Dillard's sat at a right turn in the concourse where it went south and west. To the west I noticed a shopping cart on its side. This wasn't unusual at all—there were shopping carts all over the place, most filled with all kinds of junk. This one was on its side with a manikin torso hanging out that was wrapped in a grimy tinsel garland.

I remembered seeing it. There had been a Santa hat perched where the head should be and I thought it someone's bizarre nod to the season.

But it was turned over now and I was sure it wasn't before. I approached slowly, my footfalls echoing loudly and swept my flashlight across it. I stood quietly and listened. I saw nothing. I heard nothing.

I didn't touch it, but went back to the security office and found the right camera and wound the footage back at high speed. I saw myself walk backwards to it, a ghostly form to the infrared camera, staring at it, and then walking backwards and through the doors into Dillard's.

I had been in the department store for about five minutes, and about two minutes further back, the cart just turned over on its side. All by itself.

I leaned close to the monitor, the office chair creaking eerily, and used the arrow keys to back it up one frame at a time. I was no expert on grainy infrared video, but I could see no sign of anything touching that cart.

I checked the other security feeds. There were blind spots, plenty of them, but no one could get there without them showing up on a camera.

But I didn't find anything. Nothing at all.

I suddenly became very aware of the bottle of Jim Beam in the cabinet behind me.

If I thought this abandoned mall was creepy before, it was a hell of a lot more now. I didn't stare at the security feeds until it was time to go walk through again. I walked back and found that shopping cart. I searched all around it, first at a distance and then close, looking for something... anything to explain it. Obvious footprints in the dust, a bit of fishing line used to jerk it over from behind a pillar, something jury-rigged to knock it over.

It had been three days since I had a decent night's sleep—which for me is passing out for four hours—and I was a bit hyped up on coffee and creeped out by the vast space I found myself alone in, so maybe you will forgive me if I tell you that I did wonder whether it might have been a ghost... or something else out of the ordinary.

People believe in a lot of weird shit. AA relies on turning things over to a "higher power," and believe me that can get plenty weird, really quick. I don't go in for conspiracy theories and I'm not easily spooked, but I also firmly believe that I don't know everything, that we humans sure don't know everything.

Something happened here and I didn't know what. So I was determined to investigate it and not rule out anything. Not even ghosts.

The shopping cart turning over like that, the lack of evidence, the impossibility of it was like a thorn under the saddle blanket of my psyche, causing it to get restless and try to buck me off.

And getting bucked off by your psyche to an alcoholic meant drinking. And drinking meant I couldn't see Irene—my agreement with her foster mother is that I am at least two days sober before coming over. The last drink I had had was at gunpoint on the Chupacabra case and I wanted it to be my very last drink. Something kinda romantic about that, right?

So when I got back to the security office and saw that bottle of Jim Beam with the worn ribbon sitting on the desk right where Mitch had left it bathed in the grey glow of all those monitors, my psyche started bucking harder and prickly sweat broke out all over my body.

I opened the metal cabinet and my new thermos was sitting right where the Jim Beam had been. I rubbed at my face and wished I was a whole lot better rested.

I'm not the kind of cowboy where you would put quotes around the word when describing me. My cowboy boots are earned. I grew up in rural Arizona and started riding not long after I could walk. I worked as a rodeo clown for a few years when I was flirting with more direct ways of getting myself killed than alcohol (mostly the protect the rider, bullfighter variety, not the entertaining, barrelman variety, to get technical). I even rode bulls in the rodeo for a bit but wasn't very good at it.

So I know what it feels like to be on a bucking animal that doesn't want you there, and I know what it feels like when your grip is slipping and you are about to be thrown off.

So I left that office and ran back out into the mall.

MAYBE IT WAS TOO MUCH CAFFEINE AND NOT ENOUGH sleep. That is the thin thread I held on to try not to get bucked off as I ran out into the mall. My mouth was dry and my heart was banging in my head faster than my boots were slapping against the tile as I ran down the concourse.

But I didn't go far. Part of me knew I wasn't right, that the bucking psyche was just one part of me, the fear coursing through my body had a logical explanation.

I came to a stop and stood there bent over, panting, sweating, realizing how thirsty I was. I swung the flashlight around and felt another wave coming. I was right where the B. Dalton was, not for a long time, the whole chain went down years ago, but it used to be here. You see, I left an important part out of that story, the adorable first kiss story.

I wasn't in the bookstore alone when I spotted the cute girl with curly red hair and overalls on. I was with my best friend Tommy Wilkins. He's the one that dared me to talk to her. He's the reason that first kiss happened in the first place.

And I killed Tommy. That was the big news that gripped Arizona that I mentioned: Alcohol. Teenage jealousy. Rage. Death. It was a few years after Amy and the mall and we were sixteen and out in the desert near Globe at a party. We were very drunk and fighting. About a different girl. I was trying to leave in my old Toyota pickup. He was in front of the truck banging on the hood screaming at me. I was revving the engine screaming back.

My foot slipped off the clutch and the truck lurched forward and I ran over Tommy. My best friend Tommy.

He didn't die right away, but he died. And part of me did too.

That part of my past came back to haunt me again in full force and my psyche started bucking. This time much harder. I had to get out. I had to get away. But I didn't move, the rational part of my mind trying to gain control.

But then I heard it. The revving of an engine. The sound of

someone slamming on the hood of a car. It was distant and echoed through the empty mall, or was it just echoing in my mind? I couldn't tell.

And then I heard a voice, a ghostly voice, distant and reedy, full of pain. "Evan..." it said, calling me by my given name. "Evan... you killed me. Why did you kill me?"

I ran. There was nothing else I could do.

I WOULD LIKE TO SAY THAT THE ACCIDENT IN THE DESERT explained everything that was wrong with me. Why I used to let angry Brahma bulls chase me while an audience roared and hoped they'd get to see a man gored. Why I sank so far into the bottle. Why I have trouble holding down normal jobs and staying in a relationship. Why I changed my name to Conner Bright and started wearing a crocodile claw around my neck and strapped an eleven-inch bowie knife to my belt.

Well... the last part is most certainly true, but it feels cowardly to blame it all on that slip of my foot. Alcoholism is a disease, right? And killing your best friend is going to mess you up, a lot, but isn't twenty-five years enough of blaming that for everything?

Tommy is the reason I have such a difficult relationship with sleep. I can sleep when I'm good and drunk or beyond exhausted, but rarely any time else.

Tommy wouldn't want me to be like this. We fought, yes, we were like brothers, but we loved each other too, just like brothers.

But that's not what filled my head as I ran as fast as I could down the concourse away from the long ago home of B. Dalton. The revving of the engine and taunting of Tommy's voice was all I could hear.

I wasn't even in a rational enough state to wonder if it was a ghost or not. I was officially haunted. I was running from my past.

I ran to the south, turned the corner to the east and was approaching the spot where that troublesome shopping cart was. I was vaguely aware of the fact, but I still heard the rev-rev of the engine. I still heard someone banging on the hood of the truck. I still heard Tommy saying, "Why did you kill me, Evan?"

And then I was flying through the air, it felt like something had grabbed my foot. Like a skeletal hand. Like Tommy back from the grave.

My flashlight was facing forward and I could see that I was flying towards that shopping cart but something had changed about it. The web of metal had been cut and bent up, sharp prongs pointing at me.

It was just a flash in my mind but my survival instincts took over. I have the aches and pains from my time as a real cowboy and a rodeo clown, but I still have a modicum of the reflexes too. I twisted in the air, my side crashing into the cart just past the bent prongs. The cart slid under my weight and the breath was knocked out of me as I rolled off the cart.

I hit the tile hard on the flat of my back and couldn't breathe at all. My head banged into the tile and blossomed in pain. I heard the cart sliding across the floor and crashing into the doors of the shuttered Dillard's.

I was pretty sure I had cracked a rib or two, that I might have a concussion, and I hurt everywhere. But I wasn't bleeding and I was very much awake.

I was also very, very angry.

I kept being a rodeo clown longer than made sense. Through broken bones and a torn rotator cuff and several concussions.

I used to stuff straw into my waist, neck, and wrists and the announcers would call me scarecrow. This is before the clown makeup costuming went out of style.

I did it because the only thing that felt better than getting so drunk that I couldn't think was surviving a close brush with death.

I did it until the private investigator thing just kind of fell into my lap.

On the cold tile floor of that big empty mall, I just breathed in the stale, dirty scent of the floor and didn't move. I pretended I had myself safe in a steel barrel at the rodeo and the bull was just a few feet away, its horns ready to ram into me if I left.

And while it's true I didn't think us humans knew even a tenth as much about the real world as we think we do, I knew this wasn't a ghost doing this.

"Odd thing is," Sanchez had said when she called, "they asked for you by name."

"I will say that your reputation precedes you but... you are even more than I expected," Mitch Jones had said when he met me.

Surviving had given me clarity and focus and had stopped my psyche from bucking. This case was a whole lot simpler than I thought. It was a setup.

"Evan..." the voice said, seemingly from all around me. "Are you okay, Evan? You're not bleeding, are you?"

If this was an inside job, there was nothing about the security feeds I could trust. If this was an inside job, then the goal of it was for me to end up bleeding and dead on top of that shopping cart after the whole haunted mall thing had been established.

The police would look at the security feeds, which would be

doctored so that cart never fell over by itself and had always been that way, and call it an accident.

"Evan... are you dead yet?"

There would be a few lurid stories that dragged up my past and highlighted my ignoble end, but that would be it.

That's why I didn't move. Because this was all about me. And I wasn't dead yet.

WHEN I WAS A RODEO CLOWN, I SPENT A LOT OF TIME WITH the athletes. We camped together, we followed the circuit together, we drank together.

This meant that I knew who had drunk too much the night before and had a good chance of underperforming. Or who had just lost their girl and wouldn't be focusing. I knew who was flush with cash and who barely had enough to eat. And I knew who had a fire burning in their hearts and something to prove.

I'm sure it will come as no surprise to you that there were bookies skulking about, laying odds and taking bets. I didn't make a lot of money betting on the rodeos I worked, but enough for it to count. Enough for me to be in the flow of it. Enough for me to know when something was off and people started losing more than they should have, people that really needed some cash.

At the height of my game as a rodeo clown / bullfighter, I worked the National Finals Rodeo in Las Vegas in December. NFR is considered the Super Bowl of rodeo and it was an honor to be there. The whole thing is Christmas themed with Santa hats abounding during the event even on some of the riders. I was only slightly irked that it had taken some injuries to pull me up to the big leagues.

This was Vegas, so the usual bookies weren't needed, but

when I saw one skulking around, when the odds-on favorite for the bronc riding lost out in the finals and I lost a ton of money, I knew something was up.

So I worked it. I got a couple of riders drunk. I got the info and confronted the bookie with a tape recorder going. I turned it over to the police and saw the guy arrested and handcuffed on Christmas Day.

He was this short little weaselly guy with shifty grey eyes and a sloppy goatee named Fred Arlington.

Yeah. Just like the guy who let me into the mall, but without the big nose and the gross mole.

And I had to hand it to him. He did the same thing I do with my Australian outfit. Distract people with something outrageous so they don't look too hard at what I don't want them to see.

"Oh, no, Evan," the voice from all around me said and now I could recognize it as Fred's. "You are still breathing. What a pity. I was hoping this was going to be easy."

Arlington went to jail but that was a long time ago. And with as much effort as he had put me into getting me here to try to kill me, there was no way that the shopping cart stunt was the only trick up his sleeve.

***

FRED ARLINGTON WAS LAUGHING AT ME. NOT THROUGH the speakers which I now knew were hidden in the random shopping carts, but close. I could hear his footfalls, I could see the beam of his flashlight on the floor all around me.

"A fake nose and seventeen years and you don't even recognize your old buddy Fred," he said mildly and then his voice raised into a yell. "Do you?"

I slipped the taser out of my pocket and held it behind me as I slowly pushed myself up, letting a painful groan escape. The mall spun around me briefly and I had at least a couple of ribs broken and my left shoulder where I landed on the shopping cart was pretty numb.

"Sorry, mate," I said, shielding my eyes from the bright light and still using my accent. "Have we met?"

"Drop the act, Evan. It's unbecoming." He lowered the flashlight so it was shining between us and I could see him. The nose prosthetic with the fake mole was gone, but he still had the Clint Black concert T-shirt on stretched over his big belly, but now the T made a whole lot more sense. Clint Black had a concert that year associated with the rodeo. Fred had left me multiple clues and I had missed them in my sleep-deprived state.

"Waddaya want, Freddy?" I asked, keeping the accent, knowing that he hated being called Freddy.

He scratched at his chin and looked me up and down. "Been watching you," he said, his face pulling into a sour pout. "Hoping you were out there breaking the law and I could return the favor. But no. You're even working for the cops."

I didn't have patience for this. When the room stopped spinning, when he took another step and was close enough, I pulled the taser from behind my back and fired.

The prongs stuck in his Clint Black concert T and... nothing. He just pulled them out and laughed.

"Oh... you thought the taser worked," he said, his voice loud and echoing in the empty space. "That is so adorable." When he stopped laughing, he pulled a snub-nosed .45 revolver from his back pocket and pointed it at me. "But don't worry there, Evan. This gun works just fine."

As Fred marched me up the dead escalator at gunpoint, my survival clarity almost fled. I was limping and in a lot of pain. The room kept spinning around me. And Tommy's screams started echoing through my head without any help from Fred.

Since starting the whole PI thing, I had tried to help people. Tried to make up for that one moment all those years ago. Fred knew about the moment because I didn't change my name until after I caught him. By then I was tired of the looks and the whispers and no one was going to hire me if they remembered those months when Arizona's media was obsessed with the tragedy. So, after his arrest I changed my name and got my private investigator's license.

But thoughts of the past weren't helpful, so I focused on the pain. It hurt to breathe and my left shoulder wasn't numb anymore but alive with sharp, prickly pain. Bulls had done worse to me, much worse, and I had gotten up out of the manure-scented loam of the rodeo arena and either faced the bull or run for cover.

Except I was a lot older now.

But I also knew that Fred didn't really want to shoot me. That would mean a murder investigation. I may not be Detective Sanchez's favorite person, but we've been through enough that she would make sure the truth was uncovered.

That thought died as soon as I had it. This was an inside job. There were no witnesses to my interview. They could claim that I didn't get the job and was furious about it. That I came back drunk and crazed, pulled my bowie knife, and he had to shoot me in self-defense.

It would take altering security footage, which was already part of the plan, and getting some alcohol down me while I was alive, but it was doable.

The bottle of Jim Beam made a whole lot more sense now. They were hoping I would fall off the wagon and drink on my own.

I felt dizzy and stopped my slow limp about halfway up the escalator. "So what's your plan here, mate?" I asked.

I twisted around and tried to look at him. As I did, I reached into my back pocket and was glad to find that my cell phone hadn't been damaged in the fall. I didn't take it out, I found the volume up button and did a long press and the phone vibrated briefly. I had an app on it to map the buttons and do custom actions. My phone was now recording audio. At least this would give Sanchez a chance of finding the truth if he shot me.

Fred snorted. "You're going to jump," he said. "Suicide, plain and simple. I'm hoping it's a slow death, but I'll take fast too. It's your Christmas present to me to make up for the one you gave me all those years ago."

He was down the escalator a few stairs and was out of my reach.

"Sorry there, Freddy," I said. "I think I'd prefer a bullet, thank ya very much."

He just smiled and shook his head. "Maybe you didn't hear me before," he said. "I've been watching you. I know what you care about... or rather, *who* you care about. That blonde medical examiner—what's her name?—Helen. And that adorable little Mexican girl, Irene."

I just stared at him. I didn't say a word. I felt a rage brewing in me that would put an angry Brahma bull to shame.

"So you're sayin' that if I don't jump, you're gonna hurt them?" I said, trying to keep the anger out of my voice.

"After we get up there, I'm going to hide," he said, gesturing with his little gun. "And you're gonna run like a ghost is after you and then you're going to jump. You put on a nice show for the cameras or I'll put a bullet in their heads."

Fred was a stupid sociopath giving me a choice like that. He couldn't imagine how that would make me feel or maybe he just didn't care and trusted that gun and my need to protect Irene and Helen too much.

"How much does your buddy Mitch Jones know about this?" I asked, trying to sound casual.

He shrugged. "He doesn't want to know too much."

"You musta paid him a lot," I said.

He shook his head and grinned. "Nah. Remembered you telling stories about this place, how you used to love coming here as a kid. So I got a job. Saw that Mitch's been skimming proceeds. Got a nice bit of evidence against him and we had a little talk."

"You're a bastard, you know that, Fred Arlington," I said. All of this was just for the recording, just for evidence.

"Takes one to know one, Evan," he said.

"Don't call me that," I hissed, letting some of the anger steam out. "My name is Conner Bright."

When he shook his head and rolled his eyes, getting ready to lecture me on my past, I moved.

My body hurts from my rodeo days, every day, but it remembers. I used to dodge angry 2,000-pound bulls and I learned a few things. The kind of things you can only learn by facing serious threat to limb and life over and over. I learned when it was time to move. I learned how to ignore my pain. And I learned how to entertain while I was at it.

I let my feet slip from under me and landed heavily on the escalator step using my right hand to cushion the fall just a bit. I let out a sharp cry of pain that was not faked in the least, and slid down a step.

Fred was laughing at me, but he was within reach now. I kicked him in the chest. Hard. With my alligator-skin boot. He went flying and tumbled down the escalator. When he got to the bottom, he didn't move.

DETECTIVE TRISHA SANCHEZ WAS NOT AT ALL HAPPY ABOUT me waking her up early on Christmas morning or having to come out to the dead Metrocenter Mall, but it was a big collar and she was ambitious, so she did it.

I'd call it a wash in terms of our relationship, but getting Sanchez involved got me out of there quicker than I would have otherwise. She took my statement. Listened to the recording on my phone. Watched the security footage of the confrontation. Had the paramedics check me out. And let me go after a loudly protesting Fred Arlington was hauled away with a broken arm and a pretty bad concussion. He deserved more.

I drove home and got to see the sun rise over the desert, yellow and orange driving back the indigo of night. It felt symbolic somehow, like this night looking at my past had changed something for the better.

I took a shower. Taped my ribs up. Ate some food. And made it to Irene's house in time for the unwrapping of presents.

Irene was dressed in purple pajamas with a unicorn print—of course—and hit me like a freight train the moment I got in the door.

It hurt like hell, broken ribs and all, but she smelled clean and soapy and I had a big smile on my face as I held her tight.

"You made it, Conner!" she said.

"For you, my Irene girl," I said. "I would do anythin'."

Her foster mother was standing in the neat, festively decorated living room in a blue robe, her black hair pulled back into a ponytail, and her round face looking tired. I could hear the other kids shouting farther in the house. Her arms were crossed and she was staring at me.

I freed one arm from Irene, pulled the three-month chip from my pocket, and tossed it to her.

She caught it deftly, her eyebrows raising when she saw what it was. This was a good place for Irene. One of the ways I knew that was all the strict rules her foster mother had placed around my visits. The girl needed me, but she needed me sober.

"For Irene," I said quietly as I still hugged the girl.

She nodded and said, "Merry Christmas, Conner."

And it was. The best Christmas I had had in years. Lack of sleep, bruises, broken ribs, and all.

And when I went home, I slept. Really slept. It seems that night in the empty mall facing my past had helped.

BACKSTORY—HAUNTED BY
THE PAST

Conner Bright and I have a couple of things in common when it comes to this story. We both grew up in Globe, Arizona, and we both thought that the Metrocenter Mall was a strange and magical place, something of a small-scale and much closer Disneyland.

I think this was mostly about growing up in a small town that doesn't provide a lot of indoor entertainment and had one, and only one, theater. If you wanted amazing Mexican food, there was plenty of it in Globe, but if you wanted to be a kid and hang out with other kids out of the desert heat, there weren't a lot of options.

This story started with reading that Metrocenter was closing and having all those memories rush back. Besides that, it was time to have fun with Conner again.

Find out more about Conner Bright mysteries at: *RobertJMc-Carter.com/series/ConnerBright*

AFTERWORD

So that's it for my contemporary musings, for now at least. Who knows when another one might pop out.

If you like short fiction, I have three other collections out as of this writing, all thematic in nature. There's more below on these.

To keep up on my stories, go to *RobertJMcCarter.com/newsletter* and sign up for my email newsletter and I'll let you know when something new comes out. And you'll get a free ebook stuffed with stories of mine, several of which you can't read anywhere else.

Thanks so much for reading!

Robert

Life After: Stories of Life, Death, and the Places in Between
A Matter of Life and Life After Death

Anomalous Readings: Thirteen Curious and Confounding Tales
Explore the curious and confounding...

Creatures Featured: Thirteen Stories of Monsters and Other Creatures

ACKNOWLEDGMENTS

It seems that I thank the same people a lot in these acknowledgements, which makes sense. My team is fairly small but they've been with me on this writing journey for a very long time.

Thanks to Dean Wesley Smith for his support, mentorship, and for believing in my stories enough to pay me money for them!

Thanks to Lisa Magnum for the lovely edits on "Laura's Magic Clock."

Hats off to my amazing beta readers that see all the things I cannot see: Peter Klein, Roni Hornstein, and Eliot Schipper.

And to Diana Cox for proofing so many stories for so many years and finding even more of my goofs.

And of course, I must thank my love, my wife, my first listener, Aleia, for your unending support of this writing adventure.

And thanks to you for reading! For what is art without an audience?

BOOKS BY ROBERT J. MCCARTER

Novels in the "Ghost's Memoir" world:

- Shuffled Off: A Ghost's Memoir, Book 1
- Drawing the Dead
- To Be a Fool: A Ghost's Memoir, Book 2
- Of Things Not Seen: A Ghost's Memoir, Book 3
- A Boy, a Girl, and a Ghost

For a complete list the "Ghost's Memoir" novels, go to ShuffledOff.com

The Wood and June versus the Apocalypse series

Find out more at WoodyAndJune.com

The Neutrinoman and Lightningirl Series

Find out more at Neutrinoman.com

Other Novels:

- Seeing Forever

Short Stores Collections

- Life After: Stories of Life, Death, and the Places in Between

- Anomalous Readings: Thirteen Curious and
  Confounding Tales
- Creatures Featured: Thirteen Stories of Monsters
  and Other Creatures

For a complete list, go to RobertJMcCarter.com